EYE FOR AN EYE

A NOVEL OF UNINTENDED CONSEQUENCES

ERIKA HOLZER

A Madison Press Book
Highlands Ranch, Colorado

This novel is a substantially revised edition of Eye for an Eye, by Erika Holzer, first published in 1980.

Cover and Formatting: Streetlight Graphics

ISBN-13: 978-0615953014
ISBN-10: 0615953018

DEDICATION

To the victims of violent crime, dead or alive

PART I

CATALYST

"Once the principle of movement has been supplied, one thing follows on after another without interruption."

—Aristotle, *Generation of Animals*

PROLOGUE

REFLECTIONS. THE DIAMOND AT HER throat, flashing splinters of orange. The crystal chandelier, out of range of her roaring fire but dancing with candlelight.

Her tight grip on the telephone?

Reflection of a holiday mood gone sour...

"Karen, for God's sake," she protested into the phone. "What are you trying to do, scare me to death? Tonight of all nights," she said, willing her voice to turn calm.

"Utter privacy is a mixed blessing, isn't it?"

"I love it now," she lied. "After three years, even a city dweller gets used to the Westchester woods."

But she never had.

"So much crime these days. It worries me. I was reading—"

"On the West Side of Manhattan, maybe," she cut in, "not out here."

But she'd been reading about it too... burglars from New York and New Jersey, heading for the suburbs. Looking for bigger game.

Burglars with wheels. And what else...guns? Knives?

"Sarah, your alarm system—"

"My security blanket, you mean," she admitted drily. "We had it upgraded while you were away. It goes off in the police station now. The cops are on the scene in five minutes, tops. Hold on while I check the roast."

On the way to the kitchen, she glanced in the mirror. The full treatment, she thought, pleased with *this* reflection, at least. Black satin lounging pajamas. Slippers with stiletto-thin heels. Blonde hair looking sleek, straight, and sexy... just the way Peter liked it.

All's well in the dinner department, she thought, sniffing and prodding, practically sailing back to the living room, her festive mood restored.

"Listen, killjoy," she said, cocking an ear to the phone, "no more raining on my parade, okay? You're supposed to say—"

"Happy First Anniversary. Don't mind me, dear. Tonight will be very special."

"Starting with my table. Wish you could see it!"

"As exquisite as that? Draw me a picture."

"My centerpiece would knock your socks off. Peter's too, I hope. Masses of tiger lilies, the most glorious shade of orange—"

"In a black vase, of course."

"What else on Halloween? Plus candlelight, crystal, and the good china." Sarah smiled. "Artfully arranged on a lace tablecloth—that wispy silvery one, remember it? Goes perfectly with my smoky-gray glasses." She touched the delicate rim of a long-stemmed champagne glass. Ran a finger along the intricate pattern of a sterling silver knife. Picked it up just to enjoy the weight of it in her hand.

"I even liberated a couple of place settings from the safe-deposit box—"

She could have bitten her tongue.

"Since when do you keep your sterling in the bank? Have there been any burglaries in your neck of the woods?"

"Don't be silly. People around here play it safe, that's all."

People around here don't want their sterling—not to

mention their jewelry—carted off in a pillowcase while they're out to dinner.

"What are you sighing about?" Sarah asked.

"I just wish Peter didn't get home so late."

"He rarely does. He had an important meeting with some Germans about his father's hedge fund. How do you think we can afford to live in this gorgeous home? Hold on again, okay? I had a hard time getting the fire started and it's looking a bit feeble."

She was having a hard time holding her temper.

She took her impatience out on a log that her robust fire didn't need, teetering on the damn heels as she struggled with the iron tongs, her hair rippling around her shoulders.

Like liquid gold, Peter would say.

Tongs back in place, she gave the radio dial a defiant twist and said into the phone, "Mood music."

"I can hear the lyrics from here. So could your neighbors, if you had any."

"Wise guy. Don't worry, I'll switch to Brahms the minute Peter walks in the door."

"When *is* he walking in?"

"Best guess? Half an hour, maybe sooner. Why don't we play catch-up while we're waiting? Tell me about your presentation. Bet you snared the account."

"Before I even took off my coat."

"They don't pay you enough, Karen," she said, meaning it. "Did I tell you about my anniversary gift to myself? I've been decorating what will become the baby's room."

"You're pregnant?"

"Not yet. Meanwhile, I'm having the time of my life! I have all the usual things—crib, bassinette, shelves full of toys—but can you guess what my biggest challenge was? The color scheme. I wanted it to be appropriate for a boy *or* a girl."

"So what did you decide on?"

She smiled. "Since Peter and I were married on Halloween, I decided on walls that were a faint pastel color of orange, with baseboards and ceilings a pale smoky-gray."

"Sounds wonderful. Reminds me of the time when you were thinking of an interior decorating career."

"That was before I met Peter," she said softly.

"Isn't that your doorbell?"

"What's on the other end of that line, an amplifier?"

"Why would Peter ring the bell? Could he have forgotten his keys?"

"Not likely. Peter's too organized. It's probably more trick-or-treaters. The kids in this neighborhood are really adorable."

"Isn't it a little late for these kids to be out and about?"

"Not around here. Unlike Manhattan, it's no home-by-eight in the suburbs. Be right back. I'll check it out."

She grinned, picking out the slightly distorted shapes. Kids draped in sheets clustered around the smallest one, who was wearing a green Muppet frog mask—all of them holding tightly to their goody bags.

Back at the phone, she said, "Would you believe old-fashioned ghosts outside my door? Oh, and one modern touch—an adorable little Muppet frog. Hang in there while I distribute the loot. Homemade candied apples this year, if you please!"

"Sarah, maybe you'd better—"

But she was already balancing a silver platter of apples in one hand while she turned a key with the other. A chip of light next to the doorknob went from unblinking red to bright yellow. She opened the door.

They pushed in on her so that she teetered precariously, almost dropping the platter. "Hey, you little roughnecks," she scolded, "I was about to hand you—"

Except for the Muppet frog, they weren't so little, she realized uneasily as seven ghosts fanned out into the foyer... the dining area... the living room.

She opened her mouth to yell at them—

And was cut off by a howl. They were howling and whooping!

A brown hand flipped the radio dial, turning up the volume.

She took an automatic step backward as one of the ghosts moved in on her. A denim sleeve shot out from under a sheet, tilting the silver platter. The candied apples went flying.

"What do you think you're doing?" she gasped when she saw where he was headed.

He was piling up her silverware.

"Put it back, damn you!"

But he didn't. Then one of them, a ghost like the others, but with a black hood, approached her table, her exquisite table. She didn't move to stop him because he had picked up a knife. A vicious yank of the tablecloth sent her crystal and china to the floor with a splintering crash. The overturned vase spilled water, drowning the flame of a candle. Black Hood advanced on her—

And stopped short while the Muppet frog took his picture.

She could almost feel Black Hood smiling under his mask posing, knife in hand, while he waited for the picture to develop

Instant results from an Instamatic... Ghosts in sneakers and running shoes. Denim legs that weaved and bobbed. Hands that grabbed. Ripped out. Piled up. Tore through. Smashed aside. And stopped. They kept stopping while the frog took their picture!

Insanity!

She snapped out of it with a jolt. Inching sideways,

11

step by indiscernible step, she moved in the direction of the front door. She was almost there when Black Hood let out a yell. She lunged. But even as her hand snaked out, her heels caught in the doormat. She missed the alarm's panic button by an inch.

She went down. Two of them dragged her toward the mess in the dining room, water seeping into black satin. Fabric tearing. And flesh—her thigh scraping across broken glass.

The howling started up again. Turned piercing. The minute Black Hood approached her, she said, "Jewelry. It's upstairs in the master bedroom to your right. My jewels. My husband's. Just open the—" He cut her off with an imperious wave. Two of them went upstairs.

But she couldn't bear the thought of her home being invaded. When they emerged from the master bedroom carrying pillowcases stuffed with jewelry, she had to turn away. She was on her feet brushing small shards of broken glass from her ruined black satin blouse when a couple of the ghosts disappeared into the kitchen. When they came out again, hoods off as they gnawed on chicken breasts, what turned her legs to rubber was that they'd let her see their faces...

Black Hood approached her again. She backed away, knowing what the bastard had noticed *this* time. The diamond pendant that had been her engagement ring. As it rose and fell with her ragged breath, she had a flash-memory of telling Peter that, as much as she loved her engagement ring, it was too many carats to wear safely in public. With a rush of bitterness at the irony, she reached for the clasp. "Take it, it's very valuable," she told Black Hood. "Take your loot and get the hell out of my home." Her hands were fumbling with the clasp when he ripped her blouse open to the waist.

They came at her like a wolf pack. Her legs were pulled apart, her body slammed against the wet floor.

When Black Hood whipped off his mask, she stared into vacant eyes. Shuddered at the thin slash of a mouth. Before she could scream, his mouth twisted and his hand shot out, knocking her senseless.

Not quite senseless... She felt the tearing pain of forced penetration. She felt it again. Again. Oh God, again and again! How much more could she endure?

"Hey, lookee, a natural blonde!"

They were gloating, howling, whooping over her while someone kept yelling at them to stop—the Muppet frog? She half raised her head in time with a flash of his camera. More flashing! More howling. She was on the verge of howling herself. She was on the brink of unconsciousness—

Her scream went off like a delayed siren.

* * *

When Karen heard the scream, the telephone in her hand clattered to the rug—a strangely muffled sound. She snatched it up again. "Sarah, tell me what's happening!"

No answer. Only the sound of raucous disco and some weird repetitive howling.

She yelled Sarah's name. She heard the rage in Sarah's voice...

"No, don't! Not on my wedding anniversary! You've got the diamond, damn you to hell! What more do you—"

A scream—agonized.

Karen heard her own scream.

She had dropped the phone again.

Hang up. Get help!

But how would she get Sarah back?

She heard Sarah sobbing.

Then another voice. "We better get outta here!"

"Shut your face and take your fuckin' pictures."

"Leave her alone! Don't hurt her!"

"Shut your face, I tole ya! Wipe those prints, you

13

little asshole."

Sarah. So close she could almost reach through the wire and touch her.

"Sarah."

It had come out a whisper.

"Sarahhhhhhhhhhhhhh!"

"Hey, boss, check out the telephone. Looks like we got us a motherfuckin' snoop!"

"... Sonofabitch."

A sound came through the phone that stopped her in mid-scream... dry, rasping—

She stared at the receiver.

What had she just heard?

"You hear that, bitch? You get yourself a fuckin' earful?"

What she heard next were the same sharp repetitive cries—a kind of whooping, like Indians on the warpath. Then a click.

She was calm when she got the Bedford police on the line. She would have stayed calm if they hadn't kept badgering her, wasting precious minutes with their questions—

Who's this calling? Where you calling from, lady? Manhattan? How come it was *you* who called in the emergency? They kept at it until she had to scream at them to shut them up, she couldn't stop screaming.

"I'm her mother!"

CHAPTER 1

I'VE NEVER QUITE APPROVED OF the police. They wear their guns too easily on their hips. To be honest, it's probably because I've never approved of guns.

The Bedford police had kept Sarah too long. By the time they released her, it was almost dark. All that time lost. I wanted to drive back to Manhattan and be alone with her. Not that Sarah would've regarded her husband Peter and his father as intruders. But *I* did.

I had the same feeling all morning—their intrusion in this room. Peter, with his ravaged expression, wearing bewilderment like an ill-fitting suit of clothes. My ex-husband, Alan, tight-lipped. Determined to be brave. If only I were alone with my beautiful Sarah.

"It's time, Karen."

I glanced at Alan. He looked uneasy.

"See what I've done to her gown," I told him stupidly, reaching out to smooth the satin. Hating the false look of Sarah's piously-folded hands.

Alan grabbed both of mine and pulled me away. "We can't keep people waiting," he said, insistent now. I wanted to hit him. I wanted to pull his tie askew and ruin the part in his neat blond hair. He took firm hold of my arm and led me to the door of the funeral home.

My friend Claudia was the first person to walk in the open door.

"It's a rotten shame," she said, vehemence in her eyes. They were red and swollen from crying. "God, what can I say?"

"Don't say anything."

She stood beside me like a sentry as I pressed hands and nodded gravely at murmured condolences. I felt like a bereaved hostess at a social gathering... and for a moment I loathed these people, with their muted voices and their lowered eyes. They were looking at Sarah with pity and regret. But I knew what they were feeling. An embarrassed relief. *Their* families were intact. And fear. Violence had struck too close to home.

Peter's mother grieved, her eyes little puff pastries with slits. She kept darting nervous bird-glances at Peter as he wandered through the room like the sole survivor of a shipwreck, not so much greeting people as encountering them. She wore unrelieved black and, for a change, no jewelry. "The city is one thing," I heard her whisper to Peter's father, "but the *suburbs*?" Peter's father, a tall man with distinguished silver-gray sideburns, was muffled in his response... something about the inflated value of gold and silver.

Sterling silver.

"You going to faint on me?" Claudia whispered.

"Just remembering something a homicide detective told me."

Remembering how Sarah had been stabbed to death with a sterling silver knife.

"I don't know who looks worse, you or Peter."

Claudia and I watched him trying to pull the slump out of his shoulders.

"He blames himself for not being home earlier that night," I said, thinking that the poor guy would never stop blaming himself.

Claudia's eyebrow arched. "Here comes Alan's latest."

A platinum blonde in chic cocktail-party black walked over. "Hope you don't mind my being here," she said.

We've been divorced six years. Why on earth would I mind?

I shook her hand and moved on. To friends I hadn't seen since the divorce. Friends I'd seen three days ago. People whose names I couldn't remember. I ran into a fresh round of hushed voices and mumbled condolences. I headed in the direction of the people I work with and made an attempt at talking shop until I felt it ease a little, the strain of being a constant object of pity.

When I finally drifted away, wishing everyone would get up and leave, I caught Claudia's eye. She got the message, bless her. As she went to work on the crowd, coaxing people to the exit, she kept running her fingers through her long black hair as if she'd forgotten her comb. It hurt me to see the effort it cost her—self-conscious movements as awkward as they were uncharacteristic. This was not an occasion where Claudia cared to stand out.

I stood over Sarah's coffin one last time.

"So peaceful, your lovely daughter," someone had told me.

Nothing so ruthlessly still can be peaceful.

Claudia materialized at my elbow. Placing both our hands on top of Sarah's folded ones, she said, "We'll say goodbye together."

The movement disturbed Sarah's hands, her right hand no longer covering her left. Behind me, Alan's cry of alarm rose and fell away, merging with Sarah's voice...

"No, don't! Not on my wedding anniversary! You've got the diamond, damn you to hell! What more do you—"

They had cut off her finger. She had tried to save a simple gold band with a sprinkle of diamond chips—her wedding ring—and they had cut off her finger for it.

I would have collapsed if Alan hadn't taken my arm and escorted me out of the funeral parlor. We walked

17

through unobstructed space and emerged into fresh air, sunshine, a blur of attentive faces.

"They... mutilated my daughter," I said.

Utter silence. It was so silent that I heard it again, my Sarah's agony. And something more, something worse—a sound that suddenly cut off Sarah's voice in mid-scream—

Check out the phone! Hey, boss, we got ourselves a motherfuckin' snoop!

You hear that, bitch? You get yourself a fuckin' earful?

"Monsters," I said with a shudder, letting it in for the first time. "They let me hear my daughter's death rattle."

I saw rows of shoulders, stiff with shock. My own were slumped with the small relief of unburdening.

Alan helped me with my coat, his blue eyes dark with pain. Peter gripped my hand, but only for a moment. He looked as if my words—any words—had lost their power to convey meaning. Someone asked about burial arrangements.

"Queens," I said in a monotone. "We're going to Queens to bury my daughter."

A limousine was waiting, back door open. As Alan, Peter, and I sat down, the driver caught my eye, his expression curiously attentive. I had the eerie sensation of being watched by a man in a chauffeur's cap who had eyes in the back of his head. Whatever was on the man's mind didn't affect his driving. It was so swift and controlled that we lost the funeral procession to traffic. When he pulled up at the cemetery. I got out of the car, grateful for a brief respite before the burial and went off by myself to wait. To look into a mocking clear-blue sky.

Sarah's eyes...

To turn my face to the rays of the sun.

Sarah's hair...

"They'll get away with it."

The limo driver was holding his chauffeur's cap as if it belonged to somebody else.

"Monsters, you called them," he intoned. "We call them savages."

"We?" I said faintly.

"They'll get away with gang rape... mutilation... murder. Unless?" he prompted.

I averted my face, not wanting him to see that I was suddenly filled with terror.

"Unless you fight back and avenge your daughter," he said flatly.

I looked at him then—tall, rail-thin, laconic as a cowpoke. He had blond hair, sun-bleached almost to white. His eyes were as impenetrable as thick smoke.

"Oh my Leader," he intoned, "the violent death which is as yet unavenged for him by any that is a partner in his shame, made him indignant—Dante. We betray the murdered by not taking revenge on the murderer, Ms. Newman. Keep this."

He handed me a slip of paper with a telephone number on it.

"This is ridiculous," I lashed out.

"Is it? Which will win out, I wonder, your sense of the ridiculous... or your sense of injustice?"

I looked around, hoping I'd spot a policeman—and saw my lawyer, Jon Willard, on his way over to me, his rapid strides eating up the distance.

The chauffeur took off in the opposite direction.

"Stay away from that guy, Karen. Do you hear me?" Jon said vehemently.

"Thanks for the warning but I don't even know the man's name."

I didn't mention that he had given me a phone number.

I went looking for Claudia. She stayed with me, not like a sentry this time, I thought with a rush of gratitude. Like a cane I could lean on.

When they lowered the coffin, my eyes locked with Alan's, willing him to reverse the irreversible. To grab hold of our daughter and pull her out. To make them stop!

But in the end I clung to the sight of friendship... to the love and loss that stood out on Claudia's face like a bas-relief.

Shovels full of earth. The sound—the crude finality of it—was even worse than the sight. My fists clenched in protest. When I opened them, I let go of a crumpled slip of paper and watched as it took its secret to the grave.

I abandoned the limo for a ride back with Claudia. On the way to her car, we passed a jeans-and-leather-jacket crowd—restless strutting kids with vapid expressions... just kids, I told myself. Nothing to be afraid of. But for a moment, I had felt it again. Terror. I stared out the window, barely aware of trees and houses moving past like the slipped gears of my mind. Grateful for a brief reprieve from pain and an overwhelming sense of loss.

I slipped my hands into my coat pockets—and discovered something small and square. A business card?

Claudia's eyes strayed from the highway. "What's that?"

"Haven't the faintest idea," I lied as I cast a quick glance at the card. How could I come up with an explanation that wouldn't sound ludicrous? That a total stranger, posing as a chauffeur, had slipped his calling card into my pocket?

Some calling card! No phone number, no name— *He'd known mine!*

I glanced at two words in elegant Gothic lettering before slipping it back into my pocket. Victims Anonymous.

It had a ring to it.

CHAPTER 2

ANHATTAN IS FULL OF SIRENS, an invasion of sounds crisscrossing the sky like searchlights. You learn not to notice when you've turned into an insomniac. I got out of bed and stood gazing at photographs spread across an entire wall.

I reached for a robe when I heard Peter come in, dark circles, like bruises, under his eyes.

"I've been thinking about enemies," he said, coming into the living room to take a chair opposite me.

His eyes roamed the room, sliding off familiar objects—a couch, a painting, a table lamp—as if nothing had the power to hold him more than a few seconds. "I can't find the enemy, Karen. I can't find anyone to blame. I'm not saying that I can't point a finger at the hoodlums who killed Sarah. But what I feel is more diffuse than that. I can't find a reason for her death that makes any sense."

"I've been terrified ever since Sarah's funeral," I said.

"Of what?"

"I'm not sure," I confessed, his anguish touching off my own. "Peter, you have to understand something. The moment I gave birth to Sarah, I made her a silent promise that I'd protect her. But from what?" I said with a sigh. "Bad karma? Bad luck? Bad timing? Some combination of all three?

He crossed the room and cried in my arms.

* * *

"New York is Attack City, ladies—over two hundred violent street crimes a day. It only takes a couple of seconds to lose your life."

Welcome to Angela Russo's Safety in Self-Defense, I thought dourly, arching an eyebrow at our instructor—a retired policewoman of Amazonian proportions.

As she launched into the particulars of "hard" versus "soft" martial arts, my attention wandered to a lineup of what looked like the kind of stuffed bags that a boxer, revving up before a fight, would punch the hell out of.

I was freezing, despite my perspiration-soaked leotard—it was November, after all. I checked my image in a full-length mirror and felt like I should be wearing camouflage fatigues, the better to kick, punch, and stomp my enemy to death.

I glared at Claudia.

"It'll be a good workout," she had assured me. "Which some of us need," she had added. Low blow coming from a tall, lithe-limbed ex-dancer when "some of us" are five-foot-four and have to count calories to avoid becoming borderline-plump.

The instructor polished off an "attack" demonstration and told us how to knock one's assailant off balance by screaming. The "yell of the spirit," she called it.

Feeling more than a little foolish, I decided to investigate the lineup of what Angela Russo had referred to as "heavy bags." A painfully thin young woman was circling one of them as if it were human. When she suddenly lunged at it, screaming, I whirled around to the woman in back of me.

"What's the matter with her?" I whispered.

"Rape victim."

As the thin woman hammered away at a two-hundred-pound bag, she let out a yell.

"Kiaiiiiiiiiiiiiiiiiiiiiiiiii!"

The yell of the spirit?

The bag was still swinging as I marched up to it, my hands balled into fists. I started to raise my arms—

They had turned into two-by-fours, nailed to my sides.

I noticed our instructor studying me. I signaled Claudia, my expression letting her know that I wanted to get the hell out of here.

Outside, I told her why. How I'd frozen up for no reason.

"Maybe you need a shrink," she said, biting her lip.

"Maybe I'm allergic to punching bags."

"Funny. Let's have lunch," Claudia said.

"Why don't we stop off first at a deli for some sandwiches and get Peter to join us?"

When Peter didn't answer the doorbell, I used my key. "He's been keeping very late hours at his father's hedge fund company," I explained as Claudia headed for the kitchen to drop off the groceries. "The poor guy's probably asleep."

Peter was sound asleep, all right. Lying on top of the bed, he hadn't even bothered to pull the covers up. Smiling, I reached for a blanket to cover him.

His cheek was unnaturally cold. My hand automatically shifted to his wrist. I shouted for Claudia.

"I can't find a pulse!" I told her as she burst into the room.

I virtually stopped breathing as Claudia checked Peter's pulse.

She looked at me and shook her head.

"He's *dead*?" I said, horrified.

Claudia reached for a bottle on a night table. "Sleeping pills," she said grimly.

As soon as she'd called the police, I left word with Peter's father's administrative assistant, telling her it was urgent.

Only then did I permit myself to weep.

CHAPTER 3

TWO GRAVESTONES NOW.

I stood facing the window of a Manhattan skyscraper—my boss Larry Quinn's penthouse apartment. I could still picture Peter's coffin being lowered into the ground in Queens only a few hours ago.

Behind me, Larry said, "Take some time off, Karen."

I turned around to face him His eyes behind his horn-rim glasses—brown, gold-flecked, and warm— were wide with concern.

Time off? A stunning offer from a man devoted to twelve-hour workdays. Had he heard about my ongoing battle with depression?

"It was sweet of you to turn your lovely penthouse into a post-funeral place of refuge, Larry," I said gently, "but I don't want a vacation. I know it's a cliché, but work really *is* medicinal—at least for me."

I spotted a doctor friend talking to Claudia and walked over. "You've lost weight. Are you getting any sleep?" he asked, peering at the deep circles under my eyes.

The movement caused his jacket to fall open.

"Your gun is showing, doctor," Claudia told him.

"I'm going from here to the shooting range," Rollins said. "Why don't you join me, Karen? I haven't seen you for months."

"I wish. I've just been too busy."

I happened to glance across the room and recognized

someone I hadn't seen in years.

"I didn't think you'd remember me," he said when I approached him.

"Why not?" I parried, looking him over. "It's only been half a dozen years."

He was wearing a suit under a dust-colored raincoat with a green and purple tie peeking out. I had a flash memory of a whole history of garish ties.

"M. McCann, the FBI man." I flushed. The words had come out in singsong. "Meet Dr. Rollins and my friend Claudia Cole," I said quickly to mask my embarrassment.

"You're probably wondering what I'm doing here," McCann said.

I was wondering why he hadn't let go of my hand.

"I called Larry when I read about your daughter. To lose her that way. And then your son-in-law..."

"Thanks for coming," I said, on the verge of tears.

I took a good look at McCann to see what six years had done to an old adversary. Not much on the downside, I had to admit. Tall stocky frame, with none of the usual concessions to middle-age spread. Straight sandy hair obscuring part of his forehead. Was he still pushing it away whenever he got into a heated discussion? I saw the same narrow blue eyes that squinted, as if they were trained on some vast prairie instead of a tight lineup of smog-tipped skyscrapers. It brought to mind an image on a popular brand of cigarettes—the Marlboro Man. McCann was definitely not your standard G-man image. Didn't he hail from Kokomo or Sioux City or some such?

"I overheard you say something about a shooting range. Rifles or handguns?"

"I don't know anything about rifles, but I've had some experience with handguns."

"If you'd like to learn something about rifles," McCann said, "I'd be happy to oblige. Using tree trunks instead of paper targets on motorized pulleys in some Manhattan basement," he added. "A friend of mine has some raw land—"

"I don't think so," I told him. But I had to admit I was intrigued... "Don't you live in Washington, McCann?"

"Tomorrow is Saturday. My soul is my own on weekends."

I cracked a smile. "I don't know whether to be offended or impressed. How can you possibly remember a six-year-old insult?"

His smile was easy. "'The FBI owns your soul,' you told me."

"You still married, McCann?"

"Lost my wife a few years ago."

"Divorced my husband six years ago." It had slipped out...

He glanced at Alan. "So Larry told me. Won't you reconsider? Rockland County is beautiful this time of year. After what you've been through, you could use a day in the country."

"I suppose you're right," I said.

* * *

I had just waved goodbye to Larry when Alan walked over with a chunky pipe-smoking man whose face was vaguely familiar. As he stuck out a big paw, the vision of an office-party introduction came back to me in a flash, along with his name. Corey Donahue, an assistant district attorney friend of Alan's.

"We've confirmed that your daughter's killers weren't Westchester locals," Donahue told me. "Looks like they drove out there from the Bronx."

"The police have traced Sarah's silverware. A few pieces of jewelry," Alan said.

"It took you people two weeks and all you've come up with is that one of the knives *may* have been used to stab Sarah to death?" I said, twisting over the words. "As for the killers who used it on her, do either of you even have a clue?"

"I know how you must feel," Donahue said lamely.

"The hell you do."

"Karen, *please.*" Alan said, tight-lipped.

I caught the meaningful glance he exchanged with Donahue.

Donahue cleared his throat. "Uh, Alan told me that you've refused to consult my psychiatrist friend."

"Alan is a Legal Aid lawyer, not a referring physician," I snapped.

"My friend is very experienced with traumas of this kind," Donahue persisted.

"The sick people are the ones who killed my daughter As for my psychology—"

"That's your business, of course."

"Yours is to bring Sarah's murderers to justice."

Donahue's pipe must have died on him. As he tapped it against the palm of his hand, I turned away—

And felt a flush of defiance as I replayed Jon Willard's warning...

Stay away from that guy, Karen. Do you hear me?

I was thinking that if Corey Donahue couldn't do the job, I may have met someone who could.

CHAPTER 4

"**C**OKE?"

McCann passed me a can to wash down the hard-boiled eggs.

He was dressed for a picnic—jeans, plaid shirt, and an electric-blue windbreaker with creases down the front... as if he'd just taken it out of the box. No Marlboro Man ten-gallon hat. He was eyeing my black wool pants suit and red cashmere sweater. Perhaps my "casual dress" wasn't casual enough for him.

"I was telling my friend Claudia how we met," I said. "She couldn't picture the FBI as an old Kemp & Carusone client."

"Old and short-lived. How come you sabotaged the account?"

"Clever of you to have figured that out, McCann."

"Not as clever as the FBI hiring a PR agency," he shot back.

"Why do you think I resorted to sabotage?" I countered. "I wasn't about to help the FBI improve its tarnished image—illegal wiretaps, harassing civil rights leaders."

"And I'm not about to indulge you in a bad habit of yours—jumping to conclusions. A lot of people in the agency weren't proud of what went on then. Including me."

Ouch.

"Sorry," I said.

He leaned back, eyes closed to catch the sun. A regular paleface for a Midwesterner, I thought. Nothing weathered or leathery about him. Smooth skin, big shoulders—

I looked away when I started to picture him with his plaid shirt off.

"Let's get down to business," McCann said. He opened the trunk of his car and took out a rifle and a handgun.

Handing me the rifle, he said, "This is a relic. An M-1 Garand carbine—your basic infantry weapon in World War II and Korea. Not much in use any more. It fires eight rounds from a clip, semi-automatic. Each time you pull the trigger, it sends a .30 caliber bullet."

It wasn't as heavy as I'd expected.

"Down on your belly."

The ground was mossy and pungent.

He showed me how to hold the rifle. How to aim it at the birch tree about 50 feet in front of me and the high hill just beyond, my right eye looking through the sights in the general direction.

The trigger felt smooth. All I had to do was exert a little pressure.

Pull the trigger, Karen.

I did—eight times—the sounds reverberating through the woods. Eight misses. McCann looked puzzled. "With that much fire power, you should have hit the tree at least once. What happened?"

"I have a confession to make. I have a 'lazy' right eye—20/200 vision. Most of what I see from it is blurry."

"That certainly explains it. Let's try the hand gun."

Handing me a small .38 caliber Smith & Wesson revolver, he said, "This fires five rounds. It's not an automatic. You have to pull the trigger each time."

Familiar territory for me...

I assumed the proper stance, sighted—and put all

five rounds into the birch tree.

"It's obvious you've done this before," he said drily.

I laughed.

He leaned over to brush some dry leaves from the sleeve of my jacket. "I like hearing you laugh."

"Thanks for the lesson, McCann."

"Time to go," he said.

On the ride back, he was completely relaxed.

But the instant we hit Manhattan, I sensed that he went into alert mode.

When I mentioned it, he said, "So did you."

I hadn't been aware of it.

"You used to love the city, Max. Do you still?"

He thought about it. "Guardedly. The way a man might love a wife he suspected of poisoning her first husband. How about you?"

"I've been here too long," I confessed. "I accept New York on its own terms—like Californians living with the threat of an earthquake."

He glanced at me. "How do you deal with *your* earthquake?"

"Oh, I draw a mental map of danger zones. Which streets to avoid after dark. Which ones to avoid—period. Furs are no problem. I don't wear them. When I plan on doing some shopping—say, carrying bagfuls of groceries—I tuck my jewelry out of sight."

"Do you have all the right locks on your door?"

"Of course I have locks. The 'right kind'? I'm not sure. Living in a big city means taking precautions. But the other side of that coin is that you can't afford to think about it all the time."

"You can't afford *not* to," he countered with a slow smile.

"Bad habit of yours, McCann, getting in the last word."

But the last word came at my front door, which he

31

insisted on seeing me to. He found the excuse of a grass stain to lightly touch my jacket again... as if he wanted to memorize the texture.

"I'll call you," he said—and paused, as if waiting for me to contradict him.

"I'd like that," I said, surprised to find that it was true.

*   *   *

My doorman handed me a large envelope mailer when I walked into the lobby. I dropped it into my oversized bag, deposited it on a small table in my foyer, and promptly forgot about it. After a deliciously relaxing bath, I padded into the kitchen to make myself a soothing cup of tea, and saw the mailer.

I picked it up. Curious. No canceled postage, no return address. It had been hand-delivered. I hefted it in my hand. It felt like a book. I opened the mailer and, sure enough, there was a book inside. It was a gold-leafed leather-bound copy of Dante's *The Divine Comedy*. A page from a calendar was stuck inside like a bookmark. It opened to *Inferno* and a paragraph bracketed in red. *Oh my Leader, the violent death which is as yet unavenged*—someone had crossed out "for him" and substituted "for her"—*by any that is a partner in "her" shame, made "her" indignant.* The calendar-bookmark was the month of November, with the number "2" circled in red at the top. Two funerals in November? Two unavenged deaths? A paragraph bracketed in red ink like red finger-pricked blood?

The phone made me jump. I caught it on the first ring. "Well?" Claudia demanded.

"Well what?" I said faintly.

"For heaven's sake, Karen, your G-man admirer with the gorgeous blue eyes! What's he like? How'd it go?"

"He wore a plaid shirt and a windbreaker and he

chewed on a blade of grass. I fired a revolver without disgracing myself," I said wryly.

"You seeing him again, I hope?"

"Matter of fact, I'm calling him back right now," I lied, the only way to get her off the phone like a shot.

I hung up and dialed again before I could change my mind. Before I could let myself forget whose voice I had *really* wanted to hear just now. When ADA Corey Donahue came on the line I said, "Karen Newman here. What's your psychiatrist friend's name and phone number?"

As soon as he told me, I hung up before he could ask about my change of heart. Once I'd made the appointment, I consigned Dante to another inferno— my hallway incinerator shaft. I'm no book burner, but I have to admit I didn't feel even a twinge of guilt. What I felt—pun intended—was poetic justice.

CHAPTER 5

H E HAD CHOSEN A FRENCH restaurant for our "informal chat."

As I walked in, I reflected on Claudia's skepticism about "shrinks"—my sentiments exactly. Still, I didn't see how it could hurt.

I gave the psychiatrist's name to the *maitre d'* and followed him past creamy walls that featured tastefully discreet nude drawings. I spotted a man in black pinstripe at a curved banquette in the back. He had apparently spotted me too. He stood up and waved me over. He looked to be a little over six feet tall. When I got closer and he removed his glasses, I saw chiseled features and honest-to-God silver sideburns.

"Mrs. Newman?"

"Dr. Coyne. Newman is my maiden name," I said coolly, knowing Donahue had to have filled him in on my marital status. I sat down.

"I stand corrected," he said with a disarming smile. "Call me Jim."

"You don't look like a Jim."

His grin told me I had said something clever.

"Most of the time, I don't feel like one," he admitted. "My childhood name, 'Jamie,' is more to my liking."

"It fits you better, somehow," I said slowly, "although I'm not sure why."

He laughed. "Karen Newman," he said. "It goes with tailored suits and no-nonsense shirts—or so she wants people to think."

"Truce," I told him with a wry smile. "I'm freezing to death. I should have worn a down vest under this jacket."

He casually broached the subject of my work.

Hoping to relax me?

"Look," I told him, "I'm not really sure I need to be here. It's just that I had a bad moment last weekend and—"

"And you prefer to solve your own problems. You distrust psychiatrists."

"Direct, aren't you?" I said, liking him for it. "Let me return the favor. This may be an 'icebreaker' lunch, but talking about my work won't melt any ice. Just the opposite."

"Are you implying that you're conflicted about your job?"

"Something like that."

"I'm guessing that you don't approve of some of your clients. But you're a senior vice president. You must be good at what you do. Tell me about Kemp & Carusone."

"It's a full-service public relations agency. We offer our clients a large variety of services. It includes such things as corporate communication techniques, product publicity, media relations—"

"Your strong suit, media relations."

I stared at him. We media experts in the PR business keep a very low profile. Dr. Coyne must have gotten the information from his pal Donahue, who had gotten it from Alan.

"Perceptive, aren't you?" I said, slightly annoyed because he was too damn good at his job. "Let's face it, Doctor, K & C is a glorified corporate image polisher. I make businessmen look good even when I don't approve of what they're selling. It's not exactly a line of work that goes with someone of my politically liberal leanings. I went into it with misgivings. At the time, I needed the independence."

"And?"

"I got used to the salary."

"What else do you *still* like about it?" he pressed.

"I have a feeling you already know the answer," I said drily. "I like the action."

When a waiter arrived, I let him order for both of us.

"Care to talk about your problem?" he asked.

I played with the handles of my briefcase-purse. "I called you because I was tempted to act against my better judgment. I didn't. End of problem."

"That's all of it?"

I noticed his eyes then—*really* noticed them. They were so deep a brown that they were almost black. Penetrating...

"Not quite all," I admitted. "I've been experiencing an odd sort of fear since my daughter's murder. It's been going on ever since her funeral."

For the first time I sensed that Dr. Coyne was looking at me with a psychiatrist's keen appraisal.

"I've tried to deal with it," I told him. "Just don't ask for details."

He leaned forward. "You know I have to."

"I took up self-defense—short-lived, as it turned out," I said, managing not to let him see my embarrassment. "I froze up."

"Interesting... But now you're back in control?"

A welcome wrap-up question. I assured him that I was.

The minute our lunch arrived, the psychiatrist seemed to disappear and a charmer called "Jamie" took his place. Unsettling at first, but not unpleasant. There was something quaint and old-fashioned about the way he saw to my every culinary need, from fresh rolls to refilled wine glass to dessert and coffee.

Naturally, he grabbed the check. That's when the psychiatrist returned for a parting shot. "If your problem continues, please call me," he said. "Therapy isn't a fate worse than death. It actually works if the patient brings two things to it. Intelligence and motivation."

"I'm not stellar in the motivation department," I warned him.

"True. But you don't require much for a single session. If you ever feel the need for a sounding board, be my guest."

Not bloody likely.

But lunch had served its purpose. I really did feel reassured.

I bade him a noncommittal goodbye and headed for the ladies' room. It turned out to be one of those soothing lounge-style affairs, all peach and white and dimly lit. I took advantage of a cushy lay-about, needing to close my eyes for a few minutes. It had been a hard morning at the office, topped off by my encounter with the faintly unsettling Dr. James Coyne aka Jamie. When I pried my eyes back open, I realized that I was being stared at.

How long had I dozed off?

My first reaction was to grab for my briefcase, which I'd left on the floor by my side. I sat up, trading stare for stare. The woman was youngish, thin-lipped, and uptight. Her lipstick, a lurid scarlet, was badly applied. Her small nose twitched.

"Kagan wants you to know we have proof," she said in the tone of a somnambulist.

Kagan. The name of the pseudo-chauffeur at Sarah's funeral?

I leapt to my feet. But the woman was already at the door.

She turned around, her eyes like the tiny bulbs in high-intensity lamps. "We know who killed your daughter," she told me.

I spent an impossible afternoon at Kemp & Carusone, outwardly calm but inwardly fuming. Leaving the damn book with my doorman was one thing. Having me followed to a restaurant so someone could drop a bombshell of a message on me was another. Outrageous!

I was leaving the office when my secretary handed me a message from McCann. Was I free for dinner? I started to tell her I'd be out of town for a while, then changed my mind. "Just tell him I'm busy, Colleen."

Bad timing, Max. Some other lifetime.

I took a cab. As soon as I set foot in my apartment, I walked to the window, eager to take in my soothing Central Park view, needing the sense of privacy it always gave me—

Utter privacy is a mixed blessing...

The urge for a double bourbon was overwhelming. Refusing to give in to it, I headed for the den, briefcase in hand. It was heavy—full of the work I hadn't been able to do all afternoon. Emptying the briefcase onto my desk, I reached into a side pouch for a yellow legal pad—

And pulled out more than the pad. A thick envelope with my name on it. The woman in the restaurant must have slipped what felt like a bunch of photographs into my briefcase.

We have proof...

I slit the envelope open with care, as if it had a bomb inside that might go off. Stacking the photographs neatly on my desk, I checked out the photograph on top. It was okay. Something I might have taken myself—the table Sarah had set for her anniversary dinner with Peter, from the porcelain dishes to the silverware to the smoky-gray glassware. But the next photo showed a couple of white ghost-figures with holes cut out for the eyes. One of them was holding a portable TV set. The one Sarah had kept in her bedroom...

I forced myself to keep going through the stack. Photographs of more ghosts clutching things. A stereo. A silver platter and matching cigarette box.

A Christmas present. A wedding gift.

I turned the photographs over more rapidly now and watched them blur into a kind of ghastly montage. Ghosts that seemed to be everywhere, leaving behind a trail of wreckage. A crystal vase, shattered. A Tiffany floor lamp, overturned. A lace tablecloth, in wild disarray. I saw candied apples and chicken breasts scattered all over the place.

My hand shook. I was running out of photographs— which meant proof of something much worse than vandalism and robbery was coming up.

Proof of Sarah being gang-raped...

I felt a stabbing pain even as I forced myself to turn over the next photograph.

Sarah's face, full of terror and revulsion.

I kept my eyes on her face, not wanting to move down to naked backs and buttocks. Moving down finally.

I had to stop again as I lost my breath and ran, choking, to the bathroom and the taste of vomit.

I went back to my desk, knowing that I needed to see this through to the end.

The ghost, this time, unlike his pals, was wearing a black hood. He stood with one of Sarah's sterling silver knives in his upraised hand.

One more photograph to go. I paused abruptly. Stared at it before turning it over.

We know who killed your daughter...

And now, so did I.

He was posing, knife in one hand, black hood in the other.

His face was a vacant lot. His mouth might have been

fashioned by the slit of a razor. He had shoulder-length black hair, a thin black band around his forehead, and a birthmark under his left eye in the shape of a tear.

I held the phone in my lap while I thought about the man with the chauffeur's cap. Jon Willard's face intruded. Jon, an associate of Barry Slotnick, the defense attorney who was currently representing Bernhard Goetz in Manhattan's most sensational murder trial. Jon, who fervently believed in courts of law, rules of evidence, judges and juries.

Kagan? Or Jon?

It wasn't even close.

Corey Donahue was working late. I told him there was something new. I told him about the photographs. The last thing I told him was "You'd better come and get them."

I hung up, knowing that I needed to make one more call.

Dr. James Coyne recognized my voice. When he added things up for me, I knew that I had been right to call him.

CHAPTER 6

"FIRST TERROR, THEN RAGE. WHAT in God's name is happening to me?" I asked.

"In a word? Displacement," Dr. Coyne said. "Your daughter is murdered. You feel rage. You feel it again when you meet this so-called chauffeur. His offer is tempting—a prospect that frightens you to the point where your mind blanks it out. That's when the process we psychiatrists call 'displacement' kicks in. You began to shift the fear of your own rage onto whatever person or object provoked it. Fear of the vigilante because of what this man's offer made you feel. Fear of the punching bag and all those rage-filled women. Fear of the jeans-and-leather-jacket crowd because those kids were vivid reminders of your daughter's killers. You were afraid of what you secretly wanted to do to them."

For the first time in my life, I grasped what my Catholic friends take for granted—the relief of the confessional. "Are you saying my fears weren't real? That what I was *really* experiencing was... was what?"

"A desire to avenge your daughter's death."

"But I abhor violence!" I protested. "I always have."

"You're thinking that your rage is abnormal. It isn't. Not under these circumstances. Only really sick individuals act out their murderous impulses."

He had such a gently reassuring voice that I wanted to believe him. I couldn't keep my hands from shaking...

He frowned. "Use your common sense. Should a victim of violent crime *not* feel outrage? If so, what's the alternative? Drive it underground?"

"What am I supposed to do with it?" I said, feeling desperate.

"Give in to your rage. Give it room to dissipate. Take comfort from the knowledge that you *didn't* act out the impulse."

He was right, I thought. Hadn't I resisted giving in to this vigilante character? Hadn't I called Alan's ADA pal Donahue and turned the photographs over to him?

The door to the reception room opened. I caught a glimpse of a young boy.

"Be back in a minute," Dr. Coyne told me.

It gave me a chance to scan his office, which up to now I'd barely noticed. His taste clearly ran to the opulent. An elaborately carved mahogany desk, handsomely fitted with antique brass. Heavy drapes in green-and-gold brocade. The drapes were complemented by an inviting emerald-green couch that actually looked comfortable. And was.

I stood up from the couch to check out the bookshelves. Along with all the expected technical tomes, I saw the swashbuckling novels of Dumas and Sabatini.

Dr. Coyne returned just as I was admiring a sensuous companion to his couch—a coffee table that was a gently curving slab of malachite.

He smiled. 'You're wondering what kind of a practice merits all this."

I took in his gold lion's-head cufflinks, the mauve Christian Dior tie, the cut of his three-piece suit. "Obviously, a very successful one."

"It was. Until I got bored with being the 'in' Manhattan guru for the idle rich."

"The female idle rich?" I teased, eyeing his couch.

"You're wondering how I've kept it professional? These help," he told me. Removing his glasses, he handed them to me.

I looked at them. Then through them. "Pure glass," I said, startled.

"I have twenty-twenty vision. I wear glasses to impose a kind of barrier between me and some of my... more persistent patients."

"Corey Donahue tells me that you confine your practice, these days, to the criminal-justice field. What got you into it?" I said, curious.

"A forensic psychiatrist who succumbed to ptomaine poisoning on the eve of a trial. I covered for him." He sat back, reflective. "Examining the accused gave me my first glimpse of a young killer's psyche. I've been fascinated ever since."

I felt as if I'd been slapped. I stood up. "I'll bet you have a regular rogue's gallery of fascinating patients," I said.

"The bulk of my patients are crime victims. Like yourself."

"You consider *me* a victim?"

"Not in the same way as your daughter. Not even in the same way as your son-in-law. But still, a victim."

I sat back down. "Will I ever get over the fear and the pain? This 'displacement'?"

He didn't say, "Of course you will!" or "Don't think that way." What he said was "I don't see how. Your daughter died an especially vicious and premature death."

I looked at him with new respect. "My mother and father were very much in love," I told him. "I was in college when she died of ovarian cancer. My father had a fatal heart attack less than two months later. I still remember how it made me feel. A terrible sense of isolation—as if I'd been cut off from my past. But after losing my only child, I feel..."

"As if you've been cut off from your future."

I could only stare.

"To suffer such an irrevocable loss is to lose something of ourselves," he said gently. "It's a kind of permanent death."

"You're uncanny," I marveled. "How could you know—"

"I've always known these things."

He had said it as if it were a curse, not a blessing.

"The rage," I said. "Will I ever get over that, at least?"

"In time. If you—"

The phone rang. I had no premonition as his professional voice ebbed away. He was looking at me, his expression tense. I had left his telephone number with Colleen in case my boss wanted to track me down.

"It's Corey Donahue," he said slowly. "They've got them..."

I couldn't understand why he stopped in mid-sentence and gripped my shoulders, or how a glass of brandy materialized in my hand.

"Easy," he was saying. "Take it easy."

He wouldn't say anymore until I drank. He took the glass away. "I didn't mean the police had literally arrested them—not yet. Donahue says they've identified the gang by its leader."

"Does he have a name?"

Does he belong to the human race?

"A street name synonymous with Puerto Rican macho. Indio," he said, pronouncing the word with startling contempt.

Indio. Shoulder-length black hair and a band around his head, like an Indian.

"What happens after they arrest him?"

He led me to the couch and sat me down. "If he's under sixteen, as Donahue suspects, there will be a Family Court proceeding."

"A proceeding? Not a trial?"

"Maybe. Maybe not. It's up to the Westchester County DA. New York allows him to try a juvenile killer as an adult. *If* the case is strong enough to stand up before a grand jury. I'm afraid it's the DA's call."

"With *those* photographs?" I held my glass out for more brandy. "Say this 'Indio' is tried as an adult and convicted of murder. He'll go to prison, won't he? He'll be sent away for a long time?"

"Nine to life is more likely. In which case, he wouldn't do more than nine years."

"Nine years?!"

It was surreal.

"You haven't told me what happens if he's *not* tried as an adult," I said cautiously.

"A juvenile proceeding in Family Court."

"That's another way of saying 'rehabilitation,' not 'punishment,' isn't it? Help the kids who never had a chance?"

"You've got a real problem, thanks to our former mayor Ed Koch."

"Koch?" I said, surprised. "The man earned raves for distancing politics from his judicial appointments to Family Court."

"True. But he was a diehard liberal. How much do you know about David Dinkins, his successor?"

"An African American who served only one term. Why?"

"This is a direct quote. 'For all his loud remarks,' Dinkins said, 'Ed Koch presided over a non-stop escalation of New York's crime rate and handed this mess to me on his way out the door.' "

"So what am I facing? My daughter's murderers doing time in a glorified country club complete with bunk beds, tennis courts, and unlocked doors?" I said bitterly.

He reached for my hand. "There's nothing weak about needing help. Let me help you get through this, Karen."

I pulled away and got to my feet. "Lean on you, you mean? I wouldn't know how."

"Let me be your unofficial liaison, at least, between you and the police. You and the DA's office."

"You're serious," I said with a rush of gratitude. "But why? I'm not even a patient."

"A friend?"

"I'm sorry," I told him.

"About what? I meant it, Karen. Friend, not lover."

"It's all I'm up to," I admitted. "Dr. Coyne, I don't know how to thank you."

"You can start by dropping the formalities."

"Thank you... Jamie."

Instant transformation. The infectious smile I'd seen in the restaurant was back.

I left his office wearing his words like an arm around my shoulders. Friend, not lover. How had he known I needed precisely that?

CHAPTER 7

MY CLOCK RADIO JARRED ME awake with a jazzy rendition of "I'm Dreaming of a White Christmas."

I snapped it off, hating the reminder. I took my time dressing, not eager to get where I had to go but able to face it, thanks to Dr. James Coyne. Thanks to my friend Jamie.

He hadn't wasted any time. Within two days of my office visit, he'd had me feeling useful, distracted from my own pain with the pain of others—a sort of "therapy" called Victims Aid. A growing phenomenon, apparently. Show up at the scene of some violent crime, armed with sympathy and practical advice.

What do I think of as I cradle a frail blood-spattered man in my arms while the police bear his wife's body away? *His* pain, not mine.

How do I dull the horror of a maimed or murdered child? By telling their parents about my Sarah...

Not today, though. Today I was free to focus exclusively on my own pain. Today was Indio's Family Court hearing.

The phone rang. "So it's Family Court," said a familiar voice.

"Thanks for keeping track, Jon."

"Do you want me there when they call you in to testify?"

I was sorely tempted. But Jamie had already filled

me in on what I could expect.

"The youth officer who's handling the hearing seems to know what he's doing," I said, "but thanks for volunteering."

"Do you know who the judge is? I'd probably be able to give you a heads-up."

"I've no idea. I don't mean to brush you off, but Claudia's waiting for me downstairs. She's driving me to court."

"Good luck, then."

Claudia's expression was tight, unable to make it real that the brutal murder of my daughter would not result in a conviction for murder. All the way to Westchester she kept it up. "He won't get away with it."

While she went looking for a parking space, I sized up a modern building with a sun-dappled plaza and tightly manicured grounds… even as I tried to ignore a battalion of fat red bows and holly wreaths. A prominent sign over the entrance to the building flashed away in green neon: ONLY 4 MORE DAYS UNTIL XMAS!

Family Court was on the sixth floor. Claudia and I slipped out of our coats—it was freezing out—and took a corner bench in the hall.

"Tell me again why they couldn't indict this monster as an adult," Claudia said.

I sighed. "According to the Bedford youth office assigned to the case, I didn't have any choice."

"The one photograph places him at the scene, Ms. Newman, knife in hand. But doing what? Rape? Robbery? Getting a glass of water? With that kind of evidence, you'd get laughed outta court. We figure there were six or seven punks, but which one used the knife? We need an eyewitness—one punk willing to talk."

"What can you do about finding him?"

"I'm working on it—me and the Bronx. Meanwhile, we get this Indio creep convicted in Family Court on a

lesser just so he's off the street. That way, he don't beat the shit out of his buddies or maybe bribe them. That way, we buy time to build us a case."

Suddenly uneasy, I went to a pay phone and called Jon Willard.

"Are you serious?" Jon told me. "This 'youth officer' doesn't know what the hell he's talking about! There's no question that there was a robbery. There's no question this Indio was there. There's no question your daughter was murdered. No question that this constitutes felony murder. That's Criminal Law 101."

A long pause. When he spoke again, his voice was thick with frustration.

"Let's face it," he told me, sounding tired. "If they're treating Sarah's murderer like a juvenile, a Family Court judge can do whatever the hell he wants."

"Thanks for leveling with me," I said, and hung up.

A big man with a cigarette in his mouth and a mournful slope to his shoulders stepped out of an elevator. The youth officer. I was tempted to slap his face. I waved him over and introduced him to Claudia.

"Can I go in with her?" Claudia asked him.

"Closed to the public. They don't even identify people by name in there." He ground out his cigarette. "See you inside," he told me with what sounded suspiciously like false good cheer as he headed into the courtroom.

"What did Jon say that upset you so?" Claudia whispered.

"Later. I need to think."

I was thinking that right about now, the youth officer would be making his charge to the judge. Robbery, if done by an adult. Then he'd quote some law and steer clear of murder and rape. The judge would go for the cut-and-dried—for robbery, he'd assured me.

But a Family Court judge could do whatever the hell he wanted...

When the courtroom doors finally opened again, it was my name they called. I jammed my hands into my pockets, went inside, and walked in on an argument in progress as a flustered kid from the DA's office, hair neatly parted, was on the carpet for daring to bring up the matter of previous convictions. He hadn't been able to pry the juvenile offender's criminal record out of a sister Family Court in the Bronx.

Had Jon been in the courtroom, he'd have had the file in his hand. He'd have been waving it in front of the judge's nose...

The Legal Aid lawyer—his dirty-blond hair tied into a ponytail with a festive red-and-green ribbon—spoke in righteous tones about confidentiality laws that keep a juvenile's past a secret.

Even from a district attorney?

The judge didn't fit the mold. I'd been expecting bland and irritable, not elegant and restrained. He was pale and hollow-cheeked, with silver-framed glasses riding an aquiline nose. His narrow shoulders were squared. His hands were on prominent display so you couldn't miss those long, tapered fingers. He kept issuing pronouncements from his perch like a professor gently chastising a couple of backward students.

Jamie had cautioned me to keep my eyes on the youth officer.

Pick out a focal point so you won't be tempted to look at Indio. He isn't in the room. He doesn't exist. Not yet...

"Next witness."

I walked to the stand, telling myself this poor excuse for a trial was just a way station. That eventually Indio would be tried for felony murder.

I avert my eyes from the murderer in this room. I have important testimony to give, my account of what I heard fifty-three days ago. But one glance at the "youthful offender" and I am lost. Go slowly then. Grip the arms of the witness chair if you have to...

Is he serious, this judge? How can I remember in such detail? How can I not?!

Back it down. Bite your lip until it bleeds, as long as you get it right, because this is lawyers' territory. This is what "robbery" turns on.

Repeat it? Does he know what he's asking? Words are tied to images, Your Honor. Sarah, screaming her heart out. It's when they cut off her finger! His Honor is looking pained. That's good because it gets worse, it gets lethal. The taunt at the end—the end of my Sarah. This "juvenile offender" gave me an earful. Can you hear it? Can you all hear it?

I swung around in my chair, my testimony over. Free now to look at a murderer, I saw designer jeans and high-top tennis shoes—very lightweight, very "cool." The black hip-length jacket had leather sleeves, a felt body, and a small yellow crown over the heart—a "hero jacket," it's called. There would be another crown logo on the back. I closed my eyes and saw the face of a man whose company had manufactured the jackets—jackets that had become more popular with gang members than sports heroes. It was why the CEO had signed on with Kemp & Carusone. He'd wanted to improve his company's image.

Talk about irony!

I opened my eyes and studied the face in Kagan's photograph. Juvenile with long black hair and headband who played at being an Indian brave. The eyes were as stone-cold flat as I remembered from the photograph. I stared at his slit of a mouth. At that oddly disconcerting birthmark.

Suddenly, Indio flashed a sudden smile—something special just for me!

I swung on the judge... the probation officer... the Legal Aid guy. They'd all seen it—a smile tantamount to a confession. Pride of authorship. Of murder! It sent me out of the courtroom wrapped in a dignified calm. It made the waiting easy. Nothing human could have witnessed a smile like that—could watch it pass from killer to victim—and not do what was right. In that moment I grasped the essence of justice. It wasn't luck or politics or fine print. It was common decency. I was even able to feel compassion for another mother... a woman who'd sat in the back of the courtroom, forced to listen to what her son had done.

When the courtroom doors finally swung open, Indio's mother came out, her fleece-lined coat tightly buttoned. Her son, still smiling, was one step behind her.

I must have leaped to my feet because the mother stopped for a moment to stare. I knew what she was seeing—she had seen it earlier in the courtroom. My face, indecent in its agony. What I saw in hers was blank indifference.

Mother and son disappeared into an elevator.

A hand closed over my shoulder.

"I gambled. You lost." The youth officer's face bent over mine. "Bad luck, drawing that sonofabitch judge."

"Bad luck? We lost because you didn't know what the hell you were doing!"

I stood up, fighting off nausea. Jamie had warned me about some of the judges but he hadn't been specific. He's just alluded to a judge with a nickname.

"—shoulda known the bastard would buy Legal Aid's 'humanity' pitch," the youth officer was saying. "Who wants to lock up a fifteen-year-old right before Christmas? Not Bleedin' Heart Art," he muttered, disgust etched in the lines of his mouth.

A judge with a nickname...

I rushed back into the courtroom. His Honor still sat on his perch. When he looked up and saw me coming, it was as if someone had sprinkled red pepper up that imperious nose.

"Yes?" he said in a tone designed to put an impertinent student in her place.

"You call that justice?" I said in a voice so low he couldn't hear the effort not to scream at him.

"Tempered with mercy, my dear Ms... Noonan, is it? I understand your feelings—"

I left the courtroom. I walked past Claudia, still talking to the youth officer. An elevator was closing. It struck me a solid blow as I slid inside. I stood hunched over as I visualized a stack of memories—all those incriminating photographs.

And I had turned them over to the law!

I got lucky. As I stepped out of the elevator, a killer stood in the lobby with his buddies. I heard raucous sounds of celebration among the hero jackets. Stared at Indio's back, then at a policeman who stood a few feet away, blue jacket open to a holster.

And thanks to Max McCann, I felt the shape of the revolver even before I saw it. I remembered the weight of it in my grip—

"Not this way."

I heard the low monotone, felt both arms grabbed from behind.

I collapsed like a house of cards against Kagan's chest.

The policeman, inches away, never even turned around.

"You knew how it would be," I gasped once we were outside.

"Lucky for you. Shall I show you what even the Bronx Family Court doesn't have a record of? A solid list of Indio's crimes."

I swayed a little, lost in the smoke of his eyes. "You people are very organized."

He shrugged. "It's the wave of the future. I'm here to invite you to— Let's call it a holiday encounter."

He was looking past me. "Your friend is almost upon us."

"May I bring her to this so-called encounter?"

"Suit yourself. But there are rules. We'll be in touch."

Claudia rushed over in time to be introduced to Kagan's mocking smile.

"We'll meet again," he said. "Don't make plans for Christmas Eve."

PART II

CONVERSION

"Oh my Leader, the violent death
which is as yet unavenged
for him by any that is a partner in his
shame made him indignant."

—Dante Inferno, Canto 29

CHAPTER 8

"I FEEL LIKE A DAMN FOOL, wearing these on a cold winter night," Claudia grumbled, waving her oversized dark glasses at me.

We were headed cross-town in a cab. I wore a beret. Claudia's velvet turban stressed her high cheekbones and slanted eyes—Egyptianesque, her ex-husband used to tell her. Her pants suit was velvet-trimmed elegance. Mine was plain wool. She wore a wool jacket. I had opted for a sensible down vest that made me feel like a stuffed teddy bear.

"The dark glasses make sense," I said. "If you disguise your face, you don't have to disguise your feelings. From what Kagan told me, I gather these 'encounters' can get pretty emotional."

"So besides faceless, what kind of people will we be meeting?" Claudia said into her compact mirror.

"Crime victims who find it hard to get through a holiday."

Especially Christmas Eve. I should be in Westchester right now. Sarah would be in the kitchen, whipping up everyone's sweet potato soufflé while I sipped my sherry and went about setting an elaborate table. How will I get through this night?!

"All members of this secret society?" Claudia asked, sounding uneasy.

I shrugged away my own uneasiness. "Kagan was vague about it."

"I'll bet," she sniffed.

"I appreciate your giving up a less... traditional Christmas Eve, Claudia. But please don't jump to any conclusions. I'm not joining anything."

"If you say so," she said doubtfully.

The cab pulled up before an innocuous brick building with frosted windows. By design? I wondered. You *literally* couldn't see what you were walking into. The two of us stood staring at a sign.

MEETING ROOM TWO FLIGHTS DOWN

Down we went. As we rounded a corner, Claudia gasped. "Lordy! There must be a couple hundred people here!" she marveled.

I took in the PTA-like atmosphere—understandable, given the occasion. The absence of Christmas decorations was a pleasant surprise.

"Some people are violating the dress code," Claudia groused as we made our way to a cloak room where a young woman took her jacket and my vest in exchange for numbers to retrieve them.

Kagan had cautioned us against wearing party attire. "Dark glasses and dark clothes are more appropriate, in keeping with the occasion," he'd told me. But Claudia was right. Maybe only three out of every five people had obliged.

Refreshments consisted of cookies and doughnuts. At a second counter, there were soft drinks, bottled water, coffee, and beer.

"I'll catch up with you later, Claudia," I said, and left her at the counter while I drifted off to eavesdrop.

"... been six years and I *still* can't buy a Christmas tree, let alone the trimmings."

"I haven't gotten rid of his clothes yet. I can't bear to even open the closet door..."

"It's the worst time of the year for my kids. Marianne used to make such a fuss over the whole Santa

Claus business."

"... insomnia. It's either that or the nightmares. All that blood!"

"If only she hadn't suffered. If only they hadn't shamed her that way..."

I had turned into a yellow caution signal—STOP, LOOK, LISTEN. I tuned in to tales of frustration and despair. Of stories that people were sharing with no inhibition. Strangers accosted strangers, but not with idle curiosity. What was palpable across the wide expanse of the room—a common bond—was empathy.

A Puerto Rican woman in dark glasses came up to me. She said, "I lost a son."

I took the snapshot she handed me. "So young," I murmured.

"Thirteen. He loved bicycles, my kid. Regular ones and motor scooters."

I studied the photograph. Inquisitive eyes. An impish grin.

"He spent every spare minute fooling with junk parts for one or the other," she told me. "Then they'd steal it, kids his own age—older, some of them. He died in the gutter, his chest heaving, gasping for breath. They shot my boy for a bicycle."

"I listened to my daughter die," I said, my voice as honest as hers. "I heard what was happening but I—I couldn't do a thing."

"Like a nightmare where you can't run," she said with a shudder.

It was easy to become the uninhibited stranger. To talk without reserve. To feel, afterward, a bleak relief. To realize, only after you'd started to turn away, that you were still holding a stranger's hand or she was holding yours.

"Learning anything?"

"That's the whole idea, isn't it? Where are *your* dark glasses, Kagan?"

"Some people don't need them. Either they're not among the 'committed'—family members, friends of a crime victim—or, like me, they have forgettable faces with no need to alter their appearance."

"Who said I was committed?" I shot back.

"Yes, of course. You fall into the category of fence-sitter. Care for a beer?"

"Coffee, please."

I studied him as he propelled me toward the beverage counter. His face really *was* forgettable. Not his figure, though. He was one long stretch of black in denim and open-necked shirt... the kind of sinuous shadow that lurks in nightmares.

"Care for a quick tour?" he asked. Without waiting for an answer, he held his beer in one hand and my elbow in the other as we did a slow circle around the room. He singled out individuals with a half-turn of his angular neck. A raised finger. An arched eyebrow.

"See that stout office cleaning woman—the one in the olive-drab scarf? Her teenaged daughter was stabbed to death for her lunch money. The tall guy with the dark glasses is a security guard. His kid—a son, not a daughter—was gang-raped. The man in blue pinstripe is a lawyer. A purse-snatcher shoved his wife in front of a subway train a year ago today."

"I get the idea," I said, burning my tongue on the coffee.

I noticed that Kagan hadn't even tasted his beer. "What's next?"

"I thought you'd never ask," he said. "Come with me."

I followed him into a back room, dark except for a spotlight over a narrow table and a cane-backed chair. Kagan held out the chair.

"I don't like melodrama," I snapped.

59

"You're a fence-sitter, Karen. Under the circumstances, it's better not to see faces. It's for our mutual protection."

He was right.

I sat down. With the light in my eyes, all I could see were shadowy forms.

What they let me *hear* was one eerie monotone after another...

"The aim of our organization is to avenge the unavenged."

"Victims Anonymous recruits people—victims of violent crime."

"We provide them with what no one else does in today's culture—moral support."

"Our motto—"

"Skip the ritual." Kagan's tone was impatient.

"We go after individuals who commit crimes—'savages', we call them."

"Our job is to re-educate the people who turn these savages loose. Permissives."

A woman's voice!

"We have preconditions for becoming a member of Victims Anonymous."

The door opened to a sliver of light.

"You don't belong in here, Miss Cole," Kagan said.

"Neither does Karen."

"Unless we can trust your discretion?"

Claudia saw through Kagan's ploy in a mini-second. "You mean because my ex-husband is a cop? I'm impressed with your snooping service, at least," she snapped.

The door slammed, thickening the silence.

Kagan's voice, when he resumed talking, sounded ominously loud.

"Still on the fence, Karen Newman?"

For a moment I felt as if I had fallen off. But I knew

better than to give in to my emotions. "I need time," I said as I replayed Jon Willard's warning.

Stay away from that guy, Karen. Do you hear me?

"A Mission-planning session is coming up," Kagan told me. "Care to sit in on it?"

"When?"

"In a few days. I'll let you know where."

"May I bring a male friend for moral support?"

"Suit yourself. But only if he waits outside. Party's over," he announced.

When Kagan and I emerged, Claudia was waiting for me.

"Let's go have that drink we both need," she said, just as a boy—very short, with dark curly hair and somber eyes—shifted into alert the minute he saw her. Claudia's eyes seemed to narrow in recognition. She whipped her dark glasses back on... but not before the boy shot her a cool look of appraisal. Claudia's limbs seemed to tighten and grow smaller, like a turtle pulling in its head.

What was *that* all about? I wondered.

"Meet Tony, one of our co-optees," Kagan said.

"We supposed to know what that means?" Claudia sniffed.

"It's a term borrowed from the Soviet KGB. Tony cooperates with us on certain assignments but he's not a member of the club."

He turned to me. "The photographs we planted in your briefcase—the ones you turned in to that ADA?" He let his voice drift.

"What about them?"

"It was Tony who risked his life to get them for us."

I had no words. The boy must have picked up on the gratitude in my face. He turned on a dime and ran from it.

Curious about Claudia's odd turtle-in-the-shell

reaction, I asked her where she had seen him before.

"Beats me," she said with an indifferent shrug. "What are you in the mood for besides good booze? Something cozy with patent-leather booths and not much spillover noise from the bar?"

"You know just the place, right?" I said, grinning.

She answered me with one of her tight smiles.

* * *

Claudia didn't get testy until the waitress left us alone with our drinks.

"This outfit of Kagan's," she said, swirling her Jim Beam, "it's bad news and you know it."

"Bad news for whom? If you're about to say it's illegal—"

"Karen, it's racist. You can't tell me these vigilantes don't go after a lot more blacks than whites."

"What's color got to do with anything?" I said, bewildered. "We're talking about robbers and rapists. Damn it, Claudia, we're in the middle of a—"

"Crime wave, I know."

She wasn't sipping her drink anymore. She damn near gulped it down. "I just can't turn it off."

"Turn *what* off?"

"The color of my skin. Can you guess how hard I prayed that Sarah's killer would be white? How relieved I was when it turned out that he was Hispanic? And no, it's not reverse racism, if that's what you're thinking. I'm black."

She said the word with a fierce mixture of anguish and pride. "Street crime automatically translates into 'black criminal' for a lot of people. Can you blame them? Given the crime statistics, *I* sure can't. But do you know how that makes me *feel*?"

"Not really," I said with a sigh. "I'm sorry if I seemed insensitive."

She reached for my hand. "You're the last one on my insensitivity meter, Whitey. But getting back to the business at hand—"

"I have to admit it's tempting," I confessed.

"You're seriously thinking about joining? Forget racist, Karen, it's illegal! Every cop I know takes a dim view of vigilantes, my ex included. Luke used to come home steaming."

"They're planning something. I just want to check it out. With Jamie," I added.

"So that he can maybe talk you out of it?"

"That's the idea," I told her, meaning it.

"Okay, I'll get off your case. Keep me informed?"

"You'll be the first to know," I promised.

"Drink up, Karen. It's past midnight."

Past Christmas Eve...

I couldn't help thinking that thanks to Victims Anonymous, I had gotten through the night.

CHAPTER 9

A CONVERTED BASEMENT-WAREHOUSE WITH A GARBAGE smell. I wondered what lurked inside. A gun club? A massage parlor? My hand hesitated over a rusty bell long enough for Jamie to sound a quiet alarm.

"You can still change your mind, Karen."

"Christmas Eve turned out to be harmless," I reminded him.

"Yes. But all this talk of a mission, of planning something... "

"That's why *you're* here."

I pressed the bell. A heavy wooden door opened a crack. "Film club?" I said, turning Kagan's code words into a timid question.

We were admitted into an anteroom where a little old man wearing red suspenders that held up baggy trousers put Jamie in his place with a "Wait here, bub!" and a gesture in the direction of a folding chair.

Jamie took out his newspaper and waved me away.

I found Kagan standing just on the other side of a pair of closed doors.

"Welcome to Porno Palace," he said, swinging a door wide to reveal a dark screening room. "Don't worry," he told me with a dry chuckle as he led me to a couple of rear seats. "There's no pornography on tonight's agenda. Just the same, what you're about to see is... well, obscene."

I stared at a giant screen as it began to flash bold headlines, followed by subtitles and a series of stark photographs.

YOUTHS MUG WIDOW!
Seventy-year-old woman opens door to a ruse

She had an ugly gash to show for it. The before-and-after photos zeroed in on a gold cross hanging from a chain that had been ripped off a neck as fragile as a dead branch...

MEDICAL STUDENT MURDERED!
Teens beat him to death with baseball bats after taking his wallet

RIFLE BARRAGE KILLS YOUNG MOTHER EN ROUTE TO SUPERMARKET!
Juvenile snipers free on bail.

More headlines swept by in a blur. More photographs.

GANG RAPE ON TENEMENT ROOF!

ARSON IN A TOKEN BOOTH!

I shot to my feet.
Kagan pulled me back down.
"One more, Karen. It's dramatized," he said in the tone of a man about to run the preview of a Hollywood movie.
The screen zeroed in on a disabled convertible. It was a quiet country road by a flowing river, the car filled with bags of groceries and a couple of rambunctious preschoolers. The woman behind the wheel was a curvaceous redhead who had "naïve" written all over

her face. Handsome young man with a crew cut, wearing corduroy jacket and tie, to the rescue? So the woman believed.

I jammed my eyes shut.

"Rape first," Kagan said in my ear, "then murder. He hit the woman over the head and drowned her in the river. After that, he drowned the children."

I was on my feet. Kagan's grip on my shoulder was part barrier, part support.

"Too many of these 'troubled youths' end up serving time in juvenile facilities. This guy was one of them. He was there for only two and a half years. He subsequently raped and murdered again."

"He got off free and clear?" I murmured, unable to make it real.

"Not for long. Thanks to the redhead's grieving husband, the father of her children," he said softly. "According to the obituary, *this* particular youth happened to die of natural causes. He drowned."

I saw people standing in the shadows but couldn't make out their faces.

"That," Kagan said with a wave in their direction, "is *your* SD Team—SD as in 'self-defense.' These teams are an integral part of our Mission planning. What you've seen, what you're about to hear, we call it Fueling. Sit down, Karen, and listen to a pro."

A man stood up, his face in shadow.

"The statistics on violent crime committed by males under twenty-five? Sixty percent. Our target group—the ones who broke the old lady's nose—were teenagers, ten to fifteen years old. They're the ones who murdered the medical student."

The voice was as matter-of-fact as a bookkeeper's.

"The ten-year-old got his first .45 automatic out of a store he broke into. He got his second from his thirteen-year-old brother, who had upgraded to a Magnum. The street price is a bargain—"

"If I had a buck for every punk with a three-hundred-dollar handgun he got for fifty, I'd be rich," Kagan drawled in my ear.

"—and crimes of this particular gang are random and pointlessly brutal. Typical of what's going down today."

"Punks!" someone yelled.

"Punks with oversize macho complexes," the voice continued. "Their leader pistol-whips grocers and liquor store clerks for the fun of it."

"This guy is beginning to sound like a retired cop," I whispered.

"You're half correct."

"Retired," I asked, "or—"

We were plunged into darkness again.

"These photographs," the police-voice went on, sounding like a cord pulled tight, "are less than a week old. They depict our targeted gang on a holiday crime spree."

One by one they flashed on the screen. A viciously beaten young man, blood spilling from his nostrils. A woman so old her face was like a finely stitched lace handkerchief—with a broken jaw. More broken bones and bloody heads. Then, "Profile of a gang leader," the police-voice continued as the pictures rolled on. "Chronic truant from grade one. Graduated from fistfights to purse-snatcher and cash-register sneak."

Not retired, I decided. This guy sounded like a cop reading from a rap sheet.

"—and by the age of eight, he'd taught his buddies how to steal. At ten he had his own gang. Life became a series of assaults, armed robberies, spending sprees, and a street rep that said 'Anyone hurts my feelings is dead meat.' Dozens of arrests after that, each one ending the same way. Send him back to mother. Mother lives well on her son's earnings. No complaints from *that* quarter. The juvenile court judges keep setting this hoodlum and his gang free—and God knows how many others like him. One of the worst offenders, the permissive who set in motion the carnage you saw just now, is Judge Arthur Younger, better known as—"

"Bleeding Heart Art!" I swung on Kagan.

"—released him right after seeing *these*."

Ghosts with denim legs.

I leapt to my feet.

"—free to rape and rob," the police-voice continued relentlessly. "Free to murder. Unless we stop them."

"Stop them! I want you to stop them!"

"Do you?" Kagan asked.

Had I said it out loud?

"This is *my* Mission, isn't it?" I whispered.

"Tomorrow night, seven o'clock. Are you with us?"

"I won't do it, Kagan. I can't."

He sat me down again and threw some photographs on the table—piles of them. My hand shook as I looked at one atrocity after another.

I closed my eyes for a moment and saw an old lady with a broken nose. A medical student robbed of his future. A young mother on her way back from the supermarket with her two children. Then I saw the sanctimonious face of Judge Arthur Younger.

I pushed the stills aside.

"Well?"

"No!" Then, "Yes. Oh God, I'm not sure... " I murmured, at war with myself.

"Last chance, Karen. Yes or no? If it's a 'no,' you'd better get used to living with these indelible memories. I'm thinking of the photographs of your daughter. You're welcome to keep them, of course, along with these photos. I'm not about to run out of disturbing images. Unfortunately, there are plenty more just like them."

I wanted to rip every photograph in two and toss the

pieces in Kagan's face.

I burst into tears, fumbling for a handkerchief in my bag.

Kagan sat there, waiting me out.

Eyes closed again, I saw what Kagan wanted me to see. Not just Sarah anymore. Not just the suicide of my son-in-law. I saw a cold-blooded killer who had to be stopped. I heard the words Kagan never tired of repeating...

What about all the other Sarahs?

I could help some of them. I could spare them the agony I had endured.

"I'll do it." It had come out a whisper.

Kagan was silent for a moment, as if waiting for me to change my mind.

"Better convince your boyfriend otherwise," he said finally.

"You've gone to a great deal of trouble to convince me," I said slowly—and caught the flicker of an emotion in his eyes. Annoyance? Resentment?

"I have, haven't I? Tell your friend that what you saw just now sickened you. Brought you back to your senses about having anything to do with Victims Anonymous."

How could it *not* sicken me?

"He'll believe you," Kagan reassured me. "Psychiatrists go for that bullshit."

Would Jamie?

"Tomorrow?" Kagan pressed.

"Tomorrow," I agreed—and caught myself wishing tomorrow would never come.

CHAPTER 10

I LEFT MY BUILDING AND SPOTTED Kagan's dark blue Oldsmobile just down the street.

"My own doorman didn't recognize me," I announced, pleased with Kagan's sloping half-smile as I slid in next to him.

I had made a gum-chewing march through the lobby in tight jeans, pea jacket, a dark wool watch cap over my new gamin haircut, and dark glasses.

"You could be Puerto Rican," Kagan said.

I thought of the Puerto Rican mother of a boy who'd been killed for his bicycle—the woman I'd met at the Christmas Eve "encounter."

"I used makeup," I told him. "I also happen to have Sephardic ancestors."

He started the engine, his eyes returning to the road—or, more precisely, to his rearview mirror.

"You must have spoiled the boyfriend's plans," he said.

Friend, not boyfriend—not that it's any of your business.

"What did you tell him?" Kagan pressed.

"That I was spending New Year's Eve with Claudia."

"What did you tell friend Claudia?"

"A couple of white lies."

"Good. We don't want curious boyfriends and girlfriends on our tail."

"That why you keep checking your rearview mirror?"

No answer.

"Where are we headed, Kagan?"

"A place you once called home.".

"... The South Bronx?"

He nodded. We drove in silence the rest of the way.

"Quite a change since you left thirty years ago," Kagan said.

"Quite a change since my parents moved here in the twenties," I admitted, staring at what was left of some once-sturdy brick and limestone buildings—the pre-war Art Deco apartment houses I'd grown up with.

He pulled over to the curb and we got out.

It took me a minute before I saw what he was up to. "I was born right over there," I said slowly, recognizing the building... or what was left of it. The door was still intact. I opened it and we went in. Was there a window that wasn't smashed? A door not gaping open? A sink or a tub that hadn't been ripped out, as if some mad dentist had been let loose on all that porcelain?

"Let's get out of here," I muttered.

Back in the car, I told Kagan that I'd spotted signs of occupants.

"Not for long," he told me. "The best way to rid a place of squatters is to set a fire. That brings firemen with axes. Once they're gone, a bunch of 'strippers' rush in, eager to pick clean derelict buildings like this one. What they're after mostly is metal—pipes, wires, fixtures. Pretty soon the druggies move in and turn what's left of the building into a crack house. Until the city shuts off the water. No more pipes. The ceilings go, then the walls—"

"I get the picture," I snapped, wondering why he liked me angry.

We drove past piles of debris. Empty lots. Emptier buildings.

Postwar East Berlin had come to the Bronx...

Kagan handed me an envelope. "My antidote to cold feet," he said.

A duplicate set of photographs! "Kagan, ·how did you—"

"Remember the Puerto Rican kid—Tony? He stole them for us."

"But who took the photographs? *Why* would anyone take them?"

"Pedro Luis Ortiz, alias Indio, is macho. Whenever he makes a big score, he wants mementos. Look at the photographs, Karen," he urged softly.

One last time, I promised myself. One by one...

Give in to rage, Jamie? That's like giving it a home, a place of refuge in your own body. Do you know how it tastes? Like bile. How it feels? Like blood pounding in your head, ready to burst.

"We're here," Kagan said, pulling over to the curb and we got out of the car.

I saw men wearing black and matching wraparound glasses. They looked fit and a little restless, as if eager to get on with the job. We followed the SD Team to a derelict building. Walked up six flights of stairs. Grouped outside a solid door, locked against intruders.

"Gang headquarters," Kagan announced.

One of the burly figures used a two-by-four to smash through the wooden door. Splinters flew. As the rest of the team moved around and past me, I was reduced to staring. I saw electricity from a rusting generator. An oil painting of the Manhattan skyline was hung on a crumbling wall. An Oriental rug in brilliant crimson lay over some cracked floorboards. I gaped at garment racks of clothing that looked expensive. Edging closer, I saw a couple of Saint Laurent suits. A velvet and sequined Oscar de la Renta gown. A stunning Bill Blass jacket—silk with purple and orange stripes.

And furs! Piles of them served as bedspreads for a

couple of sagging mattresses.

Broken furniture groaned with the weight of stereos. Television sets. All kinds of cameras. I spotted a Hasselblad. A gigantic Mitsubishi rear-projection job.

I peered into a peeling bathtub filled with gold and silver objects and coins right up to its dirty ring. I reached into the tub for a woman's gold chain. A man's Rolex watch. I dropped both items and backed away, wiping my hands on my slacks.

"Phase one," Kagan said behind me. "Attack and destroy."

I leaned against a wall and watched as the SD Team smashed—ripped—battered away. They were ruthlessly efficient. Cracks appeared on shattered TV screens. Someone sent a stack of circular silver trays and platters sailing through an open window. I picked up one of the platters that had fallen to the floor. It had an intricate basket-weave pattern—a smaller version of the one Sarah had filled with candied apples on Halloween...

It was like touching a hot stove. I hurled it out the window.

I headed for the pile of furs and stood staring at ermine and sable. A glut of mink. But the leather coat I reached for was trimmed and lined with reddish fur. The image of a bright-eyed creature smart enough to outwit hound, horse, and two-legged creatures in riding clothes only to end up as a coat made my mouth curl. I headed for the nearest window, the coat in hand.

Kagan stopped me. "That's not what we do with furs," he chided. "Start bagging the furs!" he called out loudly to the room at large.

He pointed out a safe almost out of sight behind a large pool table. "Phase two," he told me. "Reparations. Where possible, of course. Also expenses. Ours are considerable. The safe of a thief is a real jackpot. Cash, diamond rings—"

"So *that's* how you finance your operations!"

"Only partly."

I noticed a few crack pipes scattered across the floor. "Not just diamond rings," I said. "You people in the drug business too?"

"Only when it's easily convertible into hard cash. Care to stick around and see how much coke and angel dust Indio has stashed away?"

"No thanks."

"I didn't think so.

As we headed for the staircase, an SD guy asked Kagan how soon we'd be back.

"After phase three," he answered.

"With all that loot," I said, "you'd think Indio would've left someone behind to sound the alarm."

"He did. But his 'lookout' wasn't literally *inside* before we broke in just now. He'd have kept his eye on the entrance from a short distance away. He's probably alerting Indio from a nearby phone booth as we speak. Gangs like Indio's *have* to worry about being raided by rival gangs. It's what we want this to look like. Unfortunately, it will take Indio and his 'braves' a while to get back here," he said cheerfully.

"Back here from where?" I asked.

"The West Side of Manhattan, where the upper and middle class roam," he said in a tone that mimicked "where the deer and the buffalo roam."

"But *why*?"

"Indio's counting on a lot of people being all liquored up and careless. It's New Year's Eve, after all."

He started the engine and we drove off.

"Where are we going?"

"To the same general area."

"Upper Manhattan?"

"It's as good a place as any," he said.

"What are you up to, Kagan?" I said slowly.

"Just marking time so you won't be around until phase three is over."

"What's phase three?" I said cautiously.

"Trust me, you don't want to know. Nice area," he observed.

I looked around and had to agree. Not too many people on the street—too cold and windy. But you could hear music and the sounds of partying. I saw brownstones. Restaurants. Apartment houses. Most of the buildings were draped with cheerfully blinking holiday lights.

"How would Indio and his crew operate?" I asked. "I mean, no one is about to invite him and his gang to a party."

"They'll prowl the side streets. Not all of them are well lit. See for yourself."

He swung down a side street. Passed through another.

I saw a couple of Indio's brothers-in-spirit in thermal jackets and sneakers, their limbs moving with pointless energy. Even more unsettling was what I heard from time to time... the sound of wailing sirens, like a woman in a fit of hysterics.

Kagan glanced at his watch. "Time to go."

"You going to level with me about phase three?" I said irritably.

"Why not? Gang rape," he said cheerfully. "Happening even as we speak."

"Men raping men?" I gasped, unable to make it real. "My Self-Defense Team—"

"Is just standing by. As for the rapists, we leave that level of retaliation to hired studs we call C-Teams—all co-optees. All very well paid."

"How come you keep checking your rearview mirror, Kagan?"

"Jealous boyfriends make me nervous."

"Jamie's not the jealous type," I snapped.

"Is he the worrying type? That could be worse."

I turned away so Kagan wouldn't see what he had inadvertently touched off. Jamie, my self-appointed protector. Jamie, definitely the worrying type. Me worrying about Jamie worrying about me... .

Needlessly, as it turned out. We made it back without incident, let alone conversation.

This time I crept up the six flights, not wanting to hear what apparently was still going on. The unmistakable sounds of rage and pain.

"When the word goes out they were buggered, Indio and his punks can kiss their tough-guy image goodbye," Kagan observed. "After that—"

The sudden silence, followed by footsteps, was startling.

"The C-Team just left by the fire escape," Kagan told me.

I shuddered. "Going where?"

He shrugged. "Back to whatever gutter they crawled out of. It's time, Karen."

He took my hand as if he were about to lead me onto a dance floor, then handed me a small automatic.

I sat down on the top step like a recalcitrant child.

"We have preconditions." Kagan snapped. "The one that's inspired by the mafia is called 'making your bones.' "

It's called killing someone.

He resorted to the old ploy. "Sarah was stabbed to death. Her rapist-murderer is on the other side of this door."

"I can't go in there," I said hoarsely.

"First Judge Arthur Younger and now you. So Indio walks, free to kill someone else's daughter? He will, you know. He has before. Think your Sarah was the first?"

Desperately wanting her to be the last, I stood up.

"I've neglected to mention VA's informal motto," Kagan said with discernible relish. "Vengeance is ours."

I followed him into the room. There they stood, my elite Self-Defense Team. Men who hid their identity behind dark glasses and spoke only when necessary. My instincts are good, but I couldn't even sense a hint of emotion. No hate. No pleasure. No fear. They had a job to do—period.

Two of them held a big-chested, narrow-waisted boy-man with skin the color of wet sand and straight black hair that hung to his shoulders.

Two of them held Sarah's murderer.

Was there no justice? Where was the fear in those spaced-out black-marble eyes? What would it take to wipe the "fuck you" expression off his face? His arms were pinned back, red silk shirt ripped to the waist. Open to the garish hues of a tattoo—an Apache brave with a dripping knife in one upraised fist. What made me move closer was the way the tattoo moved. Too damn rhythmically...

My breath was coming in spurts, like blood pumping through an artery. "Murderer," I rasped. "You killed my daughter. I was on the phone. I heard—"

"You hear that, bitch? You get yourself a fuckin' earful?"

To hear the same voice, the same words—

My first impulse was to punch that slit of a mouth.

I stepped closer, pausing on the odd-shaped birthmark above his cheek. It was small, dark brown... something a child might have drawn to depict a single tear.

Indio's face receded as his earring came into focus.

Not an earring. A ring.

It was plain and wide. A sprinkle of diamonds winked at me. They kept winking as I yanked and tugged until I held the earring in the palm of my hand, my bloody hand, and I could hear Sarah howling. Why was she howling? I had her ring back!

I had torn it from his ear—the earring Indio had made of Sarah's wedding band. His earlobe hung like two pieces of limp macaroni and he was howling.

I noticed a knife on the table next to him. "Hold his hand down—his left hand," I told them, picking up the knife. "Not so tight. Spread the fingers. I want his ring finger, I want—"

A knot of flesh flew at me like a well-aimed baseball.

Someone caught his fist an inch from my face.

I dropped the knife and backed away, gagging.

"We got company," a voice warned.

"Karen, for the love of God!"

"Hold it right there."

I whirled in time to see Kagan's gun come whipping out, Jamie in his sights.

"Are you *crazy*?" I cried, flinging myself between them.

I clutched Jamie's arm. "What are you doing here?"

Jamie bent over me as a scowling Kagan put his gun on the flat arm of a nearby chair.

"You didn't sound right on the phone," Jamie said. "Neither did Claudia. The first New Year's Eve you two ever missed, she told me."

"So you rushed right over to your girlfriend's place in time to see her leave. You followed us," Kagan snapped. "We have business, Dr. Coyne." He took rough hold of Jamie's arm and eased him forward.

The S-D team surrounded Jamie as he inched his way into the room.

Something made me whirl around.

With his free hand, Indio had picked up the knife I'd dropped, ready to plunge it into the nearest person's back. Into Jamie!

I grabbed Kagan's gun and squeezed the trigger. I

squeezed it two more times.

Kagan took the gun away.

"Better get her out of here fast," I heard him tell Jamie. "We'll clean up."

My eyes cleared. "Clean what up?" I whispered.

Jamie grabbed hold of me, too late to block my view.

I stared at a prone figure in tight-fitting jeans and a silk shirt. At Pedro Luis Ortiz, alias Indio, one sand-brown arm outstretched, lying in blood as red as his shirt.

* * *

On the way to Jamie's place, I let him talk me out of giving myself up. I was *not* a killer. I had saved his life.

"Take a life to protect a life—that's a classic case of self-defense," he said over and over. "Look it up if you don't believe me."

I didn't have to. I knew in my heart of hearts that my guilt trip was unwarranted. That it really *was* self-defense.

"You're in shock," Jamie soothed. "Kagan will have Sarah's ring cleaned up. Shall I have it restored?"

"Please," I said gratefully. How long will it take Kagan to—"

I stared at him. "I don't remember telling you his name."

"You didn't, love. You called him a cowpoke vigilante."

"I don't understand."

He put a crystal glass in my hand and filled it to the brim with champagne.

"Time for a midnight toast," he said with a glance at the clock. He filled his own glass and raised it.

I looked into the brooding eyes of a stranger.

"Welcome to Victims Anonymous," Jamie said, banishing the stranger with one of his dazzling smiles.

"*Now* do you understand?"

I wanted to toss the champagne in his face.
I wanted to close my eyes and disappear.
I wanted to give him a medal, God help me!
We touched glasses and drank.

CHAPTER 11

"**N**ervous?" Jamie asked.

"Numb. You keep telling me that you people need my help. How?"

"Later," he said, putting me off again.

"I'd be less nervous if you'd give me a brief overview of your so-called inner circle before I meet them."

"I'll make it quick," he said, relenting. "You'll like Denzel Johnson. He's a working cop. You won't like Brian O'Neal—your typical hard-hat type. He owns a construction company. Chuck Polanski, a corrections officer, is a decent enough fellow. Timothy Hogan's a self-made businessman who heads his own accounting firm—used to, I should say. Our advertising executive is an ex-patient. Kagan you know. You do and you don't," he added with a crooked grin.

The doorbell rang. Jamie ushered everyone inside with a flourish.

A muscular black guy in jeans and navy wool jacket crossed the room with a no-nonsense stride. Denzel Johnson?

"Hi," he said casually, his eyes grave as he sized me up.

"Say something else," I told him. "I'm doing a comparison."

"To see if I was the voice you heard at your 'Fueling'? Damn right."

And proud of it!

I liked him immediately.

The businessman walked over and shook my hand. Everything about him was short and to the point, from his roughly five-foot-four-inch frame and carefully groomed salt-and-pepper beard to his introduction. "Timothy Hogan," he said. He wore a three-piece suit that had seen better days.

"Brian O'Neal," said a man with a blatantly perfunctory nod in my direction. He had "construction worker" written all over him—battering-ram bulk, cigars sticking out of his breast pocket, and a surly confidence that boasts of maleness. Definitely not my type.

Nor was the big fellow decked out in shoulder-to-toe black leather, as if he'd just slid off his trusty Harley. "Chuck Polanski," he said, sticking out his hand while I tried to keep my eyes off his silver belt buckle—a screaming eagle with talons extended. But he said "Welcome to the club" as if he meant it before sauntering off—a strutting package of virility.

Kagan came in and gave me an idle wave.

Missing: one advertising executive.

An animated Jamie, wearing a tailored blue open-neck shirt, his slacks a deeper blue, seated everyone at a round table of sturdy oak and served up cheddar-cheese-laden scrambled eggs and sautéed potatoes on gold-plated china. A long bread basket was full of fresh croissants, half plain, half chocolate-filled. As I watched him fill and refill coffee in crystal mugs, I was struck by his boyish eagerness to see to everyone's needs.

"So you're here," Kagan said to me.

"I'm still not sure why," I said.

"Jamie's idea. Which may or may not make sense."

Kagan's mouth flattened with obvious disapproval. "But before we get into that, tell us how you feel about what happened last week."

I took a few moments to think about my answer. "Uneasy," I admitted. "But grateful, too. When I needed help, Victims Anonymous jumped right in. Still, I can't help wondering whether I've lost my reason by agreeing to meet with you."

"Maybe you need to know why each of us is here," Timothy Hogan chimed in.

Kagan snapped him a make-it-brief glance.

"I had to close my business after over a dozen years in the same place," Hogan said, gray eyes clouding with the memory. "It wasn't bad judgment or competition that knocked me out of the box—hell, I'd have accepted that. It goes with the territory. But when some of your people start coming in late all the time, when others stop coming in at all—scared off by muggers—when some of them show up bleeding after trying to hold onto their wallet or their dignity..." He patted his silver-gray vest. "I'm here because *this* is what a businessman ought to be wearing to the office, not the bulletproof variety I was starting to get used to."

Denzel Johnson stretched out in his chair—but not in the manner of someone taking his ease. A man releasing tension. His wrestler's body didn't go with the face, and his face didn't match my preconceptions of a cop. Not with those ceaselessly questioning eyes and the perpetual frown of a scholar.

"I'm here," he said, "because I got tired of being half bureaucrat, half combat soldier. When the police spend more time filling out forms and cooling their heels in court than they do on the street—" He shrugged. "Don't get me wrong. I don't mind combat as long as I can trust the generals," he added with a tight smile. "But with this turn-'em-loose crowd... Let me put it this way. I can't do my job any more than Timothy could do his. Know what really gets to me? The old people. I can't look them in the eye. I can't stand to see the fear," he said, his smile twisting out of sight.

Polanski got to his feet. Everything about the man was dark, from his shirt and his black leather suit to his slick hair and hooded eyes. But there was something disarming about the grin that prompted me to grin back.

"Our prison system sucks," he said simply.

The door opened and an ethereal blonde beauty let herself in... with a key to Jamie's apartment in her hand, I noticed.

"Meet Lee Emerson, advertising executive," Jamie told me.

She breezed across the room, the slant of her skirt merging with the subtle movement of her hips. Her suit was so pale a beige that her skin flowed into it. Her ruffled blouse was as light and airy-looking as ocean foam. She had that soft clingy hair men want to touch, like the old-fashioned girl in shampoo commercials. Just when I'd decided that something about her whole floating look was oddly purposeful, not to mention unfair (I was dressed for the office in charcoal-gray severe), she extended a conciliatory hand. "Hello, Karen Newman."

I shook her hand, liking her smile.

So did Polanski, who practically fell all over himself to serve her breakfast. As she eased into the general conversation with an eager rush of words, I zeroed in on her eyes—the color of everyone's favorite afternoon sky.

"Have you told her?" she asked Jamie. "Has Karen agreed?"

But it was Kagan who picked up the ball. "Jamie thinks your PR expertise could be crucial to us," he told me. "The name of the game is recruitment."

"Wrong," Jamie bristled. "What we need is more visibility."

Locked horns. I could see that it was an old fight...

"Can't we have both?" asked Lee Emerson, playing the role of conciliator.

"A campaign to swell the ranks *and* mold public opinion.Why not?" Jamie mused. "It's time we took credit for the past three years. The public doesn't know we exist."

"Neither does the law," Denzel said pointedly.

"Visibility as an end in itself?" Kagan said. "A dangerous notion, Jamie."

"I don't get it," I interjected. "If you're talking about some kind of a PR campaign, you'll buy yourself a lot more than increased visibility. What happens to the 'anonymous' in Victims Anonymous?"

"Gone with the wind," said hard-hat O'Neal. He lit up a smelly Havana and eyed his bread plate. Jamie got there in time to whisk away the plate and make room for an ashtray.

"Is it time, then?" Denzel was leaning forward.

"I have a better question," Timothy Hogan said. "Is it suicide time?"

"Think what a popular image could do for your money-raising efforts, Tim. You keep telling me we're too dependent on my foundation grants," Jamie said cheerfully.

"We all knew we'd go public one day," Denzel said slowly, sounding as if he was picking his way across a minefield. "It was only a question of when." He looked to Jamie for confirmation.

"Maybe you're right," Kagan mused, his eyes making a slow survey around the table as if he were taking its pulse.

"It's time to take on this culture!" Polanski enthused.

Lee Emerson, looking as if she wanted to hug him, was up out of her chair. "We'll mobilize people!" she enthused.

"We'll start slowly," Kagan said, doling out each word,

his tone bringing caution back into the room. "It's time to focus on our priorities. I think we should ease up on recruitment efforts while we go after mass sympathy."

He swung on me. "Can you give it to us, Karen?"

Shocking that the question didn't shock...

"Your Sarah is avenged," he said, misreading my reaction.

"You don't have to nail me by my Jewish guilt," I said irritably. "I told you I was grateful." I looked around at the others. "I'm grateful to all of you, but I can't join your organization. I won't. Here's my offer," I said in a take-it-or-leave-it tone. "I'll use my best efforts to launch an advertising campaign on behalf of Victims Anonymous. In return, I want a guarantee up front—"

"That you'd be quits? You've got it," Kagan said, grasping what I hadn't even told Jamie yet. "I'm sure everyone in this room will sign off on your guarantee."

Denzel Johnson refilled my mug. "Before you decide, Karen, you should make it real—what you'd be doing for us, and why. I think I can safely say that none of us in this room feel shame or guilt. We're proud of what we're fighting for in spite of the way we've been forced to go about it. For now, at least," he added with a glance at Kagan, as if to underscore his words.

"What *are* you people fighting for?" I asked.

"Justice," Jamie answered fervently.

Kagan didn't hesitate. "Survival."

"Compassion for the people who need it most," Denzel said in the dark tone of a man who'd seen too little of it in his line of work.

"You're a policeman," I said, "yet you—"

"Operate outside the law? Only for as long as the law forces the police to act with one hand tied behind their collective backs. I want to help them function again. That's why I'm convinced that Victims Anonymous is only temporary."

"It will take time for our message to sink in," Jamie said, picking up the ball. "Once we have widespread support and Victims Anonymous becomes a force to be reckoned with, the politicians and the lawmakers will pay attention. Only then will we witness real change," he predicted. He squeezed my hand. "Karen, the day we all look forward to is the day we can stop being surrogate lawmen."

"Who needs vengeance once the criminal justice system starts dispensing justice?" Kagan asked, softly rhetorical.

"It's a terrible thing, force as the solution to anything," I said to no one in particular. To everyone in the room. "Yet I can't shake the feeling that what happened last week to my daughter's murderer was just. Okay, then, let's get down to business so I can cover a few preliminaries," I told them, feeling for the first time all morning that I wasn't Alice in Wonderland. "Question. What do you people mean by 'going public'? Leave your calling card at the scene? 'Victims Anonymous' in elegant Gothic lettering?"

Jamie smiled. "It *is* elegant, isn't it?"

Spoken like the proud designer of the card Kagan had slipped into my coat pocket.

"What we need now is a new calling card..." Jamie mused. "Something symbolic that the public can identify with."

Lee laid a proprietary hand on Jamie's arm. "What about a reckless Englishman who rescued French aristocrats from the guillotine?"

"The emblem Dumas used in *The Scarlet Pimpernel*... a small red flower. Not bad," he said. "Or the fleur-de-lis in *The Three Musketeers*—"

"How about Sabatini's consummate swashbuckler,

87

Scaramouch!" Lee's arms went out like a cheerleader.

Gleeful children, the two of them...

Jamie was fingering a medallion he always wore on a gold chain. It gave me an idea. "I'm thinking of a lovely creature that's been exploited by man's 'sporting instinct' for centuries," I said as the image of a leather-trimmed fur coat came back to me. "What if the target of a fox hunt were to turn the tables and hunt the hunter?"

Jamie pulled his medallion out for all to see, a slow smile softening his features.

I glanced at Kagan—according to Jamie, a reputed animal lover.

"The fox is clever, quick-witted. An animal that has learned how to outsmart man. I like it," Kagan said.

"To our new symbol," Jamie announced, his voice grave. "Karen, you have no idea how appropriate it is! We'll use the same stylized design—curved body, with the tip of the tail a hair's breadth from the head." He slipped medallion and chain back under his shirt.

Then he slipped his arm around my shoulders.

Bringing a look of resignation to Lee's lovely face and a look of interest to Kagan's.

I was about to shake Jamie's arm loose when O'Neal, of all people, raised his mug of coffee in the air and said, "Here's to one foxy lady!"

Kagan was looking at me with heightened alertness, almost as if he were sizing up an opponent. "Let's not get sidetracked by details," he said. "Karen asked us what it means to go public. Risk is what it means. New dangers. How do we keep the law from tracing us through the victims we avenge once our calling card—however disguised—is left behind? We could get away with it a couple of times. But as the incidents pile up, even the cops—no offense, Denzel—will grasp a pattern."

"No offense taken," Denzel said wrily.

"We can handle the locals," Kagan continued. "But I'd hate to have the FBI breathing down our necks until we're ready."

How could we ever be ready for *that*?! I tried to blot out the image of Max McCann.

Denzel must have picked up on my bleak expression.

"It wouldn't surprise me if people in the FBI were sympathetic," he told me. "I doubt that there's a man wearing a badge today who isn't as frustrated as we are."

"O'Neal?" Jamie pressed.

"Works for me," he said between mouthfuls of scrambled egg—his third helping.

Kagan scanned the faces around the table. "A fox is adept at keeping his pursuers off the scent. But getting back to the dangers, suppose we pull back in the beginning and only target Savages with no connection to VA membership?"

"We avenge perfect strangers?" Denzel said with a frown. "Yeah," he said slowly, his frown dissolving, "I see where you're going with this."

"Do the rest of you?" Kagan asked. "Even with a calling card, we won't be traced as long as we stay careful on the job. The cops know we're out there but they can't predict who, how, or where—not if there's no discernible pattern to our Missions. Then *gradually*, we go back to avenging members and—"

"Continue the mix as long as necessary!" Jamie's burst of enthusiasm was untainted by even the slightest hint of fear.

The buzz of conversation went on for another quarter of an hour.

As everyone finally got ready to leave, Denzel walked over. "We really do know what we're doing, Karen," he reassured me. "We've built a very impressive organization."

Kagan overheard. "Jamie wins the prize for sheer ingenuity, all right. Ask our leader about VA's structure."

"Jamie is your *leader*?" I said, stunned.

"I told you I didn't have the face for it."

I barely noticed when Lee Emerson, with a graceful shrug in my direction, dropped a key into Jamie's palm and made a dignified exit.

CHAPTER 12

JAMIE EYEBALLED HIS WATCH. "You'll be late for your meeting," he warned.

"My boss is getting used to it. Talk to me, Jamie."

"About my role in all this? Forget leaders. Victims Anonymous is only as good as its inner circle."

"Which *you* organized. Why didn't you tell me?"

"Modesty," he told me, looking immodest as hell. "It happened because..."

"Don't stop there."

He shrugged. "Because of something that happened to *me*. Afterward, I toyed with the idea of victims fighting back. But not alone, not isolated. Organized. I mapped out some strategy for over a year. Ran some tests. Then I met Kagan, who pushed me over the edge."

"Into what, exactly?"

"Missions like yours," he admitted. "But I have to admit they keep me in shape. I'm forced to practice my karate, lift weights, and go horseback riding in Central Park on a regular basis," he said with a grin.

"What else are you 'forced' to do?"

"Join committees."

"Like what?"

"Penal reform," he said, looking bored. "Victims' rights."

"Why?"

"Because those kinds of credentials buy me

foundation status with legitimate groups. It's where the bulk of our financing comes from, in case you were wondering."

"Kagan said VA raised money by selling off stolen merchandise. When you can't trace the original owner," I added as his eyebrows shot up in protest. "Reparations first."

"It's an ironclad rule. But the money left over is a drop in the bucket compared to what I get in grants. Every year or so I come up with a new anticrime program and give it a sexy title. Then I turn all the money over to Timothy Hogan, who funnels the bulk of it into Victims Anonymous."

"I gather Hogan keeps two sets of books."

"You *are* a foxy lady."

I pulled out a pad and made a few notes. "What do you people spend your money on besides Missions?"

"Travel expenses for our handpicked recruiting units. The start-up costs for each new local cell."

"You were teasing Hogan about his money-raising efforts. What's that all about?"

"My friend Timothy is a bit of a doomsayer. He worries about the grants drying up on us even as he continues to persuade a lot of well-heeled business contacts to make cash contributions. Men of conscience, he calls them."

"Don't tell me you're making these 'business contacts' privy to VA's crime-fighting activities!"

He laughed. "We're bold, love, not foolhardy. Every businessman-donor is under the impression that he's contributing to something civic-minded—like bulletproof vests for cops in patrol cars."

"How long has Victims Anonymous been in business?"

"Officially? Three years. Unofficially? Closer to five. It's all on tape. I'm compiling a record for posterity. I like to think out loud."

"I hope you're joking," I said. "All that data—"

"Won't fall into the wrong hands, don't worry. I've worked out an effective self-destruct system," he said cheerfully. "What else?"

"Kagan said to ask you about structure."

"It's cellular. It's also national in scope."

"How many cells are we talking about?"

"At last count? At least one in every major city in the country. In big crime centers like Cleveland, Chicago, Atlanta, Detroit—and our own New York, of course—we have as many as five or six. The basic idea is to keep every cell a self-motivated unit, but with guidelines from the top. That way, opening new cells across the country requires a minimum of effort. We don't tell the local cell leaders who to go after—or how. All they get are the three P's—principles, prototypes, and precautions."

"Four P's now," I said drily. "Propaganda."

"Is that what they call good PR in your business?" he teased.

"Tell me about Lee Emerson, ad exec and former patient."

"A frustrated romantic living in the wrong century. An aspiring novelist until I helped her realize she wanted to *be* a writer, not do a writer's work. After that, she got serious about advertising and turned herself into a superb businesswoman."

"End of doctor-patient relationship," I said. And waited...

"We'd been having an affair," he admitted. "But that's not why I brought her in. She came up with a good idea—so good we made her our administrative expert. Over O'Neal's male-chauvinist objections, of course. Chuck Polanski's, too, until he got a good look at her."

"He's still looking."

Jamie turned thoughtful. "Maybe now she'll start to notice."

"Now that you have your key back. I gather you want everyone to think we're having a torrid love affair?"

"Thanks for not giving me away. Despite my professional efforts, Lee is not without problems. We... She's not good for me."

Something in his face stopped me from asking why.

"*You'd* be good for me," he quipped. "Witty, wonderful, and wise."

"Not so wise," I said ruefully. "Not after what I just signed on to do. I feel something lurking in my stomach—a 'fear-ball,' I guess you could call it," I said, thinking of cats who get fur balls from licking loose hair.

He grinned. "I think you just coined a phrase."

"What *really* scares me is the prospect of investigative reporters, whistle-blowers—or worse, psychos—infiltrating your ranks. How does VA keep them out?"

"The same way an airline keeps would-be terrorists and skyjackers off its planes. We supply every cell leader with psychological profiles of people to watch out for."

"Smart. But not foolproof. Take whistle-blowers. Suppose someone who, with the best of intentions, signs on but later has a change of heart?"

"You worry too much," he said.

A little too abruptly, I thought.

He handed me a thick envelope, clearly eager to change the subject.

"Spare-time reading?" I asked.

"Profiles of some recent recruits. They're on a par with a Stephen King novel, they tell me. Any more questions?" he said as I got to my feet.

"Just one for now. That incident you alluded to about something that sparked Victims Anonymous.

You seem reluctant to talk about it. Why?"

"Because it's too painful," he admitted.

"Tell me about it," I pressed, sensing that he wanted to.

He looked away for a moment. "I was obsessed with the criminal mind—with the prospect of retraining it. So I read up on the literature. Here was the key that might unlock the problems of a society caving in on itself! I went after a new kind of patient," he said in the uneasy tone of a guilty confession. "Inmates of reform schools. Graduates of penal institutions. I paid them just to show up and kept tabs on as many of them as I could after office hours. Not very professional, I admit."

I'll say!

"Let's go downstairs," he said, and guided me to an elevator that took us two floors down to his office.

A tape recorder sat on his desk. He removed a tape from a desk drawer and placed it on the recorder, then waved me to a chair.

"*The culture is laced with antisocial amoral psychopaths.*"

The voice was unmistakably Jamie's.

"*Personality characteristics? Typically young and male. No conscience development. Manipulative and irresponsible. They reject authority and don't profit from experience. They live in a series of present moments with no sense of the future. Anyone standing in the way of their immediate gratification—a grocer defending his cash box, a woman holding onto her gold chain or her virginity—is expendable.*"

He stopped the tape, shot me a pointed look. "The hostile psychopath is a sub-category, Karen. You met him on New Year's Eve."

I killed him on New Year's Eve...

"I had a patient just like that. It wasn't long after one of our sessions that I decided to follow him, armed with a tape recorder and a miniature amplifier—instead of the licensed .45 I *should* have been carrying," he said, mouth tightening like the pull of a drawstring.

He sat back in his desk chair, his eyes hall closed. "He murdered a girl that night."

"You blame yourself? Jamie," I said gently, "you of all people should know better. "You're an excellent psychiatrist—"

"You're missing the point," he said flatly. "If I hadn't acted like a detached scientist engrossed in collecting valuable insights, I might have saved her. I'll never forget the girl's family after they learned what I'd done to their daughter's murderer. There I stood, their white knight. Their instrument of deliverance. The parents were Puerto Rican poor. What I gave them... Let's just say it was something they couldn't have afforded to buy."

"Empathy?" I asked. "Compassion?"

"Justice. I disemboweled the bastard."

I felt the color draining from my face.

Jamie began to unbutton his shirt.

"As soon as I heard the girl scream, I slid down from my 'Olympian' perch on a construction crane—not a well-thought-out plan, as it turned out. My patient recognized me as soon as I hit the ground—and lunged."

His shirt fell open to a six-inch scar across his stomach.

I could only stare as he slipped on another tape. Something in the set of his jaw made me want to clamp my hands over my ears.

"Sunday, the tenth. The Brooklyn waterfront in mid-November. Deserted. Cold. What is this guy after? He's nothing but a stick figure from up here. Find something lower, then. Get moving before you lose the twilight. A construction crane? Why not? Easy does it, now. Hand over... hand... over hand.. Test the rope. Perfect. My

psychopath is now a fleshed-out silhouette alongside his movin' groovin' buddy.

Why the arched necks?

Why the hell are they sniffing the air like predators sensing prey?Not at this late hour. Who'd be fool enough to—

Two of them. Two damn fools walking arm in arm, oblivious to the danger—

Sweet Jesus!

"Aheeeeeeeeeeeeeeeeeeeeeeeeeeeee!"

"The sound that launched Victims Anonymous," Jamie said, killing the tape. "The girl's parents gifted me with something their daughter was wearing on a chain the night that my patient stabbed her to death while his pal disposed of the girl's boyfriend."

He slipped something small, flat, and cold into my shaking hand.

It was a gold medallion in the shape of a fox.

CHAPTER 13

MY BOSS CAME IN WEARING a three-piece suit and looking more buttoned-down than usual. Larry was in ill humor.

Mine wasn't much better. I had been making "top priority" piles on my desk, and the lineup was depressing. A CEO whose speeches needed polishing—not to mention a few original ideas. An airline about to be plunged into a gargantuan labor dispute. A cosmetics manufacturer with a staid image "in dire need of a facelift," some joker had scrawled on a post-it note.

I was in dire need of a shot in the arm and a magic pill to keep my eyes from glazing over. If only I could work on one project at a time, like a problem child you could devote all your energies to.

"The Christmas holidays are long gone," Larry complained, albeit mildly. "Are you really all right?"

"I'm not up to one of your crack-of-dawn strategy sessions or last-minute travel orders, if that's what you're getting at," I snapped, "but I can still function. Sorry," I said as Larry placed a calming hand over mine. I gestured at the files piled on my desk. "I think I'm having a concentration problem."

"I think you need more time off."

The old refrain. My shoulders sagged. "How about a year or two to get my life back in shape?"

His eyebrows rose a good half-inch, letting me see the mournful look in his eyes.

He didn't say, *For God's sake, Karen, don't do this to me! I need you!* But work for someone long enough and you can read his mind.

"Make me a counteroffer," I joked, wondering if ten days and a modest raise might make me feel guilty enough to get the creative juices flowing again.

"Six months," he said, chewing on his horn-rims.

"Six months?" I stared at him. "A six-month leave of absence?"

He was up and pacing. "I don't know how I'll manage without you but, frankly, you look like hell. Take some time off, Karen. Meet some people. Fall in love."

I stared out the window. "Six months?" I repeated— and knew suddenly that that was *precisely* what I wanted. "Starting now?"

He faked a groan, my cue to say, "Don't worry, I'll clean off my desk before I leave. Thanks, Larry." We hugged, making it official.

I thought about the luxury of devoting all my energy in the next six months to a single mind-blowing project.

I also thought of a loose end. I hadn't seen Claudia since Christmas Eve. I didn't expect her blessing exactly, but I wanted her to understand.

* * *

"Why the disappearing act?" Claudia asked, leaning forward, her gold-loop earrings swinging. "Having a hot romance with the gorgeous Dr. James Coyne?"

"We're friends, not lovers," I said.

"He's part of it, isn't he?" Claudia asked. "His timing was too damn good," she said to the surprise in my face. "So he slick-talked you into joining?"

"If Jamie hadn't picked me up, so to speak, I'd still be flat on my face," I admitted.

"Don't you think I know that? It's why I can't dislike him."

"It's why I've come to depend on him."

"We never used to sidestep each other's questions."

"Then drink up and don't ask any more."

I reached for my bourbon but she seized my hand before it got there.

"Just one question, Karen. Why?"

How do I describe a scream in the night, like an overlay on my thoughts? Replay it often enough and it starts to merge with another scream in the night... Sarah's. How do I explain a phenomenon like Kagan, a man who never lets me forget that my Sarah was avenged, but what about all the other Sarahs?

I could tell Claudia only a small part of what I'd signed on for, so I settled on a clue she couldn't miss.

"This is the wrong time in my life for corporate image-polishing," I told her—and saw agreement in her eyes—partly because she had always held my job in mild contempt. "Our streets have turned into nightmare alley," I said. "How can I sit at a desk and write pep talks for top management or make creative contributions to some fat cat's profit-and-loss statement? Victims Anonymous wants to change things. As for my joining the organization, you happen to be wrong. I've taken a six-month leave of absence from Kemp & Carusone."

Her voice softened. "I understand, Karen, I really do. I didn't lose a daughter."

"That's why I can't condemn the people in Victims Anonymous," I told her. "Because I did."

PART III

COMMITMENT

*"The art of our necessities is strange,
That can make vile things precious."*

—Shakespeare, *King Lear*, Act III

CHAPTER 14

PUSHING ASIDE THE PAPERS ON my desk, I stretched and looked around at the ash-gray walls and mismatched furniture of my new office. I stole a glance at my new officemates. All women. A wide range of ages. And like me, a sweater-and-slacks crowd, from the middle-aged woman who peered back at me through pink-tinted oversize frames to an elderly lady in a red jumpsuit with rouged cheeks and powder-white skin.

I flashed the women a warm smile. Not one of them acknowledged it.

Pity. They were polite enough, but wary. I saw myself as a PR consultant with a job to do, but thanks to a thoughtless Lee Emerson they had tagged me as one of the elite.

I went back to the files on new VA recruits—the one Jamie had labeled his "horror file." A woman whose fiancé had second thoughts about marrying her after she'd been raped by two men, both of whom plea-bargained their way to short prison terms. A man who'd served time for voluntary manslaughter after firing in the dark at a burglar in his bedroom. A couple who were "smash and grab" victims—smash the display window of their coffee shop with a garbage can, grab the loot, and take off running. Then there were people I'd dubbed the "mad as hell" recruits. I reread one that, frankly, made *me* made as hell...

You know what the judge asked me before he tossed

my case out of court? Did I see the penetration. How, with the bastard's jacket over my face?

Lee Emerson swept in and pulled up an anemic-looking chair. The expensive cut of her clothes scored a double whammy, underscoring both our drab office landscape and my own typical way of dressing for work. Lee, a puff of raspberry chiffon at her throat, wore a burgundy leather pants suit that fit her like a coat of armor. I wore black corduroy pants and a baggy sweatshirt with CORNELL in faded red letters across the front.

"Got time for a quick briefing?" she asked.

"Actually, you're a relief," I told her. "After spending a couple of weeks immersed in Jamie's 'horror file' of new recruits, I'm ready to swing a bat at somebody."

She shrugged. "Why do you think it's called the horror file? Our calculating Jamie brings a psychiatrist's frame of reference to everything he touches."

"Jamie is an excellent psychiatrist," I countered. "Frankly, I think that's exactly what he *ought* to be doing."

She lost her smile. "Why don't I fill you in on the major differences between Passives and Actives," she suggested. "I'm the one who came up with the whole idea," she couldn't resist adding.

Lee's "good idea" that got her into the club's inner circle?

And it *was* good. When she was through, I couldn't resist teasing her a little, asking if the distinction between Actives and Passives wasn't just another way of saying moderates versus bat-swingers.

She shrugged. "Whatever. The point is, we Passives do the administrative work."

I pulled out a notepad. "Such as?"

"We keep records of every VA cell in the country, not to mention every member of every cell. We also keep tabs on Missions and local recruitment through a series of post office boxes—"

I must have frowned because she continued in a patronizing tone. "Not to worry. It's strictly one-way visibility."

"What else?" I said, annoyed at the way everyone kept urging me not to worry.

"We distribute crime statistics. Pull together data on potential targets—Permissives, mostly. They're the soft-on-crime people. The actual criminals we call Savages."

"Right," I said, not bothering to write it down. Sorely tempted to remind her that I had heard everything she was describing at that Christmas Eve "encounter."

"Say a local cell wants to publicize the sentencing habits of some criminal court judge," Lee continued. "Or how many times a bleeding-heart governor commuted a sentence or vetoed the death penalty. We provide the figures."

"Impressive," I said, meaning it. "You're the administrative head of all this?"

"General Lee Emerson, Chuck calls me."

Just when I thought that maybe I was being too hard on her, Lee added, with a casual wave at the women in the room, "My troops."

All of the women were within hearing distance.

"Any other military allusions I should be aware of?" I said coolly.

"Yes, as a matter of fact. R and R. Recruiting and revenging, Kagan calls it. That's Actives' territory. Nothing that concerns you."

Translation: Stick to your files until further orders, Private Newman.

Lee did a quick mirror-check. Blonde hair in place, quick ruffling of a chiffon scarf. "Well I'm off!" she announced.

I stared at two weeks' worth of Jamie's horror file and decided that I had had enough for one day. What I needed was something physical—a good workout. Maybe more than a good workout, I thought...

I didn't even bother to make my usual semi-neat piles. "Well, I'm off!" I said loftily to the room at large in mocking imitation of General Lee Emerson—and got smiles all around. Camaraderie at last!

* * *

The sign said **SAFETY IN SELF-DEFENSE.**

I had barely walked in the front door when she spotted me and came striding over—retired policewoman Angela Russo, Amazonian instructor of SIS.

"I like a person who doesn't quit," she smiled, clearly recognizing me from the one time I'd come here with Claudia. She looked down on me from her awesome height—close to six feet? The last time she'd looked down on me, I'd been scared off by a punching bag.

I said, "I like a person who likes a person—"

She laughed, a deep, rich sound. "My favorite Sydney Greenstreet line of dialogue in one of my favorite flicks. What's your pleasure?"

Anyone who liked *The Maltese Falcon* was my kind of person. This was going to be easier than I thought.

"How about some instruction on what I wasn't paying much attention to the last time I was here—your basic strikes, kicks, and escapes?" I said.

"You got it. This way..."

"I don't expect you to remember my name. It's Karen. Karen Newman."

She said what I hoped she'd say.

"Call me Angela."

Angela Russo proved to be a darn good teacher—and this time I was a good pupil.

"You're a quick study. Don't be afraid to admit that

you're enjoying yourself," she told me, and went off to help someone else.

I'm not here for enjoyment, Angela Russo. I'm here to pick your brain.

I wandered over to the "heavy bags" and got in line, wondering what it would feel like to punch away. It felt good. More than good. I wondered how long you could keep punching before your hands got tired or your fists came undone but they didn't, they couldn't, they had a will of their own—

"Next, please!" A voice of impatience broke the spell.

I started to walk away, my leotard clinging to my body like a damp bathing suit.

"You've really got it down pat," said another woman in line.

"What, the punching bag?"

She shot me a puzzled look. "No, I was talking about the yell of the spirit."

I hadn't been aware that I'd opened my mouth, let alone yelled out loud.

Embarrassed, I relinquished my place in line and looked around.

Angela Russo was staring at me.

She accepted my invitation to lunch, choosing a coffee shop just down the street. I almost wished she hadn't. She'd been puffing away on a thin cigar—cigarillo?—through ten minutes of warm-up talk and emitting smoke like a faulty chimney, but with such obvious enjoyment that I hadn't the heart to object. She was big and easy in her gestures, a Mother Earth type with dark brown eyes, shoulder-length hair, and the wholesome good looks that inspire trust in men and admiration without envy in women.

I steered her in the direction I wanted to go.

"The self-defense business? It's booming," she told me. "If you turn to the Manhattan yellow pages, you'll see for yourself."

"I guess. But is it profitable?"

"It can be," she said, looking chagrined. "If you're not a sucker for hard-luck stories, that is. A lot of my clientele consists of single mothers from lousy neighborhoods with two-plus kids to support."

"Turning the fainthearted into street warriors must be very satisfying," I told her. "It's a way to fight back. Tell me more about your clients and how they—"

"Fight whom?"

"Fight *what* is more to the point," I said casually. "The crime wave. The breakdown in our criminal justice system."

"Interesting..." She extinguished her cigarillo and wiped a bit of ash from the front of her rust-colored sweater. "The first time you came here, the friend who brought you took me aside. She wanted to explain why you froze up that day. She told me how your daughter had been murdered by a street gang. They ever catch them?"

"The police?" I said, caught short. "No, I— They told me she'd been killed by some rival gang," I lied.

"Ever heard of a guy named Denzel Johnson?"

I didn't trust my voice.

"So it's still going on... " she mused. "Are you one of them, Karen?"

Just a fellow traveler, I wanted to say. What I said sounded pretty lame. "I don't know what you're talking about."

"Let me put it this way. Two months ago you couldn't stomach the idea of self-defense. Today you make mincemeat out of one of my heavy bags, after which you outdo over half the women here with your cry of the spirit. What happened between now and then? Are we going to play games or are you going to tell me why you really asked me to lunch?"

"So I had an ulterior motive," I admitted. "But who the hell is Denzel—"

"Playing games. Okay, Denzel Johnson's a cop, an old friend. He tried to recruit me once. He had a lot to say about violent crime and fighting back and how the criminal justice system was breaking down. Sound familiar?" She grinned. "You here to recruit me, Karen?"

"No, but you're warm," I said, matching her grin. "I'm here to pick your brain. Self-defense is big business, you said. I was hoping you could fill me in on a lot of details that would impress a friend of mine."

"Because self-defense courses are breeding grounds for new recruits? Hell, half my students are fighting mad and the other half are mad at how scared they are."

"Let's clear the air about one thing," I told her. "No one sent me and I am *not* one of them. I'm helping them out with something for a limited period of time."

She looked at me with narrowed eyes before lighting up another of her cigarillos. "I chose not to 'help out' a couple of years ago," she said. "It was a few months after I'd left the force. My buddy Denzel thought I'd be ripe for the picking, but he'd miscalculated. I handed in my badge for two reasons. Denzel knew the first."

"Which was?"

"The only man I've ever loved had just been shot to death."

The more matter-of-fact the tone, the more frightening the words!

Angela let them sink in before telling me the second reason.

"When you hand in your badge, your gun goes with it," she said. "I knew my gun had to go. I was so raw inside that I was ready to shoot the first druggie who looked at me cross-eyed. What if I'd managed to track down the one who'd shot Joe?"

"He got away? You weren't able to find him?"

"I didn't even try."

"But how—"

"The 'how' is a Technicolor picture in my head. Everybody who knew Joe was in shock. I mean, the guy had a sixth sense the way a Geiger counter picks up radiation—a liquor store around the corner, a fire escape two stories up. Every cop he'd ever partnered with—and I was one—never lost any sleep being on the job with an 'active' cop because Joe didn't just watch his own back. He also watched yours."

My brows had shot up at the words "active cop."

She said, "That's police parlance for the cops who volunteer for the toughest calls. The guy who knocks his precinct's arrest statistics out of the park by making more collars in a month than most cops make over a much longer span of time. That was Joe. Denzel, too. They were a team once. What killed Joe was his uniform."

Her eyes turned inward to that Technicolor picture. "Some trigger-happy punk, high on drugs, was waving a gun under a pharmacist's nose and looking for more to feed his habit. Joe had been in a deli just down the street picking up a tuna fish sandwich and a Coke. He was half in, half out of his patrol car just as the druggie burst out of the pharmacy waving his piece. The druggie saw 'cop' and shot him in the back." Angela sucked in her breath. "Lucky for me he was never identified."

"I don't blame Denzel for trying to recruit you," I said, tight-lipped. "Maybe he ought to try again."

She tilted her head, considering it. "You may not have had recruitment in mind, but your timing is a lot better than his. Who am I kidding? Helping people defend themselves is a drop in the bucket. You hear things, doing what I do. You see the scars—and not just the physical ones. Guess you know what I'm talking about," she said with such sympathy in those narrowed eyes that it brought tears to mine. "I'm getting to be as frustrated as the man in the street," she admitted. "When sixty percent of the six million emergency calls in this city are too 'low priority' for cops to respond to—"

"But doesn't 'low priority' mean petty stuff?"

"You tell me. 'Petty' stuff like burglaries in progress? Thefts under five grand where your only recourse is to notify the insurance company and grease your windowsills?"

The waitress came by with a check. Angela grabbed it. "So you owe me," she said. "I like making important decisions from a position of strength. How's lunch next Monday at the bar two doors down? Your treat."

We sealed the bargain with a handshake.

CHAPTER 15

I SHOWED UP EARLY, SNAGGED A corner booth, and sat down on the "bad" side where the seat was spilling its white stuffing... as if someone had slit the cherry-red vinyl with a razor blade.

They came inside together. I can't say I was surprised.

"Who invited me to the party, right?" Denzel grinned.

He slid in opposite me, made room for Angela, and plopped a notebook on the table.

"Guilty as charged," Angela said, lighting up one of her cigarillos.

"Congratulations, Karen," Denzel said. "My failure is your success."

"How to succeed in recruitment without really trying," I quipped, feeling lightheaded about what I had inadvertently pulled off. The three of us pumped hands. Denzel ordered beer all around, along with our sandwiches.

"Angie, Angie," he said, turning those grave eyes on her. "Do you know what a hole you've left in my life? In the lives of all the guys in our precinct? How are you doing?"

She shrugged. "Getting by. Keeping busy." She touched his cheek. "And you?"

"Same as you, keeping busy. Still on the force. Divorced and lonely, in case you hadn't heard. Ellie got tired of being a cop's wife and married an engineer who's home every night for dinner," he said, eyes solemn with pain. "I see my two boys on weekends, holidays, summertime..."

I tuned out, feeling like a Peeping Tom as their fingers touched and their voices fell into soft reminiscence.

But I saw him too, the man they had both loved— Joe, half in, half out of a patrol car with a tuna fish sandwich in his hand.

Denzel looked up. "I had a gut feeling about you, Karen. When Angie and I talked on the phone last night, she filled me in on your discussion about self-defense clientele being ripe for recruitment in Victims Anonymous. Very astute of you."

"Denzel is a variation of the hero worshipper," Angela said. "He worships brains,"

I grinned. "In that case, let me run a few more ideas past you. Ever notice that with every article about a really brutal crime, outraged citizens surface like swimmers who've been holding their breath too long and express their outrage in letters to the editor?"

"I'll say!" Angela interjected. "Anyone happen to catch *The Wall Street Journal*'s editorial page on the latest stabbings in Central Park about a month ago? Someone penned an irate letter to the editor complaining about the standard bureaucratic 'don't scream, don't resist' advice. 'Appeasement,' the letter writer called it."

"No question about it..." Denzel mused. "People like that are ripe for recruiting. Easy enough for Lee Emerson's Passives to track them down." He scribbled a reminder in his notepad and looked up at me again. "Don't stop now."

"Citizen crime patrols," I said. "They're sprouting like weeds in a vacant lot. But for various reasons, a large percentage of such patrols fall apart and—"

"People angry enough to have organized in the first place are ripe for recruitment!" Denzel made another note.

I sat back for a moment. "Before my leave of absence from Kemp & Carusone, I happened to run across some interesting figures. Guess what one of America's newest growth industries is. Denzel?"

"Don't have a clue."

"Bulletproof vests?" Angela said.

"No cigar—pun intended. Burglar-alarm companies. There are thousands of them all across the country."

Denzel wrote another entry in his trusty notepad.

As soon as a waitress appeared with the sandwiches and beer, he raised his mug. "I wish it were champagne, ladies. Welcome aboard, both of you."

I had to force myself not to tell him that I wasn't "aboard" anything. That I had just taken a six-month leave of absence from Kemp & Carusone—more than enough time for someone with my experience to launch this or any other PR campaign.

Angela must have sensed my discomfort. Steering the conversation onto safer ground, she said, "Tell Karen exactly what pushed you into joining Victims Anonymous."

"Frustration." He pushed his beer away. His tone said, I don't want to talk about it.

"It had to do with a case that cost Denzel six months of meticulous police work—mostly false leads and dead ends," Angela said. "He put in so much overtime that the guys at the precinct had him pegged for a distant relative of the deceased."

Denzel sighed. "Picture a man who grew up to the Harlem night sounds of a different era—Duke Ellington, Cab Calloway, Billy Eckstein, the Apollo Theater," he said slowly in a voice so low you knew the pictures were already there for him. "No education, this dude. Just a man with a passion who had saved every nickel he and his family could spare until he had enough to buy a club. Nothing fancy. Just a small place with an intimate feel to it, top-drawer acoustics, and the best talent he could afford for a Harlem that had lost track of its musical heritage."

He paused, as if to gather the strength to continue.

"Picture the grand opening. Good music, good friends, champagne toasts, and a *'Pinch me, I'm dreaming!'* look in his eyes as he sits through his first Saturday night jam session—a huge success, according to the cash register receipts. Now picture—"

He took his beer back. Drank it without seeing us.

"The only picture I'm left with," he said, wiping his mouth with the back of his hand, "is what the poor guy looked like later after a couple of slugs sliced through his chest."

"He put up a big fight for the money," I whispered.

"Not even a small one. They killed him for sport. They *felt* like blowing him away."

Angela mashed out her cigarillo.

"I couldn't let go of it even after everyone else did," Denzel said bleakly. "I found his killers eventually. Saw them convicted of second-degree murder and first-degree robbery. Only it didn't stick. An appeals court ordered a new trial because a detective with a hot tip and no time or good sense to get a warrant beat me to the murder weapon that was stashed in their car."

"The DA's office 'lost' its key witnesses before a new trial date could be set." Angela bit off the words.

"They had to let them go," Denzel said grimly. "I didn't."

I opened my mouth—and clamped it shut again.

"We have company," Angela said softly.

I looked up to see a somber little face ringed with dark curls even as I heard Kagan's insinuating voice...

Those photographs we planted in your briefcase? Tony risked his life to get them.

What was a child doing even on the fringes of this

EYE FOR AN EYE

deadly business?

Denzel introduced us as the boy edged closer. "Tony Montes, meet Karen Newman," he said, beaming. "You've been waiting outside all this time, Tony?" he frowned.

A shrug. "Yeah, but I got cold."

"How'd you know where to find me, pardner? I never—"

"I followed you right from the precinct."

"That's not possible," Denzel said in slow disbelief. "How on earth did you keep up?"

"Chuck Polanski gave me cab fare but I changed for a Broadway bus. It's easier to see a patrol car from a bus." Tony grinned. "I saved money on the cab."

"He's some piece of work, isn't he, Angie? A word of advice, my young friend," Denzel told him, warmth in his smile. "Next time, get the cabbie to light up his off-duty sign in case the guy you're following looks back. Got a message for me?"

"Chuck says to please call him," Tony said, eyeing the remnants of Denzel's roast beef on rye.

"Hungry?" I asked him, moving over to make room.

But Denzel, all business now, had already signaled our waiter for the check.

The boy took the hint and turned away. I saw that he was wearing one of those garish iron-on decals across the back of his denim jacket... a flame-colored bushy-tailed fox.

"For God's sake," I said as soon as Tony was out of hearing, "That boy is how old?"

"I'm not sure. Older than he looks," Denzel said. "About thirteen by now. But you're right. Tony is too damn young for Victims Anonymous. And if you're thinking of blaming me," he added as if he had a sudden case of lockjaw, "don't. Sometimes our mutual friend shows an appalling lack of judgment."

"Jamie?"

"Sorry," Denzel said to the dismay in my face. "Your reaction was appropriate. Mine was defensive. I worry about that kid. I don't know for certain how old Tony is but I'm guessing he's roughly the same age as my youngest."

"Thirteen..." I shook my head. "Appalling is right."

"A man who makes the kind of judgment that brought *you* into the fold is entitled to an occasional lapse—hell, maybe a dozen," Denzel said with a wry grin. "We still friends?"

I grinned back. "Right from the start, Denzel, and you know it."

CHAPTER 16

I COULD BARELY KEEP MY EYES open. For the past two months, I had been putting in longer hours for a single client than when I was working on half a dozen Kemp & Carusone clients at once.

A PR person's biggest problem, my boss Larry liked to say, is a client who doesn't know how to sell himself to the public. I glanced over my paper-strewn desk. Unfortunately, Victims Anonymous was such a client.

"Last one to leave turns out the lights," one of the women called out in a singsong voice, but with a sympathetic smile in my direction as she walked out the door—headed, no doubt, for a hot dinner. Mine had come out of a paper bag over three hours ago.

I reached for a cigarette. Only two left in the pack? Lighting up, I consoled myself with the knowledge that my campaign was in the homestretch.

You can't "sell" a client without getting to know that client inside and out. Or, as Larry liked to say, "Probe, probe, probe." But probing the affairs of a secret organization was a brand new experience—like interviewing monks who'd taken a vow of silence.

Some things were obvious, of course. Victims Anonymous was rife with symbolism and cue words. The enemy was a "Savage," the bleeding-heart judge who set him loose on the public a "Permissive." There were "Actives" and "Passives." "Fueling" and "Missions." "The symbolism business is designed for mass appeal—a variety of IQs," Jamie had told me once, sounding a touch defensive.

Tired of getting double-talk about how big Victims Anonymous was, I had badgered Jamie until he had finally relented with a ballpark figure.

"At last count? Let's just say we've passed the five-hundred mark."

I consulted my list of the hundred most populated—correction, most crime-ridden—cities in America, from New York to Chicago. Victims Anonymous had over four hundred operating cells, with maybe another fifty to a hundred scattered throughout less-populated towns. My campaign, Jamie had predicted, would "send those figures through the roof."

Not bloody likely. My expertise doesn't consist of just research and writing. Ideally, I should be meeting with some company executives to take their measure and pick their brains. But VA's "executives" were a complex mix. Hundreds of faceless cell leaders—the angry and the frustrated—looked to their parent organization in New York for direction and guidance. They were all waiting, now, for mine.

I scanned the papers on my desk. It was all such garden-variety Kemp & Carusone material. I mean, if this were a PR campaign for one of my clients—say, a drug company with a new cough medicine—the first rule of thumb would be to educate the public by getting the client's message across. "Our cough medicine kills congestion and tastes good."

But VA's "consumers" were victims of violent crime—past, present, and future. And as for educating the public, what was I supposed zero in on? That our Missions sweep muggers and murderers off the streets? That this is good for the collective soul of America?

Not so easy to get *that* message across!

When one of Jamie's recruiters had asked me if I

was intending to "plant stories" in newspapers, I told him crossly, "You plant flowers. If you want to educate the media, you write a series of 'pitches' about what you're selling."

A media campaign should correct false impressions, I'd told Jamie during one of our heated discussions. "Try *this* on for size. Victims Anonymous is temporary—a stopgap until people demand the kind of criminal justice system they deserve. Maybe you do a position paper. It's longer than a pitch. The idea is to throw in anything that might improve your image. Want to know the best argument Victims Anonymous has going for it, Jamie? Best because it has the added benefit of being true? VA's *moral* stance."

I hefted a thirty-two-page document in my hand—a "position paper" that was chock-full of moral stances and fortified by a brief bloody history of what had gone wrong on our city streets. I had started with our popular ultra-liberal mayor of New York, Ed Koch, then segued into a dramatic trial involving Bernhard Goetz. A trial about which I had a lot of insider information, courtesy of my friend Jon Willard, associate for Goetz's lawyer, Barry Slotnick. Current events like the Goetz trial couldn't help but galvanize victims of violent crime to want to fight back.

Best of all—at least from *my* perspective—was that I knew where the first stage of my PR campaign should start. With the personification of injustice... the Family Court system.

I turned my attention to heavy research. I had designed it for VA volunteers, along with instructions to leave copies behind for the press, as well as for any members of the public likely to be interested in Victims Anonymous or just curious about what we had to say. My research was loaded with crime statistics. How countless people were murdered on American streets or—courtesy of a National Crime Survey—the sobering statistic that more than half of all violent crimes were never even reported to the police.

I pushed the report aside, lit up my last cigarette, and followed the drift of smoke in an empty gray room that had gone cold on me. I was thinking about the most intriguing challenge—at least for me—of a public relations campaign. I had always enjoyed burnishing the image of a company that was bucking a trend. But people who take the law into their own hands were bucking much more than a trend. They were bent on uprooting an entire system. And the word "vigilante" was about as bad an image as one could get.

Still, one category of people was really hurting. It was why I had come up with yet another symbol for Victims Anonymous. Why I'd written flyers to be delivered by Actives in every state. The flyers were devoted to a specific class of people I called the Vulnerables. The elderly, fear-chained to their apartments. Neighborhoods of demoralized black citizens, hardest hit by the crime wave. Women all across the country, frightened enough to sign up for self-defense courses and hand-gun training.

I was buttoning my coat when I felt it wash over me—the uneasy sense of something important left undone. Undone, I realized, because it would have been foolhardy to do such commonplace things as schedule briefings with the top editors of prestigious newspapers and magazines so I could stuff their files full of whatever I wanted them to know about what I was selling. A poor substitute, my "advice letter." It was full of helpful tips to the leader of every VA cell. "Research the editorial policy of your local papers," I had written. "Know your individual reporters. Vary your pitch for maximum effect. Horror stories are more likely to persuade the soft-on-crime types than a columnist already sympathetic to the victims of violent crime. Deliver one basic message at a time—much more impact that way. And never forget that your top-priority goal is to educate. To raise the consciousness of the man in the street."

I flipped off the lights. But even in the dark I retained an image of what lay on my desk—and shuddered at that morass of facts and figures. At two months of immersion in a sewer.

Too many sordid crimes. Too much human suffering.

Karen Newman, corporate public relations expert, had violated a cardinal rule of her profession. No personal stake in the client's affairs. It was okay to let your client know you cared but I had gone beyond that— way beyond. In my campaign to raise the consciousness of the man in the street, I had succeeded in raising my own.

CHAPTER 17

I FELT ODD IN MY OLD office, wearing jeans as I sat behind an uncluttered desk—a broad expanse of gleaming French walnut. For most of my working life at Kemp & Carusone, my desk had been buried under mounds of paper and yellow legal pads.

I felt odd listening to Larry make small talk.

"Thanks for coming in, Karen," he said with a warm smile and a surreptitious glance at his watch. "Very sharp, your insights on the Jeff Warren matter." He straightened his tie, which wasn't the least bit crooked.

It occurred to me that the Jeff Warren matter could just as easily have been handled on the telephone. Why hadn't it occurred to Larry?

I smiled back. "You've been missing me."

"Yeah, I have. Don't be a stranger, okay?" He squeezed my hand and left the office.

I stood up and took a slow look around. Only two months into my six-month leave and already I felt alienated from the old life. From old friends. From myself, most of all.

On my way out I thanked my secretary for keeping the desk neat and dusted. "See you in four months," I told her.

"It's drizzling out," Colleen said. "Better take an umbrella."

"I like my hands free," I shot back, only half-kidding.

My spirits sank with the elevator, jammed at the

moment with the five o'clock crowd. Even the lobby struck me as one more old friend I had lost touch with.

It was the last place I'd have expected to run into an old adversary. There stood Max McCann in his FBI "uniform"—neat dark suit, belted raincoat, and one of his garish ties that barely peeked out from under the raincoat. It was obvious that he was waiting for someone, but his faux smile the minute he spotted me gave him away. I replayed Larry's voice the day he had signed off on my leave of absence. "Take some time off, Karen. Meet some people. Fall in love." Larry, calling me in today for some patently unnecessary "insights" on the Jeff Warren matter before breaking it off in time for me to meet up with his old friend McCann.

Larry, you matchmaking SOB!

"Hello," McCann said.

Not "Fancy running into you like this..."

"Larry told me about your leave of absence. I was concerned."

"Nice of you. Nice of Larry," I said drily, letting my annoyance show. "Now what?"

"Dinner?" he asked, looking crestfallen but sounding hopeful.

"What if I said I wasn't hungry?"

"You could watch me eat. I'm hungry as a mountain lion."

I zeroed in on his garish tie—that bright shade of orange that Irish haters wear on Saint Patrick's Day.

"Beats taking potshots at tree trunks, I suppose."

He laughed and offered me his arm.

As we headed out of the building, he asked about the six-month leave of absence I'd taken two months ago. How was it going? What was I doing with my time?

I wasn't about to start spending it with an FBI agent!

Which is why I suggested that we stop off first at my place while I changed out of my sweater and jeans.

"Fix yourself a drink while I change, McCann," I told him. Then, in the tone of an afterthought: "Mind hanging your raincoat in the hall closet so it won't drip on the floor?"

My devious plan had gone like clockwork. I caught his expression in a mirror as I headed for the bedroom to change. His hand had stalled in midair as he reached for a hanger in the closet, his mouth tightening at the sight of another man's charcoal-gray slacks and cashmere jacket...

What he was looking at was Jamie's comfortable change of clothes for the work-filled evenings we had been spending together lately.

I had intended to slip into a black suit—simple, severe, a little on the dull side—but my hand reached instead for a lavender dress I hadn't worn in years... a fuller softer look with sleeves that spread like wings.

Funny how clothes can set the mood. I practically floated into the living room and over to my breathtaking twilight view of the park—a hard glitter of lights softened by the pale silver-blue splash of a lake.

McCann wasn't taking in the view. He was engrossed in my bookshelves. He turned at my entrance.

"I've never thought of you in that color," he said.

"Find any interesting books?" I asked, the polite hostess.

He reached for a well-thumbed volume of Swinburne. "My favorite poet," he told me. "Yours too?"

"From the moment we met in a college library." I sighed inwardly. Swinburne and "sensuous" went hand in hand. Not what I'd had in mind for *this* dinner date. I figured that he'd follow my lead and take an easy chair while he finished his drink. Instead, he walked slowly around my living room, replying to my small talk in his typical monosyllabic style, but... touching things. The ultrasuede cushions of the couch. The texture of brocade drapes.

He was helping me on with my coat when he reached out to touch Jamie's jacket.

"I envy him," he said, voice as soft as the cashmere.

Making me ashamed of my male-in-residence ploy.

Outside, I took him on a detour—an alley where I feed neighborhood cats—mostly strays from the look of them. I emptied my ample pockets of People Crackers.

We were in a taxicab when Max wondered aloud why I didn't have cats of my own.

"The last two died on me, one right after the other. I don't want any more animals to break my heart over," I said, sounding defensive even to my own ears. "I just lost my daughter and then my son-in-law one right after the other so I'll do my loving long distance from now on, thank you very—"

I burst into tears.

At least he couldn't see my horrified expression. Not when I was sobbing in his arms.

"Happens without warning," I said, coming up for air. "Max, I'm sorry—"

He put a finger to my lips and pushed me gently back against the cushions of the taxi, as if to say, *See how comforting silence can be?* I closed my eyes, afraid to look any longer into his. Too much tenderness there. Too much "let-me-share-the-pain."

The cab pulled up. The sign outside—luminous red and white letters dancing on a bright yellow background—said MANGIA, MANGIA.

"My favorite kind of restaurant, Italian," I told him.

The restaurant was small and elegant, a family-run establishment as warm and exuberant as its outdoor sign. When I asked Max about the unusual name, he said I was about to find out.

As soon as our hostess showed us to a table, she said, "'Mangia, mangia' means 'Eat, eat.' My siblings

125

and I were brought up hearing our mother urge us to lick the platter clean, so to speak," she said with an impish grin.

I let McCann do the ordering. "As long as it's pasta," I cautioned him.

"You asked me once if I loved this city," he told me. "To a hick from Minnesota, New York meant tough, exciting, sophisticated, beautiful. You fit the profile, Karen."

"Come on, Max," I protested. "The recurring compliment of my life has always been that I have an interesting face."

"It's a matter of style, isn't it?" he said, fixing me in that narrow gaze that almost shut out the cornflower blue of his eyes. "I admire what I totally lack. Your wry sense of humor. The way you give free rein to your feelings. The way you—"

Saved by two steaming plates of linguini marinara.

"My wife used to say I buried my emotions in a subterranean vault—which, in my line of work, has its advantages," he said with a narrow smile. "You were about to tell me my spaghetti is getting cold."

"Linguini, McCann. You're back in New York." I sampled a forkful. "Delicious!"

So was the wine. And the laughter when he splattered tomato sauce on his orange tie, which we both agreed was an improvement. We were waiting for dessert when I excused myself and headed for the ladies' room. When I returned, there was a vase of pink roses and red carnations on the table next to the zabaglione. "Flower shop around the corner," he said before I could open my mouth. "Cheerful, aren't they?"

"Thoughtful, aren't you?" I said softly.

Just as the cappuccino arrived, Max excused himself.

For the men's room, I assumed.

For the checkroom, it turned out. He had come back

with a familiar paperback—my well-thumbed copy of Swinburne—and did a quick scan.

"What are you looking for?" I asked him.

"A poem appropriate to the occasion ...   Gotcha." He looked up, a finger keeping his place. "I'm about as good at reading poetry as I am at baring my soul so if I—"

"No apologies, McCann. Read on," I said with a sense of foreboding.

His voice was a steady monotone, touching in its gravity...

Before our lives divide for ever,
While time is with us and hands are free,
(Time swift to fasten and swift to sever,
Hand from hand, as we stand by the sea)
I will say no word that a man might say
Whose whole life's love goes down in a day;
For this could never have been; and never,
Though the gods and the years relent,
Shall be.

He closed the book and handed it to me.

The cab ride home was like gliding through city streets in the hush of slow motion. In the unstrained silence, it didn't occur to either of us not to hold hands. In the lobby, there was no strain as we rode an elevator to my penthouse apartment. No strain at my door because we both knew he wouldn't be going inside. He waited like a bodyguard as I rummaged in my purse for my keys, not daring to look at him, and looking. Afraid to see what I knew he was remembering. Me, in his arms. Crying, but in his arms...

As my hand closed over the keys to my apartment, I heard a footstep from inside. Before I had time to unlock my door, it opened.

"Hello," Max said. Friendly. Resigned.

Jamie stood there smiling. "Come on in," he said

to Max.

"It's late," Max protested while I toyed with my keys and wondered how the hell Jamie had gotten in without any.

"It's never too late," Jamie said. "Please come in."

My genial host.

Make some lame excuse, Max!

But he'd hesitated too long. Jamie practically had him by the elbow and Max wasn't resisting. I mentally bowed to the inevitable. Once inside, I introduced them, poured some brandy, and sat back waiting to see how the two men would react to each other.

It started out as a sort of contest, each man maneuvering with words while taking the other's measure. I seized an opening and slipped it in that Max was an FBI agent.

The effect on Jamie was as subtle as it was instantaneous. He turned on the charm. Oh, not so that Max would notice right away. It was like expensive perfume being dabbed in all the right places. A touch of exuberance here. An ingenuous remark there. A fascinating anecdote. A sad tale leavened with humor. And questions—nothing too probing, of course. The kind that a man genuinely interested in another man's work might ask.

A masterly performance. Max sat on my couch with the look of a man who'd been charmed. No way he could have resisted Jamie's special brand of openness as he sat across from Max displaying the eagerness of a boy on a lark.

Or a man flirting with danger? Both, maybe.

I had the sense that if I confronted Jamie right now, if I said, "Who the devil *are* you?" he would come up with three very different and equally persuasive answers.

The two of them went on talking until, utterly exhausted, I broke it up.

At the door, Max looked from me to Jamie and said, "I envy you both."

That's when I realized that Jamie had been wearing his cashmere jacket all evening.

"All right," I said as soon as Max had left, "what the hell's going on?"

"I told your doorman we had an appointment."

"That explains how you got in. It doesn't tell me a thing about why you were wooing that man. Max McCann is out of my life."

"As of when?" he teased.

"Now. Tonight. What difference does it make?"

"Pity. I like his style."

"So I noticed. Apparently, it was mutual."

He seemed delighted. "How's the PR campaign going?"

"Done by the end of the week," I said and steered him out the door.

"Wonderful! Get some sleep. We'll talk tomorrow."

He popped his head back in, catching me in mid-yawn.

"Did I ever tell you what I wanted to be when I grew up?"

"Your childhood dream?" I mumbled, fading fast.

For a moment he looked wistful. Then he turned on his high beams.

"An FBI agent!"

It was the way he said it that blew the cobwebs away.

CHAPTER 18

THE IDES OF MARCH. THE fifteenth of the month on the ancient Roman calendar.

"A fitting day to go public," Jamie had said gleefully, raising a glass of orange juice on the morning we had officially launched the PR campaign. "The day Julius Caesar got his," he had said with a faint smile when Brian O'Neal had looked confused. "Victims Anonymous is about to declare war on the first half of a biblical maxim. No more rendering unto Caesar."

Now, as I stood looking over the usual paraphernalia of an effective PR campaign—posters, fliers, stacks of photocopied material—I wondered why I had bothered coming here tonight. A postmortem can be the most satisfying part of a campaign... time to take stock and gloat a little. Not *this* time. Not with the sign someone had hung over my desk and, next to it, a table close to five feet long. The warning, in red block letters—USE GLOVES OR DON'T TOUCH—suggested the kind of foresight that should have given me a secure feeling. It had the opposite effect. Going public meant increased visibility, which meant more visibility with law enforcement. What *really* nagged at me was that a lot of people at risk had become good friends.

One of them walked through the door with her characteristic bounce and grinning good humor—Rosa Ramirez, the most energetic of Lee Emerson's "troops." It was always the same, our first eye contact, our joint memory of Christmas Eve...

I lost a son.

I listened to my daughter die.

Tony Montes was right behind her. "Told you we'd find Karen here," Rosa said with a grin, giving Tony an affectionate pat that sent him edging away.

Tony, the boy who kept his distance.

He walked over to me. "Jamie wants you to meet him."

The little messenger. "No hello?" I said.

He looked sheepish for a moment before making a beeline for the table of posters and fliers. "Use gloves means no fingerprints," Tony told me in case I should think he had missed the point. "Is this stuff going national?" he asked.

"All over the country," Rosa said.

"We're lending 'em some of our star recruiters from New York," Tony announced, dark eyes bright with this special piece of intelligence. "It's a lot faster than the old system of post office boxes." He looked to me for confirmation.

All he got was a frown.

How did he get this information?!

"Your idea?" Rosa asked me.

I nodded. "It gives people quick access to useful information."

"Such as?" Tony challenged.

"Such as which Permissive New Jersey judges have been handing out eighteen-month sentences for assault with a deadly weapon," I answered reluctantly, "even as the Garden State suffers from a record-breaking number of annual felonies."

"Can I see the Action Kit?" he asked.

"It's not made up yet, Tony," I said, glad it wasn't there for him to pore over.

Typically, he stood his ground, waiting for me to tell him what *was* in it. "It's just a lot of dry facts and statistics," I lied. "Some press releases, a couple of sentencing reports—"

"And posters," he said, drawn to one in particular.

"Gun murders in Washington, D.C.," he read from the top. He skipped to the bottom. "Murder rate. More than seven times the national average. Wow!"

"Time to go," I said sharply, reaching for my coat.

"The guy downstairs made me sign in. Now I have to sign out again," Tony told me. "How come Rosa didn't have to?"

Rosa flashed me a smile. "Office cleaning ladies don't need to, honey."

"But you don't clean offices!" Tony protested.

"If wearing a scarf and this battered old coat—not to mention my skin color—makes me hired help in some people's eyes, who's complaining?" she grinned. "Cleaning ladies get to wander all over with nobody wondering what they're up to."

He held his hand next to hers. Matched skin tones. "What *are* you up to?"

Not one to ignore rhetorical questions, our Tony.

"Just holding down the fort." Rosa shrugged off her coat.

I put mine on. We hugged while Tony shuffled his feet, uncomfortable with such a public display of feminine affection.

Which made sharing the backseat of a cab with him a bittersweet experience. He had squeezed his small frame into the opposite corner, sending me a clear signal.

Gloves or not, lady, don't touch.

As if he sensed how much I wanted to...

At least he was eager to talk.

"Wanna know what's on Jamie's agenda?" he asked.

For a hooky-playing street kid, his vocabulary was impressive. "I'll bite," I quipped.

"Your first Rouser, right?"

"Not yours, I'll bet."

"I've seem 'em before," he said in the bored tone of "I've seen it all."

He took out a cigarette.

"Don't," I said, ready to snatch it away. "I don't like seeing it, Tony. You're only thirteen."

"Going on fourteen," he countered. The look he gave me was ambivalent—seemingly leery of my concern, yet simultaneously drawn to it. But he put the cigarette away.

Our cab pulled up to a building that was vaguely familiar.

A man directed us to a small room off the lobby where Jamie was waiting, his Rouser not yet under way. I don't know what I'd expected—certainly not the sight of Jamie decked out like Old Hollywood's version of a dashing pirate in black buccaneer shirt, black beard, and aviator sunglasses.

Tony studied Jamie with a skeptical half-smile. I could almost hear him thinking: "Funny way for a psychiatrist to dress!"

"Well, if it isn't Blackbeard himself," I teased, tempted to give that unruly beard of his a tug. "What are you up to?"

Jamie laughed. "You'll see soon enough." He aimed a friendly jab at Tony's arm and said, "Find her a good seat, Tadpole."

Tony stiffened like a small board. Well, what boy his age likes to be reminded of how short he is?

"Lead on, Tony," I said, and followed him out of the lobby into a large auditorium. I vaguely remembered the place. A former movie theater that was now a lecture hall. Years ago, Claudia and I had viewed our favorite Bogart flicks from tenth-row center.

While Tony was busily checking row after worn-red-velvet row, I scanned the audience. Not counting a near-empty balcony, Jamie had himself a full house. I couldn't get a handle on the crowd except that people weren't dressed in fancy clothes and, other than Tony, I didn't spot any kids. We sat down in a couple of seats smack in the middle of the balcony. It was an ideal spot for a bird's-eye view. But of *what*? Peering down, I saw a few black-clad men in the ubiquitous wraparound sunglasses working the aisles with straw baskets. I thought of dark priests making their weekly collection. Maybe one person in ten tossed something into a basket.

"What's going on down there, Tony? Who *are* these people?"

"Cell members from the five boroughs—mostly from Brooklyn and Queens— Oh, you mean the guys in black? They're collecting some horror stories from people who want everybody else to hear what happened to them or someone in their family."

I zeroed in on a woman in a floppy hat with the shoulders of a linebacker as she leaned over to plant a folded sheet of paper into a passing basket.

"Jamie is about to give a public reading of unavenged crimes?" I asked.

Tony nodded.

I rolled my eyes.

Shades of a revival meeting!

"Know why Jamie calls it a Rouser?" Tony said with a hint of malice in his voice.

"No. Why?"

"I heard Lee Emerson say it's because Jamie needs it right before he goes on a Mission. It replenishes him, she said."

Like a shot in the arm? Elmer Gantry–style melodrama?

I sighed and steeled myself for an embarrassing display of theatrics.

The lights dimmed.

Seconds later Jamie appeared, pinned to the stage by a spotlight, and began to read, his voice grave. "Can you picture it? The night someone in this audience was made a widow? The night she witnessed her husband's murder? *'Give him the money, Ben. For God's sake, get away from that cash register!'* But Ben, with business bad and getting worse, hesitates. Clenches his fist. Steps away, finally. Stares with bitter resignation as the robber, still waving his .357 Magnum, heads for the cash register."

Silence. Was Jamie milking it? Gritting his teeth? Waiting for the inevitable—a woman's muffled sobs?

"What, a measly five hundred bucks in the till?" Jamie paused. "Those eight words," he lashed out, "were a death sentence! A man's brains, blown out in a mom-and-pop liquor store by a parolee who has robbed before and, yes, killed before—and thanks to our system of so-called justice, will live to rob and kill again." He crumpled the paper in his fist. "And again." He hurled it into the audience.

A hand shot out to catch it.

A shout went up. "No!"

"Yes! Unless we stop him and Savages like him!"

The crowd roared its approval.

Jamie reached for another piece of paper. Utter silence as he read it.

"Damn," he said. "Damn them," he whispered, the microphone flinging his private mutterings far and wide.

He looked up. "How many times have you heard that it's up to us to make the system work? That we private citizens have a duty to come forward and point the finger so judge and jury can see that justice is done? There is a woman who is *not* in the audience tonight. Her husband is. She was doing some late-in-the-day shopping in the back aisles of a grocery store when

135

she hears a loud sound, followed by a scream. What she witnesses—unseen—is a muscled teenager using his hands and feet on a young woman clerk, karate-chopping her almost to death before he hits the cash register. After all, he needs to feed his drug habit. But this teenager is no dummy. He gets himself a smart lawyer. And *then* what happens?"

"He gets out on bail!" A disembodied voice, full of disgust.

"Round one for the defense. Round two. The DA has to lay out his case for the smart lawyer—an eyewitness ready, willing, and brave enough to testify. Round three—"

"The shyster tracks her down!" a hoarse voice called out.

"He tells his client where to find her!" A woman's voice—part horror, part rage.

"Round four, ladies and gentlemen," Jamie said in the flat tone of an undertaker. "A campaign of terror. While the defense lawyer delays in court, winning postponement after postponement, a six-foot-two-inch drug addict weighing close to two hundred pounds is free to stalk a five-foot-four-inch housewife. To bombard her with phone calls and menacing gestures. She's seen firsthand what this person can do to a woman. Round five," he said, gripping the podium, "a nervous breakdown."

He held up a straw basket in each hand. It was a tip-of-the-iceberg gesture. We could see, all of us, that the baskets were full, the horror unending.

When he lowered the baskets and reached for another sheet of paper, it was as if a shudder rolled through the length and breadth of the auditorium.

A lecture hall had turned back into a theater.

I was tempted to get up and leave, wanting to avoid the indelible images such horror stories engender. I told myself I would have left if, like an overlong movie, there had been an intermission so I wouldn't have to disrupt the show. But I had stayed too long and I knew it. Like everyone else, I was mesmerized by the resonant sound of Jamie's voice.

"Who here hasn't been eleven years old?" Jamie said gently. "Who hasn't played marbles after school or turned his face to the sun for a moment? Even a young kid born and bred on these mean streets should be able to let down his guard on the schoolyard steps and enjoy deep breaths of city-fouled air while he gazes into the sky for a glimpse of his future. As that future literally blows up in his face..."

Horror begat horror. Anger turned to rage. All around me the crowd's emotions began to accelerate with the sound of Jamie's voice, immersed in one tragedy after another. A nine-year-old boy heading home after school, gunned down by juvenile robbers on bikes. The pain of the boy's parents. The terror of his uncomprehending siblings.

Jamie's false beard and dark glasses had vanished for me. I saw a face I knew well, but with a new dimension. A Jamie I had never even glimpsed—this man with a depth of compassion that took my breath away and who, even as I watched, had metamorphosed into a prosecutor addressing the ultimate jury... .

"By what right do they spill our blood? By whose authority do they plunder our lives? Who told them they can wipe us out of existence and go unpunished? Will we stand by while they rob our homes? Turn the other cheek while they kill our children? Wring our hands as they wield knives and baseball bats? While they *casually* take a life?"

I was on my feet with the rest, hands gripping the balcony rail.

Tony coughed, breaking the spell so that I became

part observer, part member of the audience, able to appreciate and experience Jamie's crescendo.

In that moment I grasped Jamie's essence as an avenging angel. My initial suspicion about his staging a Rouser for theatrical reasons—along with Lee Emerson's snide remark to Chuck Polanski—receded like some nocturnal creature fleeing from the sun.

CHAPTER 19

CENTERED ON THE DESK IN my den like a fat reproach sat Lee Emerson's bulky "report from the provinces," untouched by human hands since it had arrived two weeks ago. The note attached to it was from Jamie asking me for "a report on the report by the time I get back, please."

In time for tonight's dinner meeting.

A quick glance at the top sheet reminded me what I was in for as soon as I dipped into Lee's report—gushy enthusiasm. Fortified with a cigarette, I turned to the front page. Lee had "opened"—as she put it—in Philadelphia. "A has-been town," she'd written, "too dull and dirty to live up to the awesome sight of our country's Liberty Bell!"

I looked in vain for the promised "intelligence" about her Mission activity. The only thing that seemed to be happening among the Philadelphia cells was speculation about VA's mysterious leader. Was he a Vietnam vet? A disgruntled cop? A foreign mercenary? No one suspected a psychiatrist, Lee reassured us.

Baltimore was more revealing. Apparently, Chuck Polanski had been all fired up by their hotel lobby. "All video games and pinball machines—like being greeted by a roomful of winking, leering ladies of the night," Lee had written in her purple prose.

There was some good news, at least. "The leader of the Baltimore cell turned out to be a real pro," Lee had written. "We could use her brand of talent in New York! She's smart —a real organizer, not to mentin a great recruiter, and she keeps wonderful records!"

Detroit got short shrift. "Unsafe at any speed is right! You don't dare go a city block without taking a cab." On the plus side, she gave a "thumbs-up to a plucky female ADA."

It was Denver that earned Lee the purple-prose award. She went on and on about the foothills of Colorado "... humbled before a mountain range that was as vast and brown as a woman's pleated skirt."

But Chicago rang an alarm bell. Lee had made a vague allusion, buried under a lot of amiable chitchat, to a "close call with the police."

No details?!

St. Louis was worse. A close call, this time, with violence. A Victims Anonymous target—some defense lawyer—had looked the other way while his bat-wielding juvenile delinquent clients "persuaded" motorists not to testify against them for smashing their car windows. "But one outraged complainant persisted and the poor guy lost in *and* out of court," Lee wrote. "Without corroborating testimony, the juvenile delinquents were released. They wasted no time smashing the complainant's head until he was too blind to point the finger at anyone. And get this!" she went on breathlessly. "The complainant's wife went berserk. She smashed the windows of the defense lawyer's Mercedes and ended up delivering a direct hit on his bald spot that put out his lights. It's a good thing he only suffered a mild concussion."

I poured myself a stiff drink and moved on to Los Angeles.

"We were 'escorting' an appellate judge into a high-crime area," Lee had written, "when we came upon a mugging victim—a bag lady clutching her pathetic junk as the lifeblood spilled out of her belly. We duped the judge into thinking the woman had died with his name on her lips because he'd released the man who'd stabbed her on some technicality."

I didn't even bother to make notes about what was risky in "escorting" a judge into a high-crime area.

Atlanta was next. I rolled my eyes when I saw who Lee had set her sights on this time. "Targeting a top aide in a DA's office," I wrote, "means high visibility. Anyone going on such a Mission should be unobtrusive."

How in the world could a standout beauty like Lee not stand out?

Predictably, not a trace of worry showed up in her breezy account—her usual mix of statistics and melodrama...

"With Atlanta one of the most crime-ridden cities in the nation," she complained, "you'd think the DA's office would do *less* plea bargaining, not more. But this particular DA keeps putting these—these subhumans— back on the street!"

Lee's tour ended in Houston. "The people here really understand what property rights are all about!" she enthused. "According to my clipping files, Houston boasts a DA's office that gives out free booklets on handguns, and public officials who'd correct you if you said 'gun nut' rather than 'self-defense mentality.'"

Kagan would have agreed, I thought. He was fond of referring to Texas in general and Houston in particular as the place where the frontier spirit was alive and well. His tone, as well as his keen interest, had always made me uneasy. So when Lee went on to sing the praises of the Texas women she had managed to break bread with and how they had "great potential" and "real administrative talent," I decided to keep her observations out of my report. If her assessment was correct, I didn't want the names and addresses to fall into Kagan's hands.

I stashed the list in the safe I keep in my den.

When Jamie picked me up in a cab, the first thing he said was, "What do you think of our Lee?"

"Insensitive when it comes to dealing with underlings, but very gung ho. A risk-taker to the point where I have to wonder whether the woman is detached from reality. Oh, and I don't think much of her intelligence-gathering efforts. Other than that... " I said drily.

I was surprised by Jamie's reaction. I had expected him to leap to her defense, but he looked pleased.

"Your leave of absence is up when?" he asked.   .

"A couple of months. Why?" I said, suspicious. "What's tonight's dinner all about?"

"Business, what else?"

Business, it turned out, in the kind of surroundings I abhor. I've never liked places that are more bar than restaurant, with quaint private rooms laid out like log cabins. This one showed a lot of dark leather, dartboards, and man-sized beer mugs on the windowsills.

"Whose choice was this?" I sniffed.

"O'Neal's."

"I might have known. Where's Polanski?"

"Still out of town with Lee."

Which left Brian O'Neal to play official greeter. He seated the six of us around a massive table with clawed feet. When Timothy Hogan pumped Jamie's hand and Denzel put on his Dom Perignon smile—a real contrast with Kagan's subdued expression—I knew who was about to be feted even before O'Neal broke open the bottle.

"*That* successful?" I asked, enjoying the drama of a wordless toast and raised glasses.

"Your public relations campaign is a big hit, Karen." Jamie was beaming.

"We're only a few weeks into it, but I have to admit

EYE FOR AN EYE

I'm cautiously optimistic," Kagan said.

"The press is being cautious, period," Denzel observed, champagne glass turning slowly in his hand. "It's almost as if they're afraid to take us seriously. The police are baffled."

"Even with the clues you've been leaving behind?" I asked.

"Don't compare us with your usual terrorist, eager to take credit for an atrocity," Jamie sniffed. "Instead of some crude traceable slogan, our symbol—thanks to you, love—is subtler stuff. And definitely baffling," he added, patting his fox medallion which, these days, he *consistently* wore under his shirt. It was Jamie's one concession to caution.

I had to admit that during dinner, I got caught up in the general excitement. O'Neal had been on the road and couldn't stop crowing, in between puffs on his Havana cigar, about how things were starting to roll.

"All these new recruits! The country is with us all the way!"

Hogan was high on the fund-raising strides he was making.

Denzel talked about police sympathy that bordered on outright support.

Jamie was gleeful, but not too specific, about his latest Missions and Rousers.

I pressed them about which aspects of the PR campaign were paying off the most, and got a cornucopia of answers. Cells were operating more effectively. It came from being ideologically armed, Denzel told me. Whole groups of my 'Vulnerables'—from inner-city middle-class blacks to blue-collar communities in the suburbs to organizations devoted to the elderly—were voicing loud approval of VA's tactics, Jamie told me. My statistics, such as the stark blowups of crime victims, made for powerful ammunition.

It went on and on until the dessert course, which arrived with more champagne.

That's when I realized no one had asked me about Lee's report.

"Lee's department isn't working," Kagan announced. "We'd like you to whip it into shape. Take up the slack."

"You mean help with the administrative work?" I said with a cautious look around.

"Run the whole department. Unofficially," Jamie added. "No point in pushing Lee's nose out of joint. Don't frown, Karen. You're already familiar with the entire operation. It's one reason the campaign is working so well. Can you take over just until your leave is up?"

Why not? I thought. I had been feeling really useful for the last couple of months.

But I was loath to ask myself exactly why.

CHAPTER 20

I THOUGHT OF YESTERDAY'S NOTE, DROPPED off at my building, as I approached Claudia's apartment.

"Tomorrow is April Fool's Day. An apt occasion for two darn fools to stop keeping a discreet distance from each other," she'd written. "Come to lunch—just you, me, and my ex. Luke is stopping by to burglarproof my place. He'd love to see you again, he said. Me, too."

I'd always thought of Claudia's apartment as a jewel tucked away in a dirty brown bag. Look past the curbside garbage and crumbling masonry, the artfully garish graffiti, and you could still spot the graceful lines of an old brownstone. Once inside the brownstone's tiny foyer, I automatically wrinkled my nose at the stale cooking odors coming from under the doors of other occupants. But Claudia had the whole top floor to herself and she'd put rubber stripping under her door to keep any outside odors from slipping inside.

The elevator I rode to the top floor of the brownstone was fine in every respect but one. It was so small it would have made a mole claustrophobic!

I pressed her bell and the door flew open. She pulled me inside and we hugged each other, then sat down to play catch-up on health, diet, movie recommendations—everything except what was really on our minds.

"What happened to your living room?" I asked, looking around. "It has the no-nonsense look of a study."

"Exactly what I was after. Think Luke will go for it?"

she asked.

"Absolutely." But I was already missing her lushly overpowering reds, oranges, and yellows. Gone were the plump floor cushions and carnivorous-looking plants.

"When is Luke due?"

"Any minute now. What do you think?" She did a small, nervous pirouette. Her hand swept out to a perfectly appointed table and the telltale odors of Luke's all-time favorite—oyster stew.

"Menu and décor, a ten," I told her. "Ten-plus for the hostess."

She gave my hand a grateful squeeze before hurrying off to the kitchen, looking sensational in a billowy cocoa-and-cream pants suit topped off by an exquisite turban.

I was tempted to remind her that burglarproofing, not romance, was in the air. It was typical of Luke to worry about "his careless Claudia" and her deteriorating neighborhood, even if she wasn't *his* anymore—Luke's choice, not hers.

So she hadn't given up on trying to get him back, I thought with a sense of uneasiness bordering on dread. What else but wishful thinking could explain a redecorated living room, the full makeup treatment, and this big fuss of a lunch?

Through a haze of cigarette smoke, I contemplated the good old days—old, anyway. How she and I had met through our husbands (Luke, a savvy cop and Alan, an equally savvy Legal Aid lawyer) at a New Year's Eve party. And how my unlikely friendship with Luke's "dancer-wife" (Alan's put-down description of Claudia) had outlasted both our marriages. "Dancer" had turned out to be the least relevant thing about her, as I'd discovered that first night. She had been looking around at a roomful of assorted Legal Aiders who, when they weren't posing for their annual group photographs, were railing against some crime statistics that had eroded their public mandate.

"Smug," she'd said, lowering her voice. "The smugness of people on the defensive."

I saw what she meant.

"Not my kind of party," said this outspoken irreverent creature.

That's when I knew that Claudia was my kind of person.

"Well, look who's smoking again," she said, noticing. "It's been what, six years?"

"You have a good memory. I quit the day of my divorce."

"What got you going again... as if I didn't know?"

"Stress, what else?" I said drily.

The doorbell rang. Both of us went to let Luke in.

"Let me look at you," I said, taking his hand.

Luke was wearing chinos and an aviator jacket. "A little more gray in the beard, Luke, but still slim and sturdy," I teased.

Still melancholy in the eyes and tough around the mouth.

Lunch with a detective, old friend or no, produced my first fear-ball of the day. But it melted away with red wine and thick Italian bread dunked in Claudia's delicious stew. What came back in a rush was how much I had always liked Luke.

How much Claudia still loved him...

"—makes sense after the rash of break-ins," Luke was saying.

"I said 'yes' to an extra lock," Claudia grumbled, "but *bars* on my windows?!"

"It's because of the fire escape," I reminded her. "It makes you vulnerable."

"No bars then," Luke said, capitulating. "How about a solidly anchored metal grille? I could install two of them next week."

She went for it. It would mean another lunch.

I let Claudia clear the table as I followed Luke into the foyer for a mini-education on the art of burglarproofing.

"Claud's rim lock is only a deterrent, but it's not secure against a weak door. This barricade lock adds real strength—or will, once I anchor it with a steel rod," he explained.

While he went to work on the lock, Luke and I caught up on the years. Which made it a little easier to pry...

"Jan still with Legal Aid?" I asked.

"Best damn lawyer on Alan's staff—or so he tells me."

Spoken with the pride of a man still in love with his wife.

By the time Claudia's famous lemon meringue pie was quivering on our plates, I had thought of a way to pry a little.

"So much crime, these days," I said with a sigh. "And not just in neighborhoods like this one."

"Tell me about it!" Luke shot back. "In the old days you'd spot someone dirty, search him, and nine times out of ten turn up a weapon. Now you practically have to follow him around until he commits mayhem. *How*, when we don't have the manpower? Even if we're lucky enough to catch him in the act, the courts—"

"Don't put him away. Still, vigilante justice isn't the answer," Claudia sniffed.

"Hell, no," Luke said. "I was telling Claud the other day about some vigilante action we've run into..."

I half-listened while I replayed Claudia's April Fool's Day note in my head...

"Luke is stopping by. Love to see you again. Luke too."

Why? So Luke could scare some sense into me?

"—and all it would do is bring the system crashing down on our heads."

As Luke went on talking, I was relieved to learn that

he really didn't know much. He could find "no rhyme or reason" for what was happening. Why *this* vicious mugger, but not *that* one, got his wrist broken. Why an armed robber on one block, but not on the next, was wounded with his own gun. While the police had no idea how organized the vigilantes were, he told me, the propaganda they'd left behind made it clear how far they intended to go. He admitted that no profile, no real clue to their identity, had emerged. How *could* it when the would-be victims of the muggers and the robbers couldn't or wouldn't talk? He had no idea what the fox symbol meant. "But I know the true meaning of a vigilante," he said, his mouth tight. "A two-headed monster. One mouth devours the criminal, the other its own flesh."

I barely restrained a shudder at the vividness of his description.

Even so, I couldn't resist a parting shot. When Luke stood up to leave, I said, "I'm betting these vigilantes aren't a bunch of crazies—not all of them anyway. Don't you think they have a right to be frustrated?"

He turned to me with a look of such chronic weariness that his features acquired the universal look of "cop." It was something I had learned to notice these last few months.

"Yeah," he said, "they've got a right."

It did something to me, the look on his face.

It did something to Claudia.

"So Luke would sooner lose to the criminal," she mused as soon as Luke was gone. "Karen, he *is* losing. The poor guy just can't admit it."

"Not yet," I said.

Not ever.

"You mad at me?" Claudia said cautiously.

"Because this whole lunch was a setup?"

"I was worried."

She looked so chastened that I forgave her.

"If it makes you feel any better, Claudia, I haven't joined."

"You haven't gone back to work either. But I have to admit you seem calmer, less directionless. Me, I've never felt more like a leaf in the wind," she told me, twisting the jade-and-gold band she always wore on her right hand—her wedding ring. "Hell, nothing has changed. He likes me, he loves his wife," she said in the singsong voice of plucking a daisy.

"He *still* loves you, Claudia. Not that it does you any good."

"Too little too late," she said with a vehement gesture at her redecorated living room. If there'd been a book within reach, she'd have thrown it. "The new studious Claudia won't get him back. I'm wasting my time, getting a college degree."

"Don't you *dare* quit those classes," I told her. "You've earned the credits and the good marks. You're almost there. What's more, you enjoy it."

"College before law school was just a means to an end," she said slowly. "What am I trying to prove? That I have as good a mind as that husband-stealing bitch? That I could be a better lawyer?"

"It wouldn't surprise me if you *did* turn out to be a better lawyer than Jan."

"You were about to tell me you know how I feel," she said. "But you don't. You didn't lose a husband. You walked out on one."

"Not soon enough," I quipped, pulling a half-grin out of her. "We were never a great mix. Alan is handsome enough and, politically speaking, we had a lot in common. But as far as temperament was concerned, we couldn't have been less in sync. My wry brand of humor used to irritate him."

"Not Dr. James Coyne, I'll bet."

"No," I said. But I was thinking of McCann.

"Seeing much of Jamie these days?"

"Enough. Why?"

"Victims Anonymous," she said, as if she were testing the words. "They're starting to make waves. Are they making a difference?"

"Too soon to tell, but I think they will. Why?"

"Maybe I'd like to see for myself what you're all doing."

"What for?" I said, confused by what I heard in her voice—a sense of reluctance and a trace of eagerness.

"I know, I know. I was dead set against the whole idea. I still am. But if it works, if cops like Luke could regain control of the streets, isn't that what this Victims Anonymous group is all about?"

"What *this* conversation is all about falls into the category of 'do something special for Luke,'" I snapped.

"Yeah, you're right," she admitted with a shrug.

She pulled out a compact. "Karen, whatever happened to Sarah's murderer?"

The question might have been innocent. She was applying bright red lipstick when she asked it.

"A happy ending, according to Alan's ADA friend, Corey Donahue," I said, feeding just the right tone of bitter sarcasm into my voice. "It seems Indio and his gang were wiped out by a rival gang."

Claudia hunched her shoulders together as if she were cold. "So I'll stick with the books for a while longer. But Mother of God, Karen, be careful!"

That's when I knew she knew.

CHAPTER 21

I SAT IN JAMIE'S WAITING ROOM, wondering about his cryptic telephone message.

"I'll need an hour or so of your time," he'd told me.

I showed up a little early. Apparently Jamie was still closeted with a patient. Spying some newspapers on a table, I started to reach for them. I hadn't been able to read a paper for weeks and today being Friday the thirteenth, it didn't seem like a good day to start.

I couldn't resist...

We had gotten good coverage. A few papers were reporting on what facts they had, and every crime writer worthy of the title was whipping up piece after piece full of color and high drama. The scandal sheets had been having a field day with VA's calling card—the stylized depiction of a fox.

But only Daniel Henniger, savvy editorial writer with *The Wall Street Journal*, had grasped the symbolism. In a provocative headline on the Opinion Page, he had written:

Victim of the Hunt Turns Hunter

It was the "human interest" angle that worried me. Thanks to a steady stream of reports from new recruits, I knew that our campaign was working with the general public. As for increased visibility, there wasn't a paper in the country, Jamie had told me, where we hadn't made the front page.

But the *official* opinion makers? A mixed reception. To some, Victims Anonymous was the answer to their dreams. To others, a nightmare—a virus that had to be stamped out. The good news was that the press was clueless about Victims Anonymous being a national phenomenon. It was Chicago's vigilantes or Detroit's or Cleveland's.

And being perceived as local meant no FBI interest. No Max McCann.

Jamie emerged from his office. "Today's *New York Times*," he said, tossing it to me before heading for the bathroom. His patient, a young woman, fastidiously groomed except for runny mascara, nodded in my direction and made a hasty exit.

I looked at the newspaper. A headline leaped out at me.

ARE WE ALL POTENTIAL VIGILANTES?

My words! Except in the handout Victims Anonymous had left all over town, I'd made it a declarative statement, not a question. More of my words, italicized for emphasis, followed in an article about the frustrated man in the street.

It's happening all across America. A record year for pistol licenses and instruction in firearms. A proliferation of block watchers and fierce guardians of the local park. Cheers breaking out as a mugger is mercilessly punched and kicked. A newly popular "match game"—burning crack houses to the ground. Subway gunplay... menacing punk with knife shot by person or persons unknown.

Jamie walked back in and steered me into his office. "You look a little green around the gills," he observed.

"Better green than smug," I muttered.

"I'm feeling good, all right," he admitted. "Denzel called to fill me in. The criminal justice people just

153

had one of their 'coordination meetings'—police, prosecutors, judges, corrections officers."

"Sounds exciting," I said drily.

He thought I meant it. "There's nothing quite so exhilarating as infiltrating the enemy," he said, putting an eager spin on a glass paperweight. Catching it. "One of Chuck Polanski's people was there. Denzel, too—but in his case, strictly as a police department observer. The chief spokesman for the cops was a black detective."

I groaned. "Luke Cole. I hope to God they don't know each other."

Jamie grinned. "They do now. VA has become such a 'specific' crime problem that a task force has been proposed to deal with us. The goal of these meets is coordination—an inside joke, Polanski tells me. Especially after he was able to feed everyone on the task force a couple of bogus leads."

Jamie was positively gleeful. I was appalled.

"A task force? What's the matter with you people?! Victims Anonymous has been breaking the law—flagrantly—and getting away with it so far. Do you honestly think the police are *that* inept?"

"They're disorganized, Karen, not to mention demoralized. No one can agree on a damn thing. They're also vastly understaffed," he shot back, looking exasperated, almost as if I'd rained on his parade. "You of all people should have grasped our underlying principle. We're *organized*."

Tony walked in the door.

"We'd like you to sit in on Tony's session. Tell her it's okay, Tadpole."

Tony colored at the hated nickname.

"Is *this* why you need an hour of my time?" I protested.

"It's about Tony's recurring nightmare. I thought it might help him if the three of us discussed—"

"Bad idea, Jamie," I said, getting up to leave.

"He has a conflict. Between you and the person who raised him. A sister he adores."

I sat back down.

"Big sister Maria is not exactly what you'd call a nurturing mother. When she's not off somewhere making porno movies—"

"She's a topless dancer," Tony mumbled, moving his scuffed shoes back and forth as if he were rubbing firewood. "I followed her to work one night."

"Tony has been punishing himself for—in his mind— betraying Maria. For wanting the kind of mother he's never had."

... For wanting *me*?

"Tony, are you sure you want me to do this?" I said gently.

He nodded.

I spent the next hour sitting in on someone else's nightmare.

* * *

Saturday morning playing catch-up with a desk full of work at the office is my idea of relaxing. No interruptions or small talk. No well-meaning friends.

Except Rosa Ramirez, who had gotten here ahead of me.

"So you're killing yourself on weekends now?" Rosa said, disapproval in her tone.

"What about you?" I shot back.

I noticed Lee Emerson's closed door. "What brings Lee here on a Saturday?" I wondered.

Rosa shrugged. "Heavy brunch date, maybe? Too bad. We get a lot more done when she's off traveling somewhere."

"You're too hard on her. Lee's nice enough when she's not being standoffish."

"When isn't she?"

"She has problems in that department," I admitted, "but she really does have a finely tuned sense of moral outrage," I said, and went to knock on Lee's door.

Chuck Polanski was parked on the edge of her leather-topped desk while Lee, looking demure in pearls and pale pink linen, filled a briefcase with some files. Polanski, looking more lighthearted than I'd ever seen him, had apparently abandoned black leather for a blue shirt, navy sports jacket, and loafers instead of boots.

"Did you hear, Karen?" Lee said, a becoming flush on her cheeks. "Chuck and I are off tomorrow on another tour!"

I hadn't heard. I couldn't digest it. Kagan sending standout Lee on yet another round of Missions at a time when VA's visibility was at an all-time high?

"Are you sure you want to do this, Lee? With all the publicity lately—"

"I wouldn't miss it for the world!" she enthused.

Polanski apparently agreed. His hand kept returning to the back of her chair. I tried to convince myself that protecting her was his highest priority.

"Oh, I almost forgot," Lee told me. "There's a message for you. A Claudia Cole."

Curious.... Claudia had never called me here.

I went back to my desk just as the phone rang.

It was Angela Russo. "SOS, Karen," she said. "I'm at Tony's place. How fast can you get here?"

"Something's happened to Tony?"

"He's all right but..." Her voice trailed off.

"I'm on my way!"

We hung up on each other.

"What's wrong?" Rosa asked.

But I was already out the door.

I wish I knew, Rosa.

I wish there were more cabs at this hour.

I wish the damn cab would go faster.

I wish the South Bronx would stop unfolding its ugliness outside my window.

I wish Tony hadn't been born, bred, and largely unsupervised in the Bronx.

I wish he didn't live among the gutted corpses of buildings.

I wish he didn't have strippers and derelicts for neighbors.

It wasn't as bad as I'd thought it would be, Tony's building, even though it was showing its age—crumbling brick around the edges. But it was a still-sturdy specimen from another era.

I found "Montes."

Angela's voice responded to the buzzer.

I went up an elevator, hurried down an alien hall, and walked into the reassuring presence of Mother Earth.

Angela seemed to sense my relief at the mere sight of her. Reaching out a steadying hand, she steered me inside to a dining area and black coffee, as if she knew my breakfast was still in a paper bag somewhere.

"Take it easy," she said in her soothing alto. "Denzel's in the bedroom with Tony. He'll be out soon."

I saw bright curtains and scatter rugs. Shelf after shelf of knickknacks. Lace doilies on an overstuffed couch. His sister Maria's loving touches?

I looked closer and saw the dust.

I noticed photographs lining the walls and stood back to admire their stark black-and-white drama, stunned by the photographer's skill.

"Last summer, Tony's sister Maria picked up an expensive camera on one of her trips abroad," Angela told me. "Tony was ecstatic," Angela said. She pointed out one photo on a narrow strip of wall. "Either you photograph well or the kid has real talent."

A candid shot of me, deep in concentration at my desk. Tony was always snapping away. It got so everyone had stopped noticing.

Denzel emerged, shaking his head as he closed the door behind him.

"Tony's hurt?" I whispered.

"Not in the way you mean. His sister was killed last night."

Denzel grabbed my arm. "You'd better hear it all before you try battering down that wall of resistance in there," he warned. "My two kids and I have a movie night every Friday. Two flicks back to back. I've always invited Tony, but for the last few months he's been too wrapped up with Victims Anonymous. Thank God he decided to join us last night."

"Denzel brought Tony home this morning," Angela told me. "That's when the call about Maria came in."

"That she'd been killed?"

"Murdered. Some twisted sonofabitch," Denzel muttered. "Her body was cut up."

"How—"

"Bad. His sister was a topless dancer—"

"I know. He's Jamie's patient. Jamie had me sit in on a session one time. He thought it might alleviate the nightmares Tony'd been having."

"The only thing I can figure is that some yo-yo at the topless joint where she worked must have left a side door unlocked," Denzel said. "The other girls had left. It was after the last show. A woman heard the screams and called it in."

"Jamie wants to see Tony this afternoon," Angela told me. "I have to get back to SIS and Denzel is on duty. Will you stay with Tony and then drive him over to Jamie's office?"

"Of course I will! How bad *is* he?"

"All anger and no tears," Denzel said grimly. "The

doctor we'd called left some sedatives. While I was seeing him out, Tony flushed them down the toilet."

Without another word he led me into his bedroom. Angela followed us.

Tony was sitting on the bed trembling, tight-lipped with rage.

Denzel sat down beside him. "If you want me to find out what happened to Maria, Tony, you have to do something for me. You have to let Karen take you to Jamie's later tonight."

"Then you'll tell me who killed her?" he asked.

"When I know, you'll know."

"It may take a while," Angela warned him.

"If you don't find him, *I* will!" Tony exploded.

"Listen to me," Denzel said, taking hold of Tony's small shoulders. "This is not your department, so get what you're thinking out of your head right now."

Angela went over, clearly wanting to hug him, gently cupping his face instead. It was only a moment, but some of the rigidity seemed to soften under her healing touch.

As soon as she and Denzel had left, I stayed by the bedroom door, sensing that Tony didn't want me—didn't want *anyone*—near him.

One look at his face and I knew he wouldn't cry. His eyes were like the little black buttons you see on stuffed animals, pathetic in their glassiness.

Not me, though.

I sat on the floor and cried for a long time.

CHAPTER 22

THE MINUTE I OPENED JAMIE'S waiting room door, he came out of his inner office and took gentle hold of Tony's arm. I repaired to the kitchenette to make us all coffee. On my way in with it, I almost collided with Jamie.

"I'm going upstairs to call Claudia," I said. "Where's your apartment key?"

"On my desk. I'll bring Tony up afterward. I'd like him to spend the next few nights with me. After that..." He shrugged.

Tony handed me Jamie's key in exchange for his coffee.

Not bothering to wait for an elevator, I walked quickly up two flights, uneasy about why Claudia had called me earlier.

She answered on the first ring. "Sorry it took so long," I said. "We had an emergency. Tony's sister—"

"I know."

"You *know*? I don't understand. How could you possibly—"

"Later," she said tersely. "I need to see you. How's two hours from now?"

"Claudia, what's going on?"

"Just write down where we'll meet. And be forewarned. It's a noisy dive in one of the seedier environs of Broadway."

She gave me an address and hung up.

I put together a makeshift dinner from Jamie's leftovers. When he and Tony came upstairs, it was pick-at-your-food time for all three of us.

"Take yourself to the master bedroom, Tony," Jamie said. "And take your sedative. You will *not* flush it down the tubes this time."

Tony slid his chair back. "Tell her, Jamie. You promised! Tell her I'm gonna make my bones!" He ran into the bedroom.

"I presume you were humoring him?"

"Of course I was," Jamie retorted. "Not that he'll have a killer to make his bones on. Not much chance of turning the sonofabitch up in a case like this."

We were brooding over our coffee when Jamie announced that he had to go out.

"Dammit, Jamie, so do I. I have to meet Claudia. One of us should be here."

"Tony won't even know we're gone. Trust me, that sedative I gave him works like a sledgehammer," he said. "Come see for yourself."

Jamie's elaborate bed was a sea of soothing white satin with a small mound in dead center. I saw a bit of striped pajama and a tangle of dark curls. I took the added precaution of waiting another ten minutes until I heard Tony's relaxed, repetitive breathing.

* * *

I peered inside the entrance of a place called Club 66.

"Lizard Lounge" was more like it. I backed away fast. Even on the street, the heavy metal was earsplitting. Who in their right mind would want to meet here?

Unless Claudia didn't want to be heard.

A willowy black gal sporting an outrageously blonde wig, a pair of glitter-framed dark glasses, and a skintight shell of a dress sauntered past. Her arm shot out—

"Claudia?" I said as she pulled me inside.

"Shhhh. Walk with me, Karen."

To a reserved table in an obscure corner of a room the size of a barn. Some of the locals looked me over as I passed, giving my "basic black" attire a skeptical eye. The stares that followed Claudia were one step short of attempted rape.

She moved our chairs close and we sat down.

"Why the disguise?" I asked over the so-called music.

"You happen to remember what nights I teach dancing?"

"Thursdays through Sundays. To keep wine and cheese on the table, you said."

"Karen, I don't 'teach' dancing. That wouldn't even pay for the tablecloth."

"Damn it, Claudia, why didn't you tell me you needed money?"

"Not from you. Not from Luke," she said, biting off each word. "I won't be in debt to the people I love. I quit my job last night. Can you guess what my job *was*?"

Whatever it was, she couldn't get herself to name it. I leaned closer, trying to see past the camouflage. She was twisting the jade wedding ring on her right hand. Playing with the butterfly pin at her throat.

"You're in real trouble, aren't you?"

"Let's go next door," Claudia said. "Showing may be easier than telling."

She was up before I could argue the point, weaving a serpentine path for both of us through a mass of frantically gyrating bodies. We went out a side exit, crossed a narrow alley, walked through the door of the neighboring building—

And stepped into another universe.

"The job I quit last night," Claudia said, as if she were making a formal introduction.

I stared at an elevated stage, mesmerized by the primitive jungle rhythm of undulating women. Breasts all sizes, colors, and shapes. No pasties. A movie screen on stage left was competing for customer attention with hardcore porn.

"You wouldn't believe the tips around here." Claudia's mouth matched the bitter twist of her words. "I told you my dancing days weren't over."

She searched my face for a reaction.

I was searching my memory. Tony, in Jamie's office, telling me about his sister...

She's a topless dancer. I followed her to work once.

I thought of Claudia's turtle-in-the-shell reaction right after Kagan had introduced us.

"You and Tony," I sputtered. "His sister Maria—"

"Topless dancers. Both of us. It's not safe to stay here any longer," she whispered.

We cut through the alley again while I tried to unscramble my brain. The heavy metal hadn't helped. At least Claudia and I would be able to talk without fear of being overheard.

At least she was able to cry.

"Maria may have been mixed up," Claudia told me, "but she was decent person. The two of us were what you'd call arm's-length friends."

She laid it all out for me. A dance lineup of hardened professionals. Two exceptions drawn to each other, sharing jokes and problems and dreams over coffee or a couple of drinks. Maria, guilt-ridden over her neglect of Tony but determined to "go legit" someday.

Claudia sighed. "Maria told me last night that she'd had it with her pimp. She was ready to give him the kiss-off. Bad idea, I told her. She needed to do some advance planning before she walked out on her latest gig in Korea. I begged her to back off until I could help her figure out a way to make it work, but she wouldn't listen. 'I'll wait for you in Club 66,' I told her, knowing that three or four of the dancers hadn't left yet so Maria was safe enough. But after four dancers walked out about ten minutes later, I ran back inside. I heard sounds coming from the dressing room— Oh God," she whispered, succumbing to tears, "I heard Maria screaming. I tried the door but the damn thing was locked. I yelled for Maria. I yelled for her pimp to unlock the door!" She squeezed her eyes shut. "Then I ran like hell."

I couldn't keep my hands still. "So the anonymous caller—"

"Me. There wasn't a patrol car in sight and nobody on the street. I made the call and then ducked back inside in case someone was still around who could help." She sighed. "I was too late. The cops were fast, but her pimp was faster."

"Claudia, if the dressing room door was locked, the killer couldn't have seen—"

"He didn't have to. We've met. Karen, Arnie knows my voice. He knows the color of my skin. By tomorrow he'll know all about the black topless dancer who failed to show up for work tonight."

"Dammit, Claudia, you need police protection while they look for him."

"And let Luke find out? I'd die first. Remember the Paris vacation—those lovely French beaches where it was chic to go topless? Remember what straitlaced Luke did when I gave in to the urge?"

I could still see it. Under different circumstances, we'd have laughed about it. "He pulled you off the beach by your ponytail," I said.

She shivered. "This is much worse than a topless beach."

"It's Victims Anonymous then. We'll get you moved out of harm's way tonight."

"The hell we will. Arnie can't track me down so fast if he doesn't know my name. You think I used my real one?"

"But when he does, you'll have no weapon, no—"

"I do now. Luke topped off his burglarproofing efforts by giving me what he called a 'clean piece.' Even showed me how to use it."

"Put those glitter frames back on, at least," I told her, wishing I'd brought my own dark glasses.

We checked out the bar—as much of it as we could see through the thick smoke—and pushed our way to the front door.

On the street we ran into a welcoming committee of one. Tony...

I glared at him. "You didn't take your sedative. You followed me."

"I didn't! I knew where you were going."

I'm going upstairs to call Claudia.

"Eavesdropper," I snapped.

My anger had no more reality for him than the blare of heavy metal spilling into the street. He was blocking Claudia's way.

"I never told on you," he said, one hand jabbing in the general direction of the topless joint, the unstated implication hanging between them.

You owe me. You know who killed Maria.

"Claudia!" I yelled.

But my warning had no reality for her either. Sobbing, she reached for him. There was no trace of the child in Tony's face as Claudia held him close. He was looking past her.

He looked capable of anything.

CHAPTER 23

"WHAT HAPPENED?" I ASKED BEFORE Jamie was halfway in the door.

"Let's argue over tea," he said, heading for my kitchen.

"Where's Tony?" I demanded.

"Steering clear of you *and* me. Hanging out with Chuck Polanski for now."

"To hell with Polanski," I said, sorry Jamie had called him back to New York.

"Don't be mad at Chuck. It may be his Mission, but surely you know who's running the show."

"Why is Kagan running so many shows these days? Why not you?" I snapped. "I gather you weren't any help at all in this meeting you people barred me from."

"In all fairness, I think the Mission planning went well. Maria's pimp is unlikely to make his move against Claudia until he's done his own planning."

"Claudia's agreed to play decoy?"

"Oh yes."

I lit a cigarette. "How safe *is* she?"

"You're smoking too much. Not to worry. We have round-the-clock surveillance on her. Arnie too, of course."

"How come Claudia never told me?"

"She doesn't know. Once Arnie goes after her, Polanski wants him to see a nervous quarry, not someone who knows she's being protected. From a psychiatrist's point of view, I couldn't agree more. Arnie's sort smells 'setup' a mile away. At the moment the man is calm, cool, and cocky."

"What's this pimp like? Swarthy, with greasy hair and polyester suits?"

"Not Arnie. He spends big bucks on his wardrobe. You'll see what I mean when Polanski drops off some photographs for you."

"Why would he send photographs in advance?"

"Because everyone going on a Mission has to be thoroughly familiar with the target. I had to pull rank just to get you on the Self-Defense Team."

I was out of questions. The minute I dropped onto a chair, Jamie headed for a teapot.

"Victims Anonymous has an age limit," I told him. "Tony doesn't even come close!" I mashed out my cigarette.

"They're making an exception," Jamie said, handing me a cup of tea.

"Which you could have vetoed. Why didn't you?"

"In point of fact," he said, sitting down next to me, "I agree with Kagan. Tony knows too much about our operation. He's been making threats. The only way to neutralize him is to let him have his way. Then he's in no position to sound off."

"Have his way. Cute euphemism for letting a thirteen-year-old 'do' Arnie," I said glumly. "You're his therapist. Who's in a better position to know how emotionally unstable he is? Turn him into a triggerman and he'll never be the same!"

"I know."

"You know but you don't care?"

He looked at me with one of his impenetrable stares. I was learning to see through them and what I saw was pain. I seized on it. "What kind of future will Tony have after this?"

167

Jamie sighed. "The word 'future' isn't part of Tony's vocabulary," he said. "It's the price he's paid for going it alone instead of falling in with street gangs. Do you really expect a child to have a sense of the long range when he's always had his hands full with the short? With surviving day by day? He'll survive this too."

"And Claudia? How's she bearing up?"

"More angry than frightened. She resents being on constant alert. Who wouldn't?"

"When Arnie *does* make his move—"

"The SD Team will be ready for him. You'll do fine."

"I won't go. I never asked to be on Polanski's Mission."

"We discussed that, you and I. You had mixed feelings, to say the least. Claudia and Tony, the two people you love most in the world, are in serious danger. You were willing to blast away at the monster who was out to kill them, you told me."

Oh God... what if something should go wrong?"

"What if it should go right?" Jamie said, reaching for my hand. "Let me fill you in on a kid named Tony Montes, survivor."

* * *

What if it should go right?

A thought to hold onto as I sat in the backseat of Polanski's car, a grim-faced Tony a few feet away. The car pulled over to pick up another passenger who slid into the backseat between me and Tony.

"Name's Julio," he told me. "You up for tonight, Tony?"

"I'm up for it," Tony said, patting his jacket.

I took a closer look at Julio. A teenager in patched denims, his wrists protruding from a jacket he'd outgrown. Another boy too young to be here, but old enough to be giving Tony pointers on using a gun.

At least Polanski had ruled out Tony's first weapon of choice—a knife.

I couldn't help wishing it was Denzel behind the wheel, but he'd been cut from the Mission—a last-minute switch. Someone caught him reloading Tony's gun and substituting fake bullets for the real thing. All Denzel had succeeded in killing was the bond that had grown between them over the years.

The car slowed for a traffic light. I tapped Polanski on the shoulder. "Tell me again why you think Arnie will go after Claudia tonight."

"He's been tailing Claudia every day. But for the last coupla days, he let up a little, just followed her to and from the library at night. That tells us where he plans the hit. We figure he'll move on her as soon as she shortcuts through the parking lot to her cross-town bus."

"But why *there*?"

"Have you read about those two college girls who were mugged and garroted?"

"Not far from the library," I said slowly.

"The killer's still at large," Polanski said. "Arnie's no dope. He's setting it up so it'll look like Claudia is victim number three of some nutcase out to murder 'loose' women."

"But what makes you so sure he'll go after Claudia *tonight*?"

He flashed me a grin. "Lee saw it before I did. Apparently, Arnie spends big bucks on his wardrobe. According to Claudia, he ordinarily dresses like a Park Avenue lawyer. He'll probably dress differently for tonight."

"Jeans, jacket and sneakers?"

"Wouldn't be caught dead in 'em. Instead of a pinstripe suit, he'll wear off-the-rack stuff. But the kicker will be his black scarf. Lee says the well-dressed man-about-town wouldn't be caught dead in a scarf this time of year unless he was on his way to the opera in a tux. I figure Arnie will have something special in mind for the scarf."

"I get the picture," I snapped.

"Good. Now stay loose. Arnie don't know we exist but we know all about Arnie, right down to his lime aftershave and the monogram on his satin boxer shorts."

We pulled in fifteen minutes ahead of schedule—an unattended parking lot. It was deserted at this hour except for half a dozen overnight cars Arnie wouldn't have recognized.

But the snappy blue Ford and the dusty panel truck, parked side by side, were ours.

A man dressed in black got out of the Ford. Another one emerged from the truck.

The SD Team joined up in front of Polanski's red Subaru wagon on the opposite side of the lot. "Synchronize your watches," he ordered. Then, "Everyone move into position."

One man headed for the Ford, Julio and Tony for the panel truck. Polanski and the other guy stayed with me in the Subaru. As soon as we ducked out of sight. I went into a deep-breathing routine. Take a deep breath... pause. Take another... Close your eyes and pray...

"Decoy in sight." Polanski's harsh whisper was like a voice from the grave.

My eyes flew open. Claudia had left the library steps and was headed in our direction, following the same diagonal line that would take her through the lot between the Subaru on one side and the Ford and panel truck on the other.

Claudia, dressed in a long white skirt, sauntered through a parking lot on a night so full of the soft scent of spring that caution, for once, seemed to have taken a backseat to the weather.

Ready...

If Arnie followed his own script, he would move

briskly down the same diagonal path any minute now.

"Target in sight."

Get set...

My eyes flashed to the edge of the lot. I saw a figure in a tightly belted camel's hair coat and some kind of a hat with a brim.

To keep people from getting a good look at your face, Arnie?

He moved with long slow strides.

So when the cops question potential eyewitnesses they'll be less likely to have noticed a man at the crime scene who was in no particular hurry?

My eyes locked onto the black silk scarf. Arnie was fingering it as he began to close the distance.

"Cleo!" he called out.

At the sound of her phony stage name, Claudia deliberately turned, passing Arnie's final ID test. She started to run, tripped over something, went sprawling.

Go!

Everybody out of the car—three of us on one side, three on the other. Six bodies flanking Arnie like a gauntlet. Six weapons aimed at his stomach as the Target whirled around, *his* target on her feet again and out of reach.

Tony rushed forward. "You murdered my sister!"

Improvised dialogue. TV melodrama.

But I spotted a cylinder, like a metal growth, sticking out of the muzzle end of the gun in Tony's two-handed grip—the silencer Julio had given him.

Julio now held something awkwardly that would have rested so naturally in Tony's hands: a camera. His assignment was to photograph Tony while he "made his bones."

I heard a crack. *Why,* if there was a silencer?

I couldn't fathom why Arnie pitched forward instead of backward. Or why Tony's gun seemed stuck to his hand.

Polanski cut the air with a gesture that froze everyone in place. He was peering into the night—the far end of the parking lot, rimmed with low buildings. I saw a figure wave, then jump down from his perch, a rifle hanging loose as he hurried toward us.

Denzel?

The rifle in his hand didn't have a silencer, but it had a scope. He'd shot Maria's killer before Tony had had a chance to pull the trigger.

"You killed him, you lousy bastard!" Tony screamed as the realization hit him.

Tony may have been holding a gun in his hand, but he had never sounded more like a child. Suddenly he was no longer holding the gun. Denzel had whipped it out of his hand.

"I quit this lousy organization!" Tony yelled, on the verge of tears.

"Move out, all of you," Denzel ordered.

"Jesus," Polanski muttered. "When Kagan hears—"

"Save the reciminations, Polanski," Denzel hissed. "We're not supposed to leave our calling card on this one, remember? Get your team out while a policeman who just *happened* to be passing by investigates the sound of a gunshot."

"Right." Polanski hoisted a protesting Tony away.

Julio followed, shaking his head. The men in black were already racing away. I watched the Ford take off, then the panel truck.

Denzel was bent over Arnie's body. "I'm making it look like a drug sale gone wrong," he told me when he noticed that I hadn't moved. "Now what?" he snapped as Claudia came running over with Julio in tow, still holding onto the camera.

"When I say 'action'—you know, like in 'Lights, Camera, Action'"—she told an open-mouthed Julio, "I want you to take my picture."

She turned to Denzel. "A photograph is part of the deal, right?" She pulled a gun from her shoulder bag. "My 'just in case' piece," she announced. "Ready?"

Julio nodded.

"Action," Claudia said calmly. She fired into Arnie's body. "This one's for Maria, you sick sonofabitch." She turned toward Denzel. "Think of the photograph as a formal application. Tony quits Victims Anonymous, I join. Don't worry, it's an unmarked gun, courtesy of my ex. I hear you two have met."

Denzel found his tongue before I did. "I get the picture. Now move out, all of you!"

Claudia and I ran for the Subaru as if someone were in hot pursuit.

CHAPTER 24

JAMIE WALKED OVER TO MY living-room bar and poured a brandy. "I hate seeing you so depressed," he said, offering it to me.

"Who's depressed?" I said, taking the glass.

"Shall I treat that as one of your wry jokes, or should I put on my psychiatrist's hat?"

"How about launching into a description of my symptoms?"

"Better yet," he said, edging me toward a comfortable chair, "I'll guide you to the heart of the matter."

"I just got off the phone with Claudia. Know what she said when I tried to talk her out of joining? She feels like a silent partner in Luke's fight. Her ex is part of this city's anti-vigilante task force!"

"Drink your brandy. Claudia's not your real problem, love."

The minute I finished my brandy, he refilled my glass and poured one for himself. "As horrific as Sarah's murder was, Karen, followed in short order by your son-in-law's suicide, you got through it and came back swinging. Since then, you've had a need to lavish affection on more than those stray cats you feed. You've been resisting it, but Tony Montes means a lot to you. Now, when you're ready to take him in, he turns you down flat. For now at least, he wants nothing to do with Victims Anonymous."

"I'm such a damn coward," I said, starting to cry.

"Why didn't I ask him before it was too late?"

"It's not too late," Jamie said. "It's too early."

He tipped my chin up so I couldn't avoid meeting his eyes.

"Will you take my professional word for it that this latest show of rebellion is only temporary? Tony needs you, Karen. What I want you to remember is that he knows it."

"You've seen him? He's back in therapy?"

Jamie shrugged. "In body, if not in spirit. Tony's not blaming me for the unexpected outcome of that Mission. But every time he misses an appointment, he's letting me know that he blames me for other things. Like keeping him honest."

"This Julio kid he moved in with, is it a decent atmosphere?"

"It's a bed and a place to catch a meal when he feels like it. Think of it as a halfway house. A home is what he'll have with you someday. Weepy tonight, aren't we?"

He didn't attempt to comfort me, just dumped a box of Kleenex in my lap. "How do you always know the right thing to do?" I asked him.

"Long years of practice," he said, heading for the kitchen.

He made omelets and black coffee, strong.

The minute I felt better, he switched roles on me. No more psychiatrist. No more perceptive friend. I could tell just from his tone—playful bordering on merry—that he had donned another hat.

"Your six-month leave is almost up," he said. "Don't frown. I'm not asking you to extend it."

"That's good because Larry expects me back and I'm going."

"That was the deal. But we need you to do something special, and being back with Kemp & Carusone would provide excellent cover."

"Jamie, don't you *dare* manipulate me into something else."

"Just listen for a minute, okay? The nationwide pattern of our activities has finally dawned on them."

"Dawned on whom?" I said through a flood of dread.

"The FBI," he said, smiling as if his wildest dream had come true. "Are you familiar with the legend of the Trojan horse?"

I closed my eyes. I was very familiar with it.

He said, "We want you to infiltrate Troy."

* * *

I went to another breakfast at Jamie's place, elegantly served and well attended, not unlike my introduction six months ago to VA's "inner circle."

I had been nervous then, but at least I'd been able to eat.

Brian O'Neal, as usual, was stuffing himself.

Chuck Polanski was more intent on sharing private chitchat with Lee than he was in the food.

Denzel was out of uniform.

Timothy Hogan wore a three-piece suit—seersucker instead of tweed.

Angela Russo was a welcome addition. I sat next to her, drinking coffee and trying not to look at Kagan who, as usual, seemed to be presiding over the rest of us from his vantage point on a windowsill.

"Karen?" he said.

The buzz of conversation trailed off.

"I already told Jamie I won't do it," I said evenly. "I like Max McCann. I respect him. I won't—"

"We all know that. But something important is at stake."

"Jamie made it perfectly clear what's at stake."

"We're not just talking about the safety of everyone in this room, some of whom you *also* like and respect.
176

Friends you've grown close to," Kagan said.

"Not just me and Angie," Denzel reminded me. "What about Rosa Ramirez? What about most of the people you've been working with over the last six months?"

"Not to mention your closest friend," Polanski interjected. "Claudia wouldn't be alive if it hadn't been for Victims Anonymous."

"We have cells in every major city in the country. If you don't agree to do this, Karen, a lot of people you brought into the fold will suffer the consequences," Lee told me.

As if I needed reminding.

I stood up abruptly. "You neglected to toss Jamie into the mix," I said caustically. "Like Claudia, he wouldn't be alive today if it weren't for me. You'll have my decision by the end of the week."

I headed for the door.

Angela met me there. And even though I'd never said word one to her about my feelings for Max McCann, she got to the heart of the matter, her voice too low for anyone else to hear.

"Don't hate yourself too much, Karen."

PART IV

CONFLICT

"We are dead groups of matter when we hate;
But when we love, we are as gods!"

—Friedrich Schiller, *Friendship*

CHAPTER 25

SOMEONE HAD FORGOTTEN THAT I'M not big on chrysanthemums. Still, they added a cheerful splash of color and a pungent smell to the dead air in the room. I moved them off my desk and onto a windowsill. The note next to the flowers said WELCOME BACK! Back to messy labor disputes. Reams of statistics. Writing speeches for testy CEOs who tended to trip over their metaphors.

At least my secretary remembered how I took my coffee—black and espresso-strong. She'd even moved what used to be my kidney-shaped "guest" ashtray from the coffee table to my desk while frowning with disapproval because it was no longer just for guests.

I lit up and took it one file at a time.

"No calls for a couple of hours," I told her.

She grinned. "Need some time to get back to the real world?"

I just left it, Colleen...

The first thing I did was pull some old files together when the FBI, in the person of Max McCann, had been a Kemp & Carusone client. It had yielded few clues to McCann's character but turned out to be much more revealing about my own. I had summed it up in half a dozen words: "The lady doth protest too much." Besides, we were both married.

Max, on the other hand, had my number right from the start. I remember telling myself he was baiting me with all that soft-spoken good humor—that he was smug—when, in fact, I was being defensive.

Only once had he lashed out at me in anger—the incident was marked in my notes. "G-man McCann, is it?" he'd said angrily. "You think in stereotypes, Karen. Macho trigger-happy redneck, subpoena in hand, wiretap in the pocket, midnight knock at the door. Every FBI agent a chump?"

I sighed and went to work on Kemp & Carusone business. Two hours later I was feeling like a drunken sailor wondering what had happened to her sea legs. It couldn't be *this* hard to concentrate. I couldn't be *this* bored.

I made myself a "most pressing business" pile and plunged in.

A couple of hours later, I discovered that everything I was working on was one big yawn. Colleen swore that I was turning into a caffeine addict.

"How's it going?" Larry asked from the doorway as I sat contemplating my third cup in as many hours. Ever since I'd been back, he had been looking in on me from time to time like a mother hen.

"The Bill Stanley communications audit is almost done," I told Larry, stifling a yawn I didn't have to fake. I'd been at my desk since the ungodly hour of seven. "Do you want a preliminary report? Management relations are shaky across the board—distributors, dealers, media. An in-depth probe will turn up the usual company strengths and weaknesses, with a success factor—"

"Still having trouble, aren't you?"

Along with listlessness, Larry had picked up on the unmistakable sound of duty.

"Don't expect to get back in the swing of things right away," he told me. "Especially when you have other things on your mind."

Other things. An affair of the heart gone sour, I'd told him.

Setting the hook, Kagan had called it.

I didn't have to fake an awkward smile—not when I recognized the penetrating look behind those horn-rims of his. Larry's matchmaking instincts were practically reaching across the room.

"You seeing anyone now?" he asked.

I wanted to hug him for his concern. "It's probably too soon," I said.

Larry had made his move.

I just hadn't expected it to happen the minute I left work that afternoon. As I stepped out of the elevator, I spotted Max in the lobby.

I let the five o'clock crowd surge ahead of me. What I let him see as I headed in his direction was surprise on its way to becoming dismay.

"Hello, Max," I said when we were within touching distance.

"You've been letting your hair grow."

"I haven't been to a beauty parlor lately."

"I like it," he said. His eyes said, "I want to touch it."

I backed away automatically. "What are you doing here?"

"Welcoming you back."

"I happened to be in town so I thought we might have dinner."

I permitted myself a small smile. "You're persistent."

"It goes with the training."

"What brings you to New York?" I asked as we crossed the lobby.

"Special assignment in the offing."

"So Larry sent you a distress signal," I said with just the right hint of anger.

"I'm grateful to him," he said without apology.

I heard Kagan's voice in my ear.

Make contact as soon as you can.

"Okay, dinner it is, as long as it's Italian. Same deal as last time, McCann. You pick the restaurant and do the ordering."

We were sharing a platter of steamed clams when one of McCann's clams refused to open. It struck me that he was a clam when it came to opening up about the Bureau no matter how innocent my questions were—at least they sounded innocent to *me*. Even so, I detected an undercurrent of excitement when he said that, aside from me, he couldn't wait to return to Washington.

I tried again with the pasta course. "Pretty ordinary looking, the FBI's New York headquarters. I was expecting something more stately on the outside and sinister on the in."

He laughed. "You'd find our Washington headquarters more to your liking."

Don't count on it!

"Did you get the assignment you wanted?"

"Hard to tell. It would mean more time here."

Remembering Kagan's instructions ("Let him get personal but not too personal"), I led him into a guarded conversation about Jamie. About how I was still feeling bruised, even though Jamie and I had remained friends.

After dinner, Max took me home and asked for an herbal tea. "I could use less caffeine in my life right now," he told me.

"Hope you like chamomile," I said while I crossed fingers that I could dig some up. Black coffee had long ago aced tea out of my life.

I left him in the den. When I came back with the tea, he was so engrossed in a wall of photographs that he didn't even hear me. As he turned away, I saw something happening to his eyes—a slight widening. I didn't have to guess what had caused it. He was experiencing the small shock of comparing my picture—taken nine months ago—with the woman who had just walked in the door. It was your basic "before and after" phenomenon.

I glanced into the first mirror I saw. What leaped out made my heart shrink. Innocence isn't the dominant trait in the face of a woman in her late forties. Yet how else to describe what the camera had captured in my photograph taken at the end of October right before Sarah's rape and murder? It wasn't that my face was lined with wrinkles. I'd have preferred that to what I saw in the mirror.

A mask of deceit.

I managed to ask him when he'd be back from Washington. After that, I rattled on about how my enjoyment of the PR business at Kemp & Carusone had dissolved on me like a soft tablet in hot water.

Not to worry, he assured me. It was natural.

We had a nightcap in the living room.

"What's happened to your green thumb?" he asked, frowning over an untidy row of drooping plants that had dropped half their leaves on the windowsill.

How could I tell him that I hadn't even noticed?

I said, "We could use a shot in the arm, my plants and me."

"I'll call you as soon as I'm back in town," he told me.

"I'd like that, Max," I said and walked him to the door.

CHAPTER 26

"WHAT HAPPENED TO YOUR LIVING room?" Claudia decorously lowered herself onto a plump red cushion with her favorite butterfly motif. "I got bored with straight-backed chairs."

I looked around, happy to see the old arrangement. Gone was the dignified-office look—trim tight furniture in grays and tans, indirect lighting, and shelves of unread books. Back were all the knock-your-socks-off colors, the exotic plants, the cushiony chairs that forced you into a reclining position. Her lighting scheme was new, and there was nothing indirect about it—the pulsating reds, pinks, and lavenders of a fireworks display.

I pulled up a burnt-orange cushion and joined her on the floor.

"Okay, Claudia," I said, accepting a glass of Chardonnay, "why the summons? I take it Kagan wants you to be my official contact."

"Makes sense, don't you think? Now that you and McCann have gotten together, he wants you to steer clear of everybody but your old friend Claudia."

"Karen Newman, reporting in," I said with mock solemnity, taking a dim satisfaction in the fact that my report would only take a few minutes.

Blame it on a clam, Kagan.

"We have a valuable pipeline into the police," Claudia said when I'd finished.

"Thanks to Denzel and Angela?" I asked.

"You're kidding, right? Who better to pump the new head of the police task force than yours truly?"

"Claudia, it's *Luke* we're talking about!"

"The pot calling the kettle black? You don't like what you're doing with McCann? Neither do I with Luke. Given the stepped-up FBI interest, your intelligence-gathering efforts could prove vital. My intel keeps Victims Anonymous two steps ahead of the local law."

"How can you be so calm?"

"Think so?" she countered. "Look past the makeup job."

I saw it then—signs of stress, like the faint cracks in old plaster. "Are you being careful, at least?"

"Not just careful, dahling. Clevah," she said, slipping effortlessly into her Tallulah Bankhead routine from one of our favorite movies. She hugged my fears away. "Not to worry. I'm being very tactful. I have a question, by the way—and don't you dare laugh at me. What the hell is a Trojan horse?"

I couldn't help myself. I erupted into laughter. Minutes later, Claudia joined in.

When we came up for air, I explained how the ancient Greeks had schemed their way into the walled city of Troy—their fiercest enemy—by leaving a hollow wooden horse full of soldiers just outside the gates, hoping the Trojans would bring the gift inside.

"Got it! Beware of Greeks bearing gifts." She pulled a dictionary off a shelf and came up with as good a definition as any. "A subversive device insinuated within enemy ranks."

Refilling our wine glasses, she told me that Kemp & Carusone was about to receive a call from the National Corrections Association.

"Chuck Polanski's outfit? What on earth for?"

"Hell, *you're* in the image-polishing business, not me. My guess is that, from time to time, Kagan wants to give you an excuse to meet with someone besides me."

"To discuss what?"

"Tactics. We're swimming in FBI waters now."

As if I needed reminding!

"I ought to be talking to Kagan," I protested. "Polanski's more of a human being, but he doesn't exactly inspire confidence. Not after what he set Tony up to do."

"Don't sweat it. I figure Kagan really *is* calling the shots. Polanski is just the detail man."

"You're probably right."

Claudia finger-traced the butterfly pattern on her cushion. "According to my Chinese mythology professor, the butterfly—also known as *l'angelica farfala*—is a symbol of longevity. Dante's symbol for our immortal soul..." she mused.

"Interesting," I said. "The ancient Greeks used the word 'psyche' for butterflies *and* souls. Beats me why an insect that's lucky to live out the summer should be a symbol for longevity."

The quip turned sour in my mouth. Claudia had always been drawn to butterflies. It was reflected in her favorite décor, even in her choice of jewelry—from pins to barrettes. What filled me with uneasiness, I realized, was the escalating danger of our situation as we headed into our own risk-filled summer.

"Polanski's really not a bad guy," Claudia said in that same musing tone.

"Because he headed the Arnie Mission?"

"Because he helped keep me alive."

She had said it so softly that I knew she was feeling it too... the exquisite fragility of life.

* * *

I met Polanski in the East Village. It was cocktail hour or I'd never have set foot in the neighborhood, let

EYE FOR AN EYE

alone in a bar with an overflow crowd that smelled of sweat, leather, and cheap beer. On the way to a booth in back, he led me past a bunch of tattooed well-oiled muscle men.

"What's up?" I asked as soon as he'd ordered drinks, wanting to get the hell out of the area while it was still light.

"An FBI power struggle between Washington and New York," he said. "The big question is whether agent Max McCann gets to head a certain vigilante investigation." He lowered his voice. "We're with Washington on this. We *want* McCann. Your job is to give him the edge he needs."

"I'm supposed to help Max get the assignment? But that's crazy!"

"Scary maybe, but not crazy."

As he explained what Kagan had in mind, I had to admit it made a lot of sense.

"—so, as soon as McCann is 'in like Flynn,' you pull out all the stops."

"Meaning?" I said, on instant alert.

"Kagan wants you to play Mata Hari."

"No way! Kagan can go to hell and back before—"

"I told him you'd say that." Big grin. "Always figured you for a one-man woman."

"You figured right," I shot back, more than willing to cash in on my "torrid romance" with Jamie.

CHAPTER 27

SOME ORDERS GO DOWN EASIER than others.

Be wined and dined, if that's his pleasure. No more prying until you get the word. My pleasure, Kagan. Your move.

A week had passed and there'd been nothing new from Kagan.

A whole week of Max in town and me in his arms. It turned out that he loved to dance. Every time we went to dinner, he seemed to have an ear cocked, waiting for the music to begin. I never wanted it to end...

"Penny?" Max asked.

"Just enjoying the moment. I like it here."

A slick little combo swung into melody—danceable tunes with the kind of lyrics you want to croon in your partner's ear. We were about to do exactly that when a beefy fellow with a crew cut, standing at the bar, called out "McCann?" and waved him over.

"Be right back," Max said with an apologetic half-smile.

But it was about fifteen minutes later when Max came back, preoccupation in his eyes and a newspaper tucked under his arm.

"Sorry that took so long," he apologized.

"Dance?" I prodded.

"Sure."

But his mind was elsewhere.

"Who was that?" I asked.

"A business contact."

Kagan's contact... or the FBI's?

As soon as the music stopped, I said, "Ready for a cappuccino?"

He nodded. While we waited, I reached idly for the newspaper the beefy guy had given him. It fell open to a headline. THE FOX STRIKES AGAIN!

Kagan's contact. The headline confirmed it.

I leafed idly through the paper as Max sipped his coffee and I pretended mine was too hot. I looked up, finally, with a troubled frown.

"Something the matter?" he said, finally noticing.

"This news story about some vigilantes. I thought it was an aberration—that it was limited to Manhattan. But there's a reference to Chicago, Los Angeles, Detroit..."

"I know," he said.

"But *why*? Are you involved in this vigilante business?"

"Not yet, but I may be. Karen, what's the *matter*?"

"*This* is the assignment you've been after?"

"Yes," he said, puzzled.

I pushed my coffee away and lit a cigarette. "Max, if I'd thought that these people—the vigilantes—had anything to do with you, I'd have mentioned them sooner. Not that I'm eager to talk about the whole thing. It's just..."

I let him interrupt my nervous rambling. Let him guide me back to where I wanted to go. To Kagan, the chauffeur who had driven me and my ex to our daughter's funeral. "I was approached by these people. By Victims Anonymous," I told him. "Naturally, I told the bastard off. But he and his group tried again after the funeral of my son-in-law. They sent me photographs of the gang that had attacked Sarah, including a photograph of her killer. Frankly, after what happened in Family Court, I was tempted to join them. But not for long. I called an ADA I knew. After that..."

I tried not to focus on what was happening to Max's

face. I was thinking of Kagan's rule of thumb, glad he wasn't here to gloat over the results.

Build as much truth into a cover story as you can get away with.

Max's face was rigid with shock. It was followed by the slow soft smile of a man who can hardly believe his good fortune. "I have to call Washington," he said, motioning our waiter for a check.

I stole a glance at the dance floor. They were playing a waltz.

* * *

"The guessing game is over," Max explained as we emerged from Dulles Airport into the steam bath that is Washington, D.C. in July. "This gives us a *modus operandi* on how these vigilantes recruit."

"One version, at least," I said, as nervous as I sounded.

"It's a start. It could lead anywhere."

It had led me to FBI headquarters in Washington.

"The card they gave you helps," he said, hailing a cab.

"How?"

"We have a name."

He pulled it out of his pocket and we both stared at it: Victims Anonymous.

"Up to now we weren't sure. Our information has been sketchy."

Score one. Kagan had wanted to know how much the FBI knew.

In the cab he took my hand, a total departure for McCann when he had business on his mind. He proceeded to point out the sights. Washington was his adopted city now. Its clean straight lines and stark white monuments suited him, I thought. I told him I preferred the chaos of New York, which had the virtue of being true.

Our cab rolled into an ample courtyard ringed with columns, like a circular row of guardians. There were statues everywhere, I noted as we got out. I mentally compared the forty-story skyscraper that was FBI headquarters in Manhattan with its Washington D.C. counterpart—a squat stone building with sledgehammer solidity.

"I told you there was a lot about D.C. you'd like," Max said with a grin as I halted before an enormous bronze flag and, behind it, a cluster of three statues.

"Fidelity, Bravery, Integrity," I read aloud.

"This sculpture was J. Edgar's pride and joy," he told me.

"It's sexist, if you ask me—and you did. 'Bravery' stands tall—a man of action. 'Integrity' sits in thoughtful contemplation. Now take a close look at 'Fidelity' as she kneels in abject adoration—"

Joined laughter. It tore a hole in the tension I was feeling.

Inside, a somber guard checked Max's badge—an impressive bit of heraldry and gold stars. He slipped a visitor's badge-on-a-chain around my neck.

He grew away from me with each floor we passed on the elevator. With almost brisk formality, he led the way to his office on the fourth floor. It was what I had pictured—no frills. A circular desk, a couple of comfortable-looking chairs, a small leather couch, a bookcase, a small portrait of J. Edgar, and next to it, a framed golden key.

"On the occasion of my tenth anniversary with the Bureau," he said with a touch of pride. "Next year I'll pass the twenty-year mark."

I sat on a couch while Max put through a call to see if his immediate superior was ready for us, "he" being the section chief of the Criminal Investigation Division.

"He's running a little late," Max told me, replacing the phone.

It was a reprieve of sorts.

He offered me a welcome distraction. "Care for a private tour? We run them all day long. It's top-drawer image-polishing, Karen. Right up your alley," he teased as he rang for an escort.

Max introduced me to an attractive young blonde woman who arrived ten minutes later. We didn't bother with an elevator since it was just a few flights down.

The inevitable video waited—a rousing welcome by the current FBI director, a conservative-banker type.

Let the tour begin...

Ten minutes into it and I was issuing silent congratulations to the Bureau's PR staff. A stark photograph is worth a thousand words, especially when accompanied by an artful arrangement of startling facts and figures. Hadn't I introduced the same sort of format into my PR campaign for Victims Anonymous?

The FBI labs were a marvel, exploring everything from the obvious—fingerprints, blood, urine—to the not so obvious.

We can be identified by the sweat of our brow? Our tear ducts?

I saw firearms by the thousands in a display labeled "Gangster Era." A documents section that looked into fraudulent checks, anonymous letters, and stolen art. A "Crime Clock" that Jamie would have killed for—one murder, rape, burglary, robbery every few minutes.

I was cheered by the Bureau's four "priorities": crime, foreign counterintelligence, white-collar crime, terrorism.

Nothing about vigilante justice...

I was chilled by the statistics my guide reeled off. She put the total number of FBI agents at well over eight thousand. A lot of manpower.

"They operate out of sixty field offices," she told me. As to the hundreds of criminals on the FBI's ten-most-wanted list, she said that the Bureau had caught all but twenty-five.

That efficient? They'd been at it only forty years.

When my guide launched into a description of the Bureau's computer network—it was called the National Crime Information Center—I cracked a smile and pretended to look interested.

"Talk about instant information!" she exclaimed.

Talk about instant fear.

Max showed up when my tour guide was about to steer me in the direction of the FBI's firearms demonstration.

"Have you discovered our Achilles' heel?" he asked me—and showed me a statistic I had missed, all right. No female FBI agents until 1972, the year Hoover died. "We had three women in the early twenties," he pointed out with impish good humor, "but two of them resigned right after Mr. Hoover took office. The third one lasted only a couple of years."

We rode the elevator, exited on the top floor, and entered a wood-paneled office.

"Karen Newman, meet Bernard Rees," Max said.

My fear-ball started to form the minute Rees slipped into the "I know you've been over all this, sorry to put you through it again" routine. It took only a few questions before I began to appreciate how adroit this man was—a debriefing that never for an instant left the comfortable arena of an informal chat. After a while, it was hard not to go with the flow, even to the point of doodling on a yellow pad.

Unfortunately, it gave Max an idea.

"Think you could do a quick sketch of the man at the funeral?"

"I don't draw," I lied. Actually, I do a fair likeness. But even if I'd attempted it, they would have been disappointed. Kagan would have emerged as a lean-faced Everyman with not much in the way of distinguishing characteristics.

"I'm interested in the assumption that you and the police made initially," Rees said, leaning forward to show how interested he really was. "Tell me again why you assumed that these vigilantes were a strictly local operation."

"I guess because *I'm* local. I live in Manhattan. I buried my daughter in Queens, and her attackers were from the Bronx. All New York City territory. I just assumed it was their territory too."

"A national pattern has been emerging," Rees told me, and began to describe it.

Score one. Kagan had figured they didn't know much. He was right.

"What do you think of us, Karen Newman?" Rees asked as he lit my cigarette.

"What do I think of the FBI?" I forced a laugh. "Max has been telling tales out of school. That was the 'old' FBI. From what Max tells me, things have changed for the better."

Rees smiled. "It may surprise you to learn that Max and I share your views about the 'old' FBI. Illegal wiretaps. Harassment of civil rights leaders. A deplorable business."

Bernard Rees seemed such a reasonable man. He had such a reasonable face. Big cow-brown eyes and a lot of friendly wrinkles—the kind that betray how often a man laughs. He was chewing placidly on an unlit pipe.

Max, on the other hand, looked unhappy... which told me the two of them hadn't worked out this part of the scenario in advance. Rees launched into a brief description of the "new" FBI—one leery of trampling on constitutional rights. That was at odds with a certain faction within the Bureau.

"Is this wise, Bernie, making Karen privy to such information?" Max asked.

"Why I think we must. Hold your reservations in check for a moment, Max. I understand you've taken our tour, Karen. May I call you Karen? The tour gives you a fair idea of our jurisdiction—kidnapping, terrorism, and the like. All federal crimes. But what kind are making headlines?"

"Street crimes?"

"Fast becoming *the* social issue of our time," he agreed. "One no savvy politician can afford to ignore. A matter not for the FBI, in my view, but for our local police forces."

"I couldn't agree more." I said with conviction.

"Yet in the next presidential election two years hence, I can tell you with assurance that a number of politicians will be tempted to translate the public's growing impatience with escalating violence in their cities into legislation of... shall we say 'dubious validity'? Some of us worry—not unduly—about the role the Bureau might be forced to play."

"I read something somewhere about a presidential task force," I said casually.

"On violent crime. Quite so. A trial balloon to test public reaction. It's headed by a former attorney general whose task is to discover what the federal government can do about what *traditionally* has been the responsibility of the states."

"What they can do is federalize crime," Max said tightly.

"There's talk of resurrecting an old idea in FBI circles." Rees telegraphed his distaste by the sharp angle of his nose. "Create a national computerized criminal-history system—a dangerous precedent. Another trial balloon is floating about. Ambitious congressmen have been introducing 'career criminal' bills. Then there's the spectacle of anti-crime rhetoric emanating from the White House which, quite frankly, I find ominous."

"They won't be happy until they've turned the FBI into a national police force. To concentrate that much power into a single government agency," Max snapped, spilling his coffee. "What do we use for a model—a Latin American dictatorship?"

"Max is quite the fanatic on this subject," Rees said with delicacy. "What he means is that it's safer to disperse the power. Roughly ninety percent of crime is handled locally. Always has been."

"That can change," Max muttered.

"What he means," Rees said softly, "is that this vigilante outfit could be the catalyst for such a change."

"But *why*?" I asked with genuine alarm.

"The timing," Max said. "That, and the apparent scope of this vigilante organization."

"It would appear that we have a nationwide conspiracy on our hands," Rees jumped in. "Individuals committing crimes to avenge crimes. It goes without saying .that once their criminal activity crosses state borders, FBI jurisdiction kicks in."

Rees finally lit his pipe.

"It's also a good excuse for a certain faction in the Bureau to point to a breakdown in the system that our local police aren't equipped to handle—or so they'll claim," Max said. "If those eager beavers get to step in and mop up—" He broke off with a harsh laugh. "If they do, they'll make a federal case out of it."

Rees laughed in real appreciation. "It would certainly dovetail with the president's desire to get people aboard his 'federalize crime' bandwagon, wouldn't it? Worse, it would give the FBI the kind of 'hero' publicity we could do without right now. Because you see," he said gravely, "if we drag the case out just to keep making headlines—and, in the process, political capital—if we bring down Victims Anonymous with a series of big splashes, I'm afraid it could spawn that national police force we have every reason to be afraid of."

"Unless?" I said, naming what he had left unspoken.

"I like this woman," he told Max. "Unless a very different faction in the Bureau were calling the shots. Unless Max, here, were to take charge of this investigation."

Score two. Kagan had wanted to confirm that McCann would likely be heading the investigation.

I said with pasted-on calm, "What difference would Max make?"

"I'd wrap it up fast."

My skepticism must have leaped out because Max was looking slightly offended.

"It can be done. To defuse a widespread operation," Rees said, "one must ignore the little people and take out their leaders."

"Cut off the head of the snake and the body will die," I murmured.

Rees smiled. "I remember the film. A hard one to forget. *Viva Zapata!*"

"What if *only* little people are involved?" I asked.

"Not possible. There are clever brains at work here. It's too well organized."

Score three. Kagan had wanted to know their strategy.

"Where would you start?

"New York, of course," Max said.

"Evidence points to Manhattan as their base," Rees chimed in. "And as you pointed out, it's where they tried to recruit you."

Did Max know where this was leading? Did Kagan have to be right all *the time?*

"Given encouragement, they might try again," Rees said.

Max was on his feet. "No, Bernie. Karen, I swear—"

He didn't have to. I said, "It's all right, Max."

"Just the same, it must have occurred to you, Max. The logic is inescapable." Rees turned to me. "You see, our director is on the fence about this, never mind why. In his heart of hearts, he knows Max, here, has the perfect background for the job. And quite apart from sheer experience, Max works well with local law enforcement. But more important, I trust Max. Give me what I need to convince a fence-sitter, Karen. Permit me to tell my director that if your good friend Max were to be in charge, you'd agree to reestablish contact with the vigilante outfit. I gather from Max that you know how."

"I don't know what to say."

Vacillate, Kagan had told me.

"I daresay Max is eager to talk you out of it so, in fairness, let's not try to resolve the matter in one sitting. But decide soon, will you, Karen?"

He might just as well have said, "Welcome aboard!"

Max and I had planned to stop off for a drink at his place, but he wasn't in the mood to play host. We were silent on the way to the airport. But as soon as we boarded, he took my hand. "No," he said. "It's too risky. "I don't want you to do it."

"I'm tired, Max. Let's talk about it when we're back in New York."

I pretended to fall asleep even as I fought fiercely to stay awake, afraid I'd have a nightmare about Sarah that might give me away.

We had planned dinner in Manhattan after we landed but Max took me straight home and saw me to the door.

"Stop torturing yourself," I told him. "I have no choice and you know it."

I dug out my keys.

He looked as if he wanted to shove his fist through the door. "I'll call you," he said and walked away.

"Come back here and kiss me good night."

He walked back like a sleepwalker, as if giving himself time to believe what I'd said.

He didn't give me a chance to take it back.

I never wanted it to end...

Until I remembered Kagan's Mata Hari scenario and knew that it never should have begun. I pulled away from him.

I replayed my reasons for committing this unforgivable treason in the first place. It wasn't because I owed Victims Anonymous a damn thing for avenging Sarah's murder. After all, they had tricked me into joining. It was because I couldn't bring myself to put so many people I loved in harm's way.

When Max unlocked my door, I knew he wouldn't push it open without an invitation. Max didn't push. I went inside, not trusting my voice even to say good night.

Minutes later, the phone rang.

I answered, surprised that my voice sounded so normal.

Kagan's sounded smug.

"Congratulations," he said.

"If that's a joke, I'm not in the mood."

"It's no joke. I wanted to mark the occasion. The role you've just undertaken."

"What role?" I snapped.

"Karen Newman, double agent."

CHAPTER 28

M AX WALKED IN FIVE MINUTES late, looking wilted from the heat.

Thanks to the possibility, however remote, that my vigilante contacts might have me under surveillance, Max had told me, he wanted to avoid my being seen with an FBI agent.

I was eyeing the meat-loaf-and-potatoes menu from a corner booth and bemoaning the demise of our elegant dining-and-dancing days when he slid into the seat opposite me.

"August in New York," he groused, as if Washington had never heard of heat waves. "You know this place?" he asked, looking around with suspicion at pseudo-brick walls and a fake stucco ceiling. The marigolds on the tables were real.

"My once-favorite diner," I said, handing him the menu. "Let's hope the cook hasn't gone the way of the décor. It used to be comfortable red leather booths instead of these tight little tables."

"Try the egg-lemon soup and the stuffed grape leaves," I suggested. "You like moussaka? I'm getting the meatless version."

I was glad to see that the service was still fast.

Max dug in with gusto. "Now *this* is what I call down-home cooking," he said after he'd finished his soup and savored almost half of his meatless moussaka.

He put his fork aside without warning. "God, I hate

the waiting."

"It's worth waiting for if I get to meet a leader or two."

"But to risk your going on some vigilante mission—"

"Max," I said, longing to tell him it wasn't my first, "I'm not in any danger. Not as long as they want something from me."

"Beats me what they want with you when they're putting out stuff of *this* caliber," he said, producing a familiar-looking sheet of bright orange paper. He handed it to me.

"So it's come to this," I read out loud, marveling at the steadiness of my voice. "Teenagers who sweep through our subways, relieving us of our watches, wallets and chains. Teenagers who rove in bands and teach us to send our kids to school with 'stickup money' in their lunch bags."

"Not bad," I told him, handing it back as I pictured the day I had written it...

"Well, look who's here," he said with a grin.

When I saw who was headed our way I dropped my fork, which was not too far off the mark, I suppose, for a woman at the unexpected sight of a man who used to be her lover until their romance had soured.

"What have they done to our oasis of chrome and neon?" Jamie exclaimed with a sweeping gesture. "Curtains, tablecloths, and cheap carpeting instead of that glorious black-and-white tiled floor. A glitzy coffee shop pretending to be a restaurant. It's an architectural lobotomy!"

I managed a wan smile of acquiescence.

"So you're partial to old diners, are you?" Max observed, offering Jamie a chair.

"They're going the way of the dinosaurs, I'm afraid," Jamie said, sitting down next to me. "How are you, Max?"

Max was fine.

After getting over the shock of hearing Jamie call

Max by his first name, I tuned out their small talk as Jamie waved a waitress over and we waited until she returned with Jamie's order. The minute she was gone, Jamie looked from Max to me and dropped his bomb.

"This meeting isn't accidental, Max," he said. "Karen has confided in me about what she's planning to do."

Max slid his chair back, eyes narrowed, as if to get a better view of us both.

I didn't even have the luxury of digging four inches of heel into Jamie's leather boot.

"Are you upset by this... breach of security, I suppose you'd call it? You won't be after I explain," Jamie reassured him.

"I'm listening."

I listened on a different level. It was an artful blend of truth and fiction—Kagan's cover-story rule...

How, after the pseudo-chauffeur at Sarah's funeral had mailed me some graphic photographs of my daughter's ordeal shortly after a Family Court judge had released the murderer, I'd been tempted to join Victims Anonymous.

How I'd consulted Jamie professionally.

How he had zeroed in on the irrationality—the danger—inherent in vigilante solutions to injustice.

Ha!

How Jamie persuaded me to turn the photographs over to an ADA.

How, during the course of helping me over the guilt of my short-lived temptation, we had become good friends.

How it was hardly surprising that, even after our personal relationship had ended, I would confide in my friend and former psychiatrist when, once again, I found myself in the unsettling position of taking up with these vigilantes—albeit, this time, for a good cause.

Did Max blame me for confiding in him? For Jamie

being worried about me?

Max didn't blame either of us. "You should have told me how frightened you really were," he said, reaching for my hand. Holding it on the tabletop for all the world—for Jamie—to see.

"If you came here for reassurance, Jamie," he said slowly, accepting Jamie's offer of a cigarette, "all you'll get is a good supper."

"Can we talk, at least?"

"If you don't mind doing it in the night air. Security," Max reminded him.

"Bringing tension to the table is bad manners, my mother used to say. Forgive me," Jamie said, and proceeded to engage us in a merry round of entertainment while we finished our meal.

I sat back and watched it happening all over again. Max being pulled into the vortex of Jamie's charm. The small pleasure of discovering some shared experience, a common ground. A hearty laugh, sparked by jocular good humor.

... As lonely as all that, Max?

I had barely been able to pull a smile out of him since our trip to Washington.

When the check came, I grabbed it—first sense of control I'd had all evening.

It didn't last five minutes on the street. Jamie began to ask Max some questions.

Max responded as far as he could, even as a bond cemented before my eyes.

A bond constructed on the fraudulent foundation of mutual concern.

I resented being a pawn in whatever new game Jamie was playing—not that I could do anything about it

"I have to admit these vigilantes have a sharp point to their dagger, Max. Just last week I was browsing through a mail-order catalogue and four items jumped out at me," Jamie said. "A door-knob alarm that goes off at a touch. A key ring with a gas-propelled shriek canister—I'm not kidding. A woman's belt with a knife disguised as a buckle. Oh, and Italy's latest fashion accessory. A leather anti-mugging pouch."

"According to the Bureau, we have a greater chance of being mugged than of getting a divorce," Max said with a grin.

The switch to easygoing banter over the sad state of our criminal justice system was like a cool breeze in the midst of a heat wave. It blew the tensions away.

Jamie was leaning against a lamppost when Max announced that we had earned ourselves dessert— something sinful—and for one wild moment I thought Jamie was about to swing round the pole like a kid who'd been told he can stay up late.

I walked on eggshells after that, sensing more truth than fiction in Jamie's behavior.

As we left the ice cream parlor, Max said, "To be continued."

Jamie grinned. "When?"

"Next Sunday?" Max asked me.

"Why not," I said with a shrug. Did I have a choice?

We let Jamie have the first cab and spent the next twenty minutes talking about him before a second one came along. Max kept our cab waiting while he delivered me to my doorman. In unspoken agreement, we'd been avoiding my apartment door since the good-night kiss.

We avoided more than that. I walked in on Jamie enjoying a sherry on my couch. My glass awaited me on the coffee table.

"Angry with me? Or just confused, I hope?"

"How about both?" I snapped, annoyed because I needed the sherry.

"Kagan was expecting a personal slant on Max," Jamie told me. "But that's not what you handed off to

Claudia. Kagan knows damn well you don't intend to do a good job in your role as a double agent. Missed my calling," he said, pouring himself another sherry. "I should have been an actor."

"*Were* you acting, Jamie?"

"Missed your calling too, love. You should have been a therapist."

"You're glazing over," I said, looking closer. "Are you four or five drinks ahead of me? What the hell is going on?"

"Should've been an actor," he said. "Should've been *something*."

He picked up the bottle of sherry and raised it like a flag. "To my mother," he said—a lethargic toast. He refilled our glasses.

"What's wrong?" I said, alarmed.

"Mother is what's wrong."

"I thought she was dead," I said, frowning with the memory of the only other time he'd had too much to drink. He had pointed out the portrait of a beautiful young woman.

And told me what? That he was fifteen when she had died.

"Oh no," he said with a grim smile. "Mother is very much alive."

"Go home while you're still able to," I said gently.

"See you on Sunday," he said.

He got as far as the door before it dawned on me. It must have dawned on him at the same time because he reached in his pocket and placed a key on my foyer table.

"I lied to you before about the doorman letting me in."

A duplicate key, surreptitiously made. Naïve of me not to have realized what I had forfeited along with my peace of mind. What else, besides my privacy... surveillance? A tap on my telephone?

I let it go because Jamie was in no condition to give an accounting of anything, and because the problem I was wrestling with was graver than duplicate keys to my apartment.

CHAPTER 29

SUNDAY IN THE PARK HAD been a revelation. Jamie's picnic conversation was riddled with provocative asides about a host of thorny issues confronting people in the field of criminal justice. Max, it turned out, despised light sentences for rapists and murderers, was one of us on the parole issue, and had less of a problem with capital punishment than *I* did!

The conversation made me so uncomfortable that Jamie's suggestion of a movie had been a welcome relief. I should have known better. When I heard what we were going to see—the latest in a series of vigilante-style melodramas—I was fairly certain that what Jamie was after was much more than a personal slant on FBI agent Max McCann.

I was getting good at a newly developed skill—how to hide my fears. Besides, I have a history of losing sight of everything when I go to the movies. Seeing one in the Big Apple is quite an experience. What you get for the price of admission is a sort of group encounter with a lot of irreverent sidewalk philosophers. This particular movie theater full of critics expressed themselves periodically in jeers and cheers, howls and whistles, thumbs-downs, and rally-round-the-flag.

They were mostly rallying on this flick. Lots of frenzied applause each time the hero—a tough-talking, gun-toting Vietnam vet—mouthed such predictable dialogue as "By God, I didn't fight for my country just to come home and watch some foulmouthed punks take over the greatest city in the world!"

Afterward, the three of us retired to my place for beer and pizza.

"Admit it, Max, you enjoyed the film as much as I did," Jamie teased. "You couldn't witness some trigger-happy psycho getting away with the slaughter of innocents without rooting for the good guy to blow his so-called brains out. I saw it in your eyes, lawman."

"Guilty," Max said, amused.

"Keep the admissions flowing, Max. I've barely begun," Jamie said gleefully. "The rapist who buried his victims alive. You wanted him to go down."

"Makes me human, does it?"

"Makes you one of us, all right. How about the scene—"

Makes you one of us. You trying to recruit him, Jamie?

Not for long, apparently. I listened to a deeply troubled Max grope for solutions to the crime problem... and heard him concede failure.

"I don't have the answers," he said with a sigh. "But neither do they."

"No more vigilante talk," Jamie announced as he reached for my best brandy with a proprietary air not lost on Max. "A piece of my personal history, Max," he said, pouring with a flourish, "in exchange for a chunk of yours."

Brandy mellows... was that it? Or was it the impression Jamie gave Max of being a fellow loner? It was as if Jamie had found the hidden combination that opened the door to a secret room. Max's usual reticence gave way without a shudder of resistance. What came through was a man who loved the Bureau without ever losing sight of its flaws. Who, over the years, had paid a steep price, such as losing plum assignments because of his integrity.

"Been shifted all over the lot, haven't you?" Jamie said.

Max's expression was resigned, not bitter.

Jamie picked up on it. "That's what you get for being a hero worshipper," he said.

"Who, me?" Max scoffed. "Not likely."

"Not lately, you mean. I'll wager it was different growing up in the cornfields when you longed to be an FBI agent."

"No cigar, Jamie. After seeing two mounted policemen in a movie, I grew up wanting to be a New York cop on horseback."

"What an adventurous notion!" Jamie exclaimed.

"I'd have made tracks right after high school, but my old man had his own obsession. I was the first one the family could afford to educate, so his goal for me was to go for the brass ring—a profession. We struck a deal. I would attend a Midwestern college, followed by some law school in Manhattan. Then, if I *still* wanted to be a cop... " He shrugged. "Well, I was in the right city for it. If not, I could use my law degree to become another kind of cop. My dad was the J. Edgar Hoover fan, not me."

"But when things began to sour, you didn't cut and run," Jamie pointed out. "It shows admirable perseverance, Max."

"That what you shrinks call it?"

"Loyalty, then. How else could you stomach Hoover's personality cult? The power lust of a man who kept secret files—"

"Shut up, Jamie."

"Since when is the truth off limits?"

"It isn't. Just don't rub my nose in it. I've fought my battles, even won a few. But I never badmouth an employer."

"Come off it, Max. The Bureau's no employer.

It's home."

"Am I supposed to apologize for that?"

"Never apologize for love and loyalty."

What followed was a deafening silence.

"Have much in common these days with your fellow agents?" Jamie asked.

Max dropped his eyes and stared into his brandy. "Other than a few exceptions, about as much as I ever did," he admitted.

"Odd man out," Jamie mused. "What is it one's colleagues are supposed to represent? A camaraderie born of similar interests and shared values? When I was young and foolish, I joined the American Psychiatric Association. Instead of camaraderie, I discovered that most disappointing of substitutes—the functional relationship."

I couldn't help being impressed as Jamie skillfully brought us back to vigilante talk, knowing that it was only a matter of time before Max thought to ask Jamie the obvious...

"I'd like the benefit of your insights on victim psychology, Jamie. Do you mind?"

Jamie didn't mind. "All I know about Victims Anonymous, Max, is what I read in the papers," he said. After that, he switched seamlessly to "armchair psychologizing" about the sort of people he thought would be tempted to join a vigilante organization. I saw Max's idle curiosity turn to fascination as Jamie dropped a few minor revelations. I couldn't see any harm in them, but I didn't see what he hoped to accomplish either. Next on Jamie's hidden agenda was a host of general-interest questions about the FBI—the kind of questions that a man who loves his work is only too eager to answer...

"The pre-investigation stage, you mean?" Max said. "Call it an FBI probe."

"What makes it federal? When two or more persons 'conspire'—key word—to deprive you of your constitutional rights. Our catchall conspiracy laws make me uneasy."

"RICO? It's a very controversial law, Jamie. Going after a bunch of frustrated violent crime victims with a law intended to net mobsters is theoretically possible, but the Bureau would be risking a huge public outcry."

I tuned out the question-and-answer period, intent on maintaining a blank-faced calm while I asked a few silent questions of my own...

Could I be part of a "catchall conspiracy" if I hadn't been an official member of "interstate enterprise"? Could anyone in his right mind consider me a—a mobster?

"How should the FBI go about breaking the back of Victims Anonymous? That's easy," Max told Jamie. "Take out the leaders."

"Just don't lose sight of what you're up against, Max," Jamie cautioned him. "People this well organized are bound to be savvy individuals—ruthless, some of them. I'd bet my psychiatrist's license on it."

"Don't risk it," Max retorted with a grin. "Not with those impressive credentials."

"Not as impressive as yours. May I see them?" Jamie asked.

Max dug in his pocket and came up with something resembling an oversized wallet. "Not much to look at," he said, handing it over.

I'd seen it in Washington. Max's photograph and the signature of the current FBI director attesting to Max's status as an agent.

Jamie slipped the credentials into his pocket and pulled them right out again. "FBI agent James Coyne, at your service," he said, his smile on high beam,

The minute Max took his wallet back, Jamie lost his

smile and something wistful and boyish took its place...

Guess what I wanted to be when I grew up? An FBI agent!

The minute Max and Jamie left, I picked up the phone and dialed.

As soon as I heard her voice, I said, "Love to see you, Claudia. Are you free?"

CHAPTER 30

C LAUDIA WAS TEN MINUTES LATE. But so was I. I hadn't let her hear a thing in my voice last night. The code words carried their own cryptic message.

I was about to go back inside for a nostalgic cup of coffee—this was the bar where I'd had a few beers with Angela and Denzel after Angela joined Victims Anonymous—when I spotted Tony getting off a motorbike.

Tony, who had crept back to the organization "like a chastened animal returning to the feed bowl," Jamie had told me once. "Where else could he have gone for the kind of sustenance he needed?"

"Claudia won't be able to meet you. Chuck Polanski needed her to do something," he told me.

"No 'Hello, how are you'?" I chided.

"Hi." Very soft.

"I've missed you," I said, my voice tuned to his.

Claudia wanted me to tell you you're supposed to meet Kagan."

"And you know *where*?"

He nodded.

"Coffee?" I offered, pretending to be all business. Another nod.

We went inside. Tony marched over to a booth, black eyes solemn, his sturdy little frame lean and tough as a wire hanger. It was obvious that be was trying not to show what was in the air like energy—how glad he was to see me.

I wanted to crush him to my chest. I ordered two coffees, black.

Business concluded, he allowed himself the small luxury of a hot dog.

"Claudia quit school," he announced after the first bite. "She won't be going back in the fall either. She won't like me telling you."

"Thanks," I said faintly, accepting the inevitable.

"Kagan thinks you've changed," he blurted out. "That's why he wants you to honcho your own Mission planning. He said you needed a Rouser. He doesn't know I heard," Tony said, making wet rings on the table with his mug... uneasy with telling tales out of school.

He doesn't know you came here to warn me.

"I'll pay for it," he said as the waitress brought the bill. He handed her a five-dollar bill and told her to keep the change.

"Gotta get going," he told me.

I nodded. Watched, frowning, as he rode off on a motorbike in heavy traffic, even though I knew how carefully Rosa Ramirez had schooled him in bike riding...

He loved bicycles, my kid—regular ones and motor scooters. He spent every spare minute fooling with junk parts for one or the other.

I sighed, wondering if Jamie was in his office. He'd told me that Tony was keeping regular appointments again. My own appointment with Kagan wasn't scheduled until late afternoon. Plenty of time to stop off at Jamie's place first. It was supposed to be off limits to me now, but I was eager for Jamie to update me about Tony's progress.

It wasn't Jamie who opened the door to his office.

"Looks as if Jamie's corner-cutting is rubbing off on you," Kagan said drily.

I shrugged. "I wanted to talk to him about Tony.

Where's Jamie?"

"Upstairs nursing a headache."

I went inside, sensing that Kagan didn't want me to.

The door to Jamie's inner office was wide open, I noticed a scatter of tapes on Jamie's desk.

"Destroying evidence, Kagan?" I said archly.

"Just taking inventory."

Why don't I believe you?

"I won't keep you, then. See you at four-thirty?"

"Four-thirty," Kagan confirmed.

* * *

I arrived fifteen minutes early, my cab pulling up at the designated entrance to Central Park. Kagan's impeccable directions led me right to the appointed bench, empty except for a dented diet-soda can. Off in the near distance I spotted a boy, a dog, and a man. Recognizing the casual slouch and the angle of the neck, I started to walk over, but Kagan's lazy wave of acknowledgment put me on hold. Which was just as well. It turned out to be fifteen minutes of grist for my what-makes-Kagan-tick mill. It wasn't just the fascinating sight of him putting a German shepherd through its obedience-training paces. It was the odd chemistry of the situation... The boy, afraid of his own dog. The dog, afraid of Kagan. Kagan, intent on the dog's increasingly eager responses as he learned how to distinguish friend from foe. The boy, increasingly awed by Kagan's success.

But if Kagan recognized wide-eyed hero worship in the boy's glance, he seemed indifferent. I decided that Kagan was utterly incapable of relating to another human being.

The "why" continued to elude me.

He related well to the German shepherd. "The next-best thing to a burglar alarm in a high-risk neighborhood," he'd told me once. I walked toward him—close enough to hear his voice. It was firm. His gestures were authoritative, his smile easy. Any warmth in the smile? Anything personal for the dog, at least?

As soon as he had dismissed his charges, I went back to the bench, determined to catch Kagan off balance. When he ambled over, characteristically loose-limbed in khaki shirt and slacks, I said, "Kagan, the mystery man. No home. No woman. No discernible pleasures. What do you live for?"

"Victims Anonymous," he said without hesitation.

"And before that? After that?"

"Don't you know there will always be a Victims Anonymous?"

The boy and his dog were almost out of sight.

"Nice dog," Kagan said.

"What's nice about him?"

"He's predictable. It's why I like animals. Press the right buttons and you get results, not surprises. Can you honestly say the same for our unpredictable Jamie?"

"How did you know I wanted to talk about him and not McCann?"

"Because I leave nothing to chance. Mind telling me what your little threesome was all about?"

So he knows about Max and Jamie!

"I'm not sure," I said, and laid it out for him—but in the best possible light. Nothing about Jamie's emotion-laden response to the FBI—that was only a theory, after all. I limited my remarks to recruitment.

"In fairness," I concluded, "even if Jamie had some crazy notion about trying to recruit McCann, he got off it as soon as it began to look hopeless."

"He should have known it was hopeless from the start. I fear Jamie is becoming bored with the action. Or the lack of it," he added. "Nothing a few good Missions won't cure," he said with a thin coating of contempt. "I trust the strain of separation won't weigh too heavily on the big romance?"

"No sacrifice is too great for the cause," I drawled. Kagan likes his humor dry.

"The price of conviction runs high," he said with a faint smile.

"A noble sentiment," I said, thinking that in Kagan's mouth the word "conviction" lost its nobility and acquired a neutral sound, like "potatoes" or "dry-cell batteries."

"McCann seems smitten, Karen. My sources tell me the attraction looks mutual."

"Your sources are misinformed," I shot back. "Why don't we get back to the purpose of this meet? What do I do if Jamie is taking risks like this failed recruitment effort?"

"You tell *me* about it so I can defuse the situation."

"Which is exactly what I did. As for my romancing Max McCann, it's not going to happen so—"

"The closer you get to McCann, the safer we'll all be. Bed him down, Karen. You might even enjoy it."

My hand didn't even get close to his face. That's how fast his reflexes were.

"Not your style, sleeping with two men?" he said with that insolent smile. "Your loyalty is touching, though I'm not sure Jamie deserves it. Not after setting you up on your first Mission in the Bronx. He could cite mitigating circumstances, I suppose. Jamie *did* risk his life. On the other hand, a man who acts like he has nine lives and is eager to throw away half of them away doesn't deserve much credit for deliberately turning his back on a punk with a knife."

"Indio?" I gasped.

"Well, why not? You weren't about to 'make your bones' on your own. No stomach for it, remember? Jamie was counting on you to use my gun to save his life. Lucky for him you came through. Lucky for all of us. In the clamor and confusion, we got our photograph. Nobody joins the organization without it."

"Blackmail," I said bitterly as I recalled Jamie's guarded explanation about how VA kept troublemakers in line.

"So now I'm in your little black box," I said.

"Why would you be an exception?"

"Because I'm not a member of Victims Anonymous. I didn't join a damn thing."

His smile was patronizing. "A nice distinction."

Twilight in the park now. I calmed myself in its tranquility while I asked myself a couple of questions. What was Kagan's game and how did I keep from playing it? Was he trying to throw cold water on the "big romance" with Jamie so Max could catch me on the rebound? Was he letting me know I was in no position to cut and run even if I was ready to?

"Truce, Kagan," I said with a faux smile that had surrender in it. "I take it I won't be breaching security anymore by seeing Jamie occasionally, with or without McCann."

"By all means, expand your social circle by one."

What I saw in his smug glance was "Give Jamie hell!"

My very thought.

I shrugged. "Don't get your hopes up. Jamie can be a manipulative SOB but that doesn't mean we won't kiss and make up."

Why do I get the feeling that he doesn't believe me ...

The thought of Kagan's eerie perceptiveness returned abruptly when we left the park. As he updated me on some Victims Anonymous activities, he seemed to know precisely what I wanted to hear about. Not surprising if, like Kagan, you moved through life as if you were on constant alert...

Our conversation died. The streets were congested

with tourists. With people who had worked late. I noticed that, for Kagan, they didn't seem to exist.

They did and they didn't. It was as if his eyes moved over faces like a computer making rapid calculations. The man in the blue blazer, I could almost hear him thinking, how would he react under stress? The woman in the saucy red beret, how soon would she panic once she realized someone was following her? Had Kagan even noticed the exuberant swing of the woman's shoulder bag? Her possessive hold on the arm of her male companion? It was as if Kagan lacked the antennae to tune in to the whole of human behavior, let alone respond to its subtleties.

I was so engrossed in this odd display of detachment that I didn't spot a cat lurking alongside a garbage can. In a flash Kagan had dipped into my jacket pocket— everyone knew about my ongoing supply of People Crackers—and had the cat literally eating out of his hand. The contrast between this unguarded moment and Kagan's typically laconic way of moving startled me.

That's when I realized that Kagan's easygoing manner was a pose!

I confirmed it in the split second after the cat darted away and I saw what was already happening to his face. Behind the thick gray smoke of his eyes—impenetrable, I'd once thought—was a controlled tension. It was like a lightbulb with an infinite source of energy that never burns itself out. It was the tension that had made me acutely aware of his presence in a room. That made me breathe a little freer after he'd left.

It was his pseudo casualness that had made me miss it altogether.

CHAPTER 31

I WENT HOME TO SHED MY office uniform for jeans and an old shirt, tossed Jamie's slacks and cashmere jacket into a laundry bag, and called him to say I was on my way over.

When I arrived, pasta puttanesca awaited me on a candlelit table for two. Jamie was disarming in a white apron.

"I'm in no mood to break bread with you," I said, emptying the laundry bag on the floor. "Kagan told me how you deliberately turned your back on Indio so I had to shoot the bastard before he stabbed you in the back. Thanks to you, Kagan took my photograph while I 'made my bones.' Thanks to you, I ended up in his damn blackmail box."

"But I did you a favor," Jamie protested.

"Run that by me again, will you? This ought to be good," I said, pulling up a chair.

"I won't deny I was out to protect the organization and get you aboard. But I had another purpose as well. I wanted to give you the killing experience."

"But that's *horrible*," I said, believing him. "Look how much therapy you had to put me through before I got over it. I'm not over it yet!"

"Everything has a price tag. Whatever else Victims Anonymous stands for, it breeds violence. Using a gun for the second time, should the need arise, is much easier than the first. It could save your life."

"I won't eat your damn pasta," I said, standing up.

"Don't go," he pleaded. "I want to talk to you about Max."

That got my attention. The concern in his voice was genuine. I sat back down, sensing a new alliance—Max, Jamie, and me.

"It's nothing specific, you understand. I'm relying totally on instinct. But twice now, Kagan has alluded to Max as a 'worrier.' I asked myself what would Kagan's devious mind expect a worrier to do?"

He paused to fill our wine glasses.

I listened to him dissect, analyze, and probe for twenty minutes before interrupting.

"Jamie, have you switched sides?"

"Whatever else you may have told Kagan, I hope you didn't wave *that* red flag under his nose," Jamie said with a lopsided smile. "I could never be disloyal to my own creation. Victims Anonymous was *my* idea."

"You've lost control of the leadership," I told him gently.

His smile collapsed. "All the more reason not to lose sight of what it originally stood for—and still does. We're the good outlaws, Karen. That's what Victims Anonymous is all about. Justice for the crime victim was my goal," he said slowly. "What's Kagan's goal? What is he up to?"

"Best guess? He likes to manipulate people. He's after power—"

"You're wrong. Kagan is much more complex than that," Jamie reflected. "Now *there's* a man I'd like to strap to my psychiatrist's couch."

"What would you find, I wonder? Man with a cause, dedicated—"

"*Consumed.* Kagan has the soul of a revolutionary, Karen. His is a darker need…"

He slid a plate laden with pasta puttenesa—my

favorite—to my side of the table before starting on his.

He was refilling our glasses when a question occurred to me. "Kagan always has a drink of some kind in his hand but I can't remember ever seeing him drink. What's *that* all about?"

"It makes him look like he's hanging loose with the rest of us," Jamie said without hesitation. "We drop our guard but Kagan never misses a beat."

"Tell me the truth, Jamie. *Were* you trying to recruit Max?"

"Let's just say I was testing the waters," he said, looking sheepish. "Max may think the way we do on a lot of issues and he really hates what's happening, but he won't cut corners to stop it, Karen. Not even for you," he added, his eyes narrowing in sympathy.

"The company man..."

"Have you ever asked yourself why a man doesn't pursue an eight-year-old attraction?"

"I can guess. Max was married—unhappily, I'm beginning to suspect."

"Exactly. He couldn't forget you but he never looked you up until after his wife had died. Max toes the line."

"You're just full of happy insights tonight. Jamie, if he ever finds out—"

He put a comforting arm around my shoulders. "We'll have to make sure he doesn't." He stood up. "It's late and we're both exhausted. Why don't you stay the night and spare me the effort of putting you in a cab?"

I started to protest.

"Don't worry. I won't let you sleep downstairs alone. You take the bed. Tony loves it, by the way. My couch, I've discovered, is quite comfortable."

"Sure you have no romantic intentions?" I teased.

He planted a chaste kiss on my forehead. "The moment has passed us by, love."

Were Kagan's "sources" on the job, waiting for the

lights to go out? I wondered. The thought of bolstering my kiss-and-make-up fairytale, coupled with bone-weary fatigue, made Jamie's invitation irresistible. His bedroom was richly colored and heavily draped. The feel of fresh satin sheets put out my lights almost at once.

* * *

I awoke in the middle of the night. Whatever it was—strange bed, lustful thoughts of Max—I couldn't get back to sleep. Slipping into an ivory-colored robe Jamie had left for me, I padded out to the kitchen for a glass of juice to go with my cigarette. On the way back I glanced at Jamie on the couch and saw that was fast asleep.

Not asleep, I realized, moving closer. Pretending to be...

"What's the matter, Jamie?"

He sat up. "Dissecting Kagan's psyche earlier tonight put me in mind of my own," he confessed. "Children are such easy targets for an emotionally insecure parent..."

"Your mother?" I said, remembering his bitter drunken toast.

"I was five when my father left her. For the next ten years, I played substitute dad. I was her confidant, her constant escort, her worshipful little man of the house. Karen, don't you *see*? I was so busy tuning in to her neurotic needs that it whizzed right by me—those formative years when a child must discover his 'self' or risk growing up without one! In my profession, they call it being 'narcissistically deprived.' Can you begin to grasp what Victims Anonymous gave back to me? My aborted childhood. Who needs Batman and Superman when, waiting in the wings, is King Arthur and the Scarlet Pimpernel?"

It explained the novels on Jamie's bookshelf—characters out of Dumas and Sabatini —and why he'd

223

told me Lee Emerson was bad for him. Why, from time to time, he shifted without warning into a gleeful child or a man with a cape.

And for the first time, I understood why Jamie needed the artificial stimulant of a Rouser or a Mission.

"Shall I tell you my personal definition of terror?" Jamie whispered. "To search for yourself in the mirror and know that what stares back is someone else's unlived dreams. To go through life knowing that your mother has stolen your identity."

I shivered. I couldn't stop shivering in the August heat.

I spent the rest of the night holding him in my arms.

CHAPTER 32

A T THE SOUND OF MY doorbell, I opened the door and they all filed in—a faintly expectant Kagan, Lee Emerson, and Chuck Polanski, who wore a this-better-be-good expression, given the ungodly hour. It was two o'clock in the morning. I had done it knowing that the *last* thing everyone in this room wanted was to risk blowing my cover with Max.

"Getting cold feet about your Mission?" a skeptical Polanski asked.

My Mission was a week off.

"Don't jump to conclusions, Polanski. It's about Lee maybe being in danger," I snapped... and had the satisfaction of seeing his jaw tighten. "There's talk about a 'tall stunning blonde' who's been spotted on several different occasions while some 'vigilante activity' was going on—activity that could tie in with the FBI investigation of Victims Anonymous. Someone saw Lee in Chicago. St. Louis. Atlanta."

But the reproach in my voice was aimed at Kagan, who should have known better.

Polanski swung on Kagan. "Well?" he said defiantly.

"It's a near impossibility that McCann could identify Lee if he happened to run into her on some street in New York," he said. "As to Lee's visibility in other cities, that's something else, isn't it? No more out-of-town Missions, Lee."

Predictably, her reaction was mixed. I knew how

much she loved "being on the road," as she put it, but Polanski's discomfort had unnerved her.

"So I'm grounded," she said irritably. She turned to me. "How's 'Operation Feeder' coming along, Karen?"

Coy label for what I was doing.

"Ask me again next week," I snapped.

Not fully satisfied with Kagan's assessment of the danger, Polanski wanted to know if the FBI still planned to break up Victims Anonymous cell by cell.

"And indict a lot of misguided people as co-conspirators? It's not going to happen," I reassured him. "The latest bulletin out of the Bureau's Congressional and Public Affairs office says they're looking into different groups of vigilantes—so-called extremists—but with no solid evidence, so far, of a national conspiracy."

"What exactly does that mean?" Lee asked breathlessly.

"It means that the FBI is focused on the inner circle—us," Polanski said mirthlessly.

"Since we're all here, Karen, how about a progress report?" Kagan said.

"You can tell Timothy Hogan he's not the only one with budget problems. Drug enforcement being top priority, the FBI has 'limited resources for investigating a bunch of vigilantes'—that's an exact quote."

Smiles all around. Everyone got ready to leave.

Lee couldn't resist adding a personal update. "Our fox symbol is turning up all over. It's written on walls. Spray-painted in subways. People are on the offensive. *We* did that!"

Isn't it a thrill and a half? Aren't we important? Isn't my life significant?

I was tempted to caution her that with every thrill comes a danger. I wanted to say, "Go back to advertising."

"Good luck next week with your Mission," Polanski told me, sounding as if I'd need it.

* * *

I sat in a darkened screening room packed with some recent recruits. They were strangers. While I couldn't see clearly, what struck me was their body language—not just alert, but eager.

A little too eager. The whole purpose of a Mission "planning session" is to get a Self-Defense Team primed for action. These guys were on the prod before I'd even opened my mouth. I didn't bother with my notes, just signaled the projectionist and waited for the anonymity of total darkness.

"A fifteen-year-old who violates the child labor laws," I said as a muscled figure with a mop of dark hair appeared on the screen. "He works nights. I'll let him tell you at what."

"I look for the creeps with briefcases, y'know? And watches, good ones. Broads with gold chains. Hey, I got expenses!"

"As for *how* he does business, let's just say he likes waving his Magnum around," I said. "After ten arrests and two convictions, does he look worried?"

"Next." I showed them a new face, but with the same old story.

"You kiddin' me, man? I go for drunks, old ladies, anything that moves. I dig some sucker's running shoes? I take 'em."

"They all 'take 'em,' these teenaged thugs," I said, letting my listeners see one smug face after another.

I turned up the pace, film images tumbling one after another as I felt a small hard deposit pressing into my breastbone, like the residue of minerals that hard water leaves behind. By the time I got to the punch line, it had become a solid painful lump.

"The object of tomorrow's Mission," I said, "the man responsible for turning these Savages loose on the rest of the world—

—the man who set Indio and his gang free—

"—is Judge Arthur Younger. The conviction record of this Family Court judge is a sick joke. His dismissal rate is an abomination."

For a good twenty minutes I spelled it out—a kind of "rap sheet" on Judge Arthur Younger and the hoodlums he invariably released to their mothers, sisters, and big brothers. How many of these hoodlums were repeat offenders. I gave my audience a graphic picture—some of them documented on film—of the "beneficiaries" of Judge Younger's charitable outlook on law and order—a body count of crime victims that numbered well over a hundred and ran the gamut from the very young to the very old. People who had been maimed and murdered. Fractured and scarred.

The lights went on. I'd spotted Kagan earlier but apparently he had already left.

Jamie had waited, a dignified presence in the back of the room.

"Very effective," he complimented me later. "How did it feel?"

"Dirty."

"Take you home?" he offered.

I had to stop myself from clinging to his arm. We were fast turning into a mutual support society.

I couldn't stop myself from asking him a disturbing question. "Jamie, why do I despise Judge Arthur Younger even more than the criminals he releases?"

"Because you know where the real control center of evil is—in his courtroom," he answered without hesitation. "When a judge abdicates responsibility, criminals multiply into big numbers."

He stopped for a moment and took my hand. "How's Max holding up?"

"He took me to lunch and tried to make me back

out," I said.

"Interesting..."

We didn't talk the rest of the way.

When I got home I took a Valium instead of a sleeping pill.

Amd woke up in a stupor.

All day at work I avoided mirrors, determined not to look in one until I got to Claudia's apartment. I started to giggle... the onset of hysteria?

"Good thing you decided to dress at my place," Claudia observed with a wicked grin. "No way you'd have made it past your doorman this time, Whitey."

Not in a black leather miniskirt and five-inch heels.

"My rouge is redder than your lipstick," I said with a frown.

"My skirt is shorter and my beret is metallic gold."

Mine was black. I tugged it down, eyed my long-legged friend as she slowly swung a thin-strapped gold shoulder bag to some invisible beat, and said, "You win the vamp prize, Claudia." Grabbing my own shoulder bag, I said, "Let's go."

"We have plenty of time. We'll just zip up the West Side Drive—"

"What if we get stuck in traffic? It's that time of day," I said, sorry we hadn't opted for a cab.

"That time of *night*," she corrected me, adjusting the blinds over her window.

We left her apartment.

And got stuck in the elevator—me, Claudia, and a man who had joined us on the second floor. He kept hitting the button—a frantic jabbing motion. Given his mental state, I kept my panic to myself.

Stuck in an elevator on the way to my Mission!

Claudia pressed the red emergency button. Nothing. I asked her whether her building superintendent would be out at this hour.

"Out to lunch, more likely," she said drily. "We could be here all night."

"Don't say that!" The man was portly, his face getting redder by the minute.

I don't recommend a solid half hour of banging and shouting in a steel cage. That's how long it took for help to arrive in the form of a super with rum on his breath and a marijuana look in his eye. Our companion in claustrophobia chose that moment to slip, groaning, to the floor. I yelled for a doctor as Claudia bent to loosen his collar.

The super returned with a cop who assumed we were hookers. What with seeing the man to an ambulance—his color was good and he had a pulse—and giving particulars to the man in blue, it was another hour before we were on our way.

"Where to?" Claudia wondered. "The show has to be well under way by now."

"Let me think. Kagan said something about a 'slam-bang' climax. Wouldn't tell me what it was and spoil the surprise. But Tony, bless him, had the foresight to tell me *where*."

"That kid's a first-class eavesdropper," Claudia drawled as she braked for a traffic light. "How about telling *me* where we're going?"

"Twenty-sixth and the Hudson River."

"Nice neighborhood," she said acidly. "Don't worry. We'll make it," she promised, hitting the gas. "I'm a whiz at timed lights."

She was good, all right, even if she did cheat a little by going through two stop signs and the last red light.

"Bingo," she said as we slowed on Twenty-fifth Street and drove right past an untidy little procession. We went around the next corner, pulled into an empty lot, and jumped out. It was them, all right. Half a block away and headed in our direction—my Self-Defense Team moving four abreast, with Judge Arthur Younger in the middle. The Team resembled a bunch of juveniles on a late-night mugging spree, with a cover story to match. In their "drug-crazed" euphoria, they'd intercepted a Family Court judge on his way home. The judge was sandwiched between a weight-lifter type and some guy Jamie had pointed out to me a while ago—Kagan's new protégé. He was slim-hipped, fair-haired, and looked as if he ought to be herding cattle on the range instead of working the dark side of New York in sneakers and hero jacket.

What unnerved me was how surprised he looked when he saw us.

We walked up like a rear guard behind eight black hero jackets and Judge Arthur Younger in a torn navy jacket. Unless he was able to turn around, there was no way Younger could get a good look at me and little chance he'd remember my face—especially in my "tart" mode. But I'd gotten a good look at *him.* Judge Arthur Younger was blinking rapidly. Somewhere along the way he'd lost his silver-framed glasses. A blood smear had dried on his upper lip, a sort of half-mustache under that aquiline nose. There was nothing imperious about the rest of him. His eyes were glazing over. His mouth was pinched. His shoulders were hunched. Those long tapered fingers of his shook.

We were nearing Twenty-sixth Street when I noticed a couple just down the street heading in our direction. A shapely young woman in a short skirt, swaying from one drink too many. Her male companion, in suit and tie, too smitten with his date to think of crossing to the other side of the deserted street. Kagan's protégé paused, head tilting to one side, one hand slipping into his pocket.

For a knife?

"Don't you *dare*," I hissed, before he could give the

order to turn a nonviolent Mission into a mugging.

He glared at me, brown eyes flecked with gold that glinted in the lamplight. But he took his hand out of his pocket as the couple moved blithely through our midst like a small boat through a mined harbor.

It was at Twenty-sixth and the Hudson River when everyone slowed. We turned a sharp corner—

And practically walked into a police car parked at the curb!

The panicked judge broke free and made a run for the car. I heard gunshots and spun around to see a pistol in the hands of the fair-haired guy.

Claudia slammed me against the wall of a building.

I looked up to see a cop slumped over the wheel of the police car, his partner leaning into a blood-spattered windshield. The judge lay on the sidewalk in a dead faint.

"Oh... my... God," Claudia breathed.

I staggered forward on my high heels.

The policeman who'd been slumped over the wheel—a black cop—sat up.

Denzel?

The seemingly "bloodied" head of his partner snapped up off the windshield, a few strands of long dark hair escaping from under her cap.

Angela!

Kagan's "slam-bang" climax was over, complete with blanks and fake blood.

Before I could speak, let alone bring my muscles back to life, the whole scene lit up like a movie set.

"What the hell? Turn that goddamn thing off!" Denzel yelled.

Angela, one arm in front of her face, was blinking like a deer transfixed by the headlights of a car.

The "goddamn thing" was a spotlight. Kagan's protégé took his sweet time turning it off. "Sorry about that," he muttered as everything went dark again.

Sorry? If the judge hadn't fainted on us, the spotlight would have given him a good look at his would-be rescuers. At Denzel and Angela.

"Better check out Hizzoner," Kagan told Denzel. "He doesn't look so good."

Denzel was out of the patrol car and on his knees, Angela right behind him. "Cardiac arrest," Denzel confirmed, his fingers on a limp wrist. Without even looking up, he ordered the SD Team to scatter.

Claudia and I stayed put while we watched and prayed, time beating in my temples. Five chest compressions for every lungful of air. A dusky complexion—much worse than the man stuck in the elevator of my apartment building.

"I've got a pulse." Denzel's voice was matter-of-fact.

"He's coming around," Angela agreed, breathing for herself now.

"Go with Karen and Claudia," Denzel told Angela. "I'll get Younger to a hospital."

Claudia and I slipped out of our spiked heels, and the three of us made a mad dash for Claudia's car. We were on the highway, well within the speed limit, when Angela lit one of her cigarillos. "It's not as if I didn't anticipate something like this," she said with a troubled frown. "Do you realize what we flirted with tonight? Felony murder."

Claudia went through her second red light of the evening. "That judge isn't about to die on us, is he?" she asked.

"He'll be all right."

"But if he'd died?" I pressed.

"Or more precisely, if Denzel and I hadn't gotten here in time to revive him? We'd have been facing a murder charge," Angela said grimly.

We drove the rest of the way in silence.

Claudia pulled over to a cab stand to let me and Angela out. Security meant taking separate cabs home. I waved goodbye to Claudia. A cab came to a halt. Before Angela got in, I said, "We have to talk. You, me, Denzel, Jamie—"

"Claudia?"

"Why do you say it like that?"

"She's not ready to get out and you know it," Angela said.

Riding home in the next cab that came along got me thinking about what Angela had left *unsaid* even though I'd seen it in her face. It was easier getting into something like this than it would be to get out.

I was wiping off what was left of the red lipstick when I noticed the light under my apartment door. I didn't even bother digging for my keys, knowing the door would be unlocked. "Another duplicate key, Jamie?" I said drily.

"Your mascara is caked. Sit down. We have things to discuss."

"My very thought. When I tell you what happened tonight—"

"Claudia just did. I picked up when she called a few minutes ago. She'd just checked in with a couple of hospitals. The man you two encountered in the elevator checked out ten minutes after he'd checked in. Looks like the only genuine cardiac arrest patient was Judge Arthur Younger, and he's doing fine."

I lowered myself into a chair. "Jamie, what's going on?"

"A first-class game of chess, the better to checkmate *you*."

It had clicked for Jamie when I'd told him Max wanted me to back out of the Mission at the last minute. Why, with so much at stake over a Mission when no one was likely to get hurt? Max must have been approached by one of Kagan's informants with a last-minute tip that your Mission might turn ugly, even violent. It wasn't hard to predict what he would do with *that* information. Jump into the fray in order to protect you."

"But how would he know when and where?"

"Twenty-sixth Street and the Hudson River? He knew, all right. Kagan undoubtedly made sure of that. Max would have been there tonight if I hadn't tricked him."

"You called him?"

"And said you'd just called *me* when you couldn't get ahold of him. VA doesn't trust you enough yet to give you the Mission's true location, you told me. The one on Twenty-sixth was a phony, to be switched at the last minute. You gave me some vague directions in Brooklyn where the real thing was going down and hung up."

"Max bought it? How do you *know* he bought it?"

"Because I went with him on his wild-goose chase to Brooklyn, that's how. I'm exhausted. More brandy?"

"Then that portly man in the elevator—"

"A setup to keep you—and, more importantly, Claudia—away from your Mission without you suspecting anything. If Max had taken the bait and shown up as Kagan expected him to—"

"He'd have recognized her. He's met her a few times. He knows that Claudia is my closest friend."

"There's more. When Max and I took off for Brooklyn, he brought a camera. That's standard operating procedure for stake-outs. Claudia told me that when Denzel and Angela got to the scene, the police car was lit up by a spotlight."

"It seemed deliberate. What was Kagan after?"

"Photographs. They give him real bargaining power. He wants to control you through Angela and Denzel. Cross him and he's in a position to supply the

FBI with names to go with the faces he wanted Max to photograph."

"He'd expose Denzel and Angela just to keep me from quitting?!"

"And keep you from becoming a turncoat. He knows you and Max are falling in love, Karen."

"But *you're* the one I'm supposed to be in love with," I protested.

"Don't be naïve. Kagan knows better."

Jamie checked his watch. "I'd better get back to 'the worrier.'"

I leapt to my feet. "Max will wonder—"

"Wait. Think first. Before you and I talk to him, you have to back up my story and add a few details of your own. You have to be convincing about why you couldn't reach him. How you finally managed to get through to me with your SOS."

"I'll say I always know where my shrink is. That I don't go anywhere without your emergency number. Max, on the other hand, isn't always easy to track down. Especially when there's no time to leave a trail of messages."

"You're a quick study. Ironic, isn't it," he mused, "Kagan knowing we're not lovers, Max thinking we were. Or still are."

"What makes you think—"

"I sensed something in his attitude tonight."

"Jamie," I whispered, "what's going to happen to us?"

"Nothing a guardian angel can't protect you from."

He flashed me a faded smile and let himself out.

CHAPTER 33

A PICNIC WITH MAX IN A parked car was not exactly a duplicate of our first date, but it was raining out so we had no choice.

He handed me an egg salad on rye. "You look better already. A lot less strung out."

I felt worse, knowing he was due to leave for Washington.

"Are you free Monday night for dinner?" Max asked.

"How about dinner at my place for a change?" I said, glad he'd be back so soon.

He smiled and started the car.

I couldn't get used to the formality. Did he really believe Jamie and I were back together? *Why*, when I'd given him no reason?

"Dirt roads," he grumbled as he rolled us out of a pothole.

"This is horse country. They keep them unpaved to—"

The car stopped with a jolt. "Wait here," he told me, and got out.

I sighed when I saw him bend over a mound of gray fur.

"Squirrel?" I asked.

"A cat. The bastard who struck her kept right on going. Don't look, Karen. Give me a minute."

I looked anyway. Saw him turn his windbreaker into a bright blue stretcher for a dead pile of fur. Watched him carry it to the side of the road and roll it gently onto the ground. When he came back, his windbreaker had a crescent-shaped smear across the front.

"I'm sorry," he said at my expression.

"I'm so sick of the sight of death!"

He held me, dry-eyed, against his chest.

"You won't be alone while I'm away?" he asked. "Jamie will be around?"

"I guess."

Back in the car, I closed my eyes, grateful that the drive back to Manhattan was filled with companionable silence.

* * *

I didn't have to drift into the Monday-morning blues. I had lived them all weekend. Kemp & Carusone had become the discarded lover who made you wonder afterward what you'd ever seen in him. I still enjoyed attacking a thorny problem with Larry, but he was too discerning not to notice my general lack of enthusiasm for corporate public relations. I put on a good face and smoked a lot while Larry walked around the office tight-lipped, as if waiting for me to hand in my resignation.

My spirits picked up a bit as the dinner hour approached. I stopped off for sourdough bread and ice cream.

One foot into the foyer of my apartment and I realized that someone had been here. *Or still was?*

The louvered doors to the kitchen were open, but the door to my guest bathroom was closed. It should have been reversed. Yanking an umbrella from its stand, I tiptoed over. The noise from inside the bathroom was peculiar. Bread and ice cream hit the rug while I raised my improvised weapon with one hand and reached for the doorknob with the other...

Now!

I had a sense of color and shape as two balls of energy

streaked out of prison. Two little cats! My reflection in a medicine cabinet mirror—Karen Newman wielding her big bad umbrella—caused me to burst out laughing.

A message in lipstick written on the cabinet made me cry...

Loving long-distance can be a lonely business.

I half-expected what I'd find in my kitchen. I was half right. Not just a case of cat food, an entire shelf! My supply of People Crackers had been replenished, and there were a couple of lemon-yellow bowls with the words feed the cat. A note told me that my new roommates were brother and sister strays threatened with eviction from a Greek coffee shop whose lease was running out. The last line said, "They need you."

I can't afford to be needed, Max. Not by a couple of strays. Not by you.

I went looking for them, guided by dead-giveaway sounds under and behind my living-room furniture. I caught a glimpse, finally, of amber eyes and an adorable split-personality face—dark gray on one side, orange and white on the other. Tantalized by the swinging tassels of a chair cushion, she came out, as if to let me admire the split pattern in reverse that ran the length of her body. A tortoiseshell cat!

A flash of gray and white took to the air. Her brother, exploring the top of a china cabinet with long white legs that would have made him top cat in a feline basketball game. Looking down at me with bright inquisitive eyes that might have been outlined in mascara, he licked his lips. Message received.

I emerged from the kitchen bearing the yellow bowls and erupted into laughter. The boy-cat looked up at me from the mess on my rug, as if to say, "Who wants cat food when they're serving melted ice cream?"

By the time Max arrived with a semi-guilty grin and red roses, I was ready with the introductions. "Meet a couple of nonstop explorers," I said, a cat in each arm. "This is Marco and this is his sister Pola—that's feminine for 'Polo.'"

He grinned. "Marco Polo, famous explorer. I get it."

"Stop wriggling, you two, and meet a matchmaker named Max McCann."

"In love already?"

"Trying not to be. Max, they can't stay."

"Why not?" he said, following me into the kitchen while I took dinner out of the oven. "They need a home. You need—"

"Don't. I'll find them a—a more stable environment. I mean it," I said as he burst out laughing.

I burst out crying.

He pulled me into his arms. "Karen, Karen... ," he whispered, as soothing as the rain. He held me away from him—a fraction of a second—and everything changed for us.

His hand on my cheek was a resting place. I leaned into it. His fingers touched my face... the corner of my mouth.

"Oh my love..." he whispered.

I swayed but he caught me, his arm around my waist, his mouth a greedy seeker of barriers. Of hidden places. He found them all... .

I lay naked on a bed I hadn't shared for a long time and wondered why I didn't feel awkward—the usual aftermath of a first intimacy. What I felt was a sense of coming home. When I moved to get up, Max pulled me down against him, almost as if he were tucking me under his wing.

"Close your eyes," he murmured, his own half open. "Stay with me. Sleep with me."

I stayed until the easy rhythm of his breathing let me go, then slipped into a robe and fled to the den to smoke furiously and cry silently. To curse the day I'd accepted an invitation on Christmas Eve. Woman on a chessboard with no way to get off.

No way?

"Think you could do a quick sketch of the man at the funeral?" Max had asked when I'd had gone with him to Washington for the first time.

I took a folder from a locked desk drawer and reached for sketches of Kagan—caricatures, really. I'd been playing with them on and off ever since. But the work I had done on Kagan really *was* hopeless. I'd have settled for a reasonable likeness, but all I'd captured was the peculiar angle of his neck. The man with a forgettable face," he'd told me. It was true enough.

But Kagan wasn't the only game in town.

I reached for my sketch pad, drew a face, penciled in hooded eyes, thick black hair, and a toothpaste-commercial smile—Chuck Polanski. I did a full-figure of Brian O'Neal. Piece of cake when your subject resembles a battering ram. I made a methodical pile, slipped it into a folder, and dropped it into my desk drawer.

"Follow me to my microwave, Max," I said. "Unless you aren't in the mood for some reconstituted broccoli quiche."

"Zabar's or homemade?" he wanted to know.

"You tell me."

"Homemade," he said with a grin after the first couple of bites.

The grin faded as we drifted into the topic of the meeting coming up. He asked me if I was nervous about it. Only marginally, I told him.

"Bernard Rees thinks they're about to ask you to join Victims Anonymous," he said. "If we get lucky, if you *do* get to meet someone important—"

"The sooner this is over. Stop worrying, Max."

He reached for my hand. "Does Jamie worry about

you the way I do?"

The question sounded involuntary.

"I doubt it."

"I don't blame you now that I know him," Max said slowly.

"Don't blame me for what?"

"For... getting back together. What happened just now—"

"Don't you *dare* apologize for it."

He let go of my hand. "I know you're still in love with him."

"You couldn't be more wrong."

"Then why are you still sleeping with him?!"

If it hadn't been for his anguish, I'd have slapped his face.

I listened to him confirm what I hadn't wanted to believe—that I might be under FBI surveillance. Rees had insisted on it. Max had gone along reluctantly, but only because of the potential violence the Bureau had exposed me to. He told me how I had made a dull, albeit sometimes elusive, subject until the evening I had gone home and gone right out again.

The evening I'd gone to Jamie's place and spent the night cradling him in my arms.

Thank God the FBI surveillance team had pulled their men off the job on the hectic night Claudia and I had played hookers!

"FBI surveillance," I said, my voice in deep freeze. "What's next, a telephone tap?"

"I'd never approve it," Max said, looking as if he'd just been kicked in the stomach.

Talk about a quick thaw. Karen Newman, dealer in doubletalk and deceit, on her high horse! I climbed down fast.

"Forget it, Max. You did what you had to. But you're wrong about why I spent one night with Jamie. We're close friends, not lovers."

"Then tonight was... ours?"

The tears in his eyes brought tears to mine.

I walked into his arms.

There was no dam-breaking urgency in our lovemaking this time. What threatened to overwhelm me was the slow, piercing sweetness of his hands. The tenderness. The way he moaned when I touched him. The confessions, half-spoken, as if saying the words out loud made them irrevocable. The words left unsaid, as if to name what we were feeling would be to lose it forever.

In the end, I said it to myself.

I've known romance and had affairs I have no reason to regret. But you, Max dearest, are the best-loved, the inexorable climax to much more than this night.

He held me with a new kind of strength—a man without doubts or inner conflicts.

I spent the rest of the night staring at the ceiling, knowing that someday I would give him both.

PART V

CAUSALITY

*Bethink thee, how much more grievous
are the consequences of our anger
than the acts which arouse it.*

—Marcus Aurelius, *Meditations*, Book II

CHAPTER 34

CLAUDIA GREETED ME WITH A look of sharp appraisal the minute I entered her apartment. "What's going on? You haven't looked this good in years."

I checked myself out in the nearest mirror. It was true.

"How about *me*?" she said, preening.

"What have you done to your hair?" The smooth straight look had become a wild and woolly tangle cascading down her back.

"Back to basics. Luke used to say I looked like a black stand-in for Sheena, Queen of the Jungle. What do you think?"

"Wild and woolly," I said. "I really like it. Seeing much of Luke?"

"Still pumping him about the special task force, you mean? Bits and pieces are all I've been getting lately. Kagan says that means something's going down. How goes it with McCann? He the reason for the natural blush in your cheeks?"

"You don't expect me to answer that, right?"

She grinned.

"We sat down to one of Claudia's specials—spinach lasagna, arugula salad, and garlic bread. The red wine flowed.

I told her I was sorry she had quit school. She told me it was only temporary.

"Sure," I said, "like rent control in New York."

"What are you here for besides the food and the company, Karen?"

"I'm setting up a meeting. You, me, Angela and Denzel, Rosa and Jamie. It's time we talked about our options."

"We got any?"

"Only one way to find out. I'd like you to be there."

"Sure. Just don't make it before VA's next Mission. It's scheduled for Labor Day."

"Who's being targeted?"

"Legal Aid." She leaned back in her chair. "This will be the most explosive Mission that Victims Anonymous ever launched, if I have anything to say about it—and I do," she said, a touch of vehemence in her tone.

Claudia had come full circle, I thought, remembering when we'd met at a Legal Aid New Year's Eve party. "The Great Defenders" she'd dubbed the lot of them.

"You're consistent, at least," I teased, reminding her of that night. "As for Legal Aiders, you could form a club of detractors, judging from the op-ed pages."

"Thanks to our efforts, Legal Aid's popularity polls have taken a big hit. They're working their collective butts off to climb back up, but it's not gonna happen. We'll finish them off at this Labor Day rally of theirs," she said with a dark satisfaction that made me uneasy. "I wouldn't miss it if I were you."

"What do I do about being recognized by an ex-husband?"

"You'll think of something. More lasagna?"

"No thanks. Won't you have the same problem about being recognized? Luke's wife will be there."

"She'll be there, all right." Venom in her voice.

"What is this, Claudia, a personal vendetta?"

"Time for dessert," she said, sidestepping my question.

"I'm stuffed."

"It's sponge cake with lemon sauce."

My favorite... "Just a sliver," I told her.

"You could be right about this vigilante business," Claudia said slowly, refilling our wine glasses. "We used to have a lot to talk about besides the crime wave."

"Why don't we start right now?"

We touched glasses in a wordless toast.

Then it was gone—the stress, the worries, the disagreements. We zeroed in on the shared knowledge that some things sailed above problems and disagreements. Even dangers. That we were fools to ever lose sight of what we meant to each other.

When I left, I was convinced that we had already achieved the impossible. That we were back in control of our destiny.

*   *   *

By the morning of the rally I wasn't so sure. While I wanted to be on hand for what promised to be high drama—I had gotten Alan to invite me—I was having second thoughts about not spending Labor Day weekend with Max.

I started to flip through a couple of PR pitches I'd drawn up for Victims Anonymous. Question: What's the favorite activity of Legal Aid lawyers? Keeping score. Toting up a "win" each time an overworked judge buys their standard excuse. (No known criminal record, Your Honor.) Each time a mugger or an armed robber walks.

Each time a juvenile like Sarah's murderer is released into the custody of his mother.

"Too many Legal Aid lawyers," I had written, "develop some on-the-job skills, the most common being their capacity to rationalize."

I put the file away and put spending the weekend with Max out of my mind. I had to admit that Claudia had piqued my curiosity.

By high noon I was heading for a site in Central Park more accustomed to rock concerts than civic-minded rallies—Legal Aid's second mistake. Their first was to hold the rally in the first place. Why go on the defensive so publicly? Why not take out a series of ads instead, spelling out some of their real accomplishments to offset their glaring failures?

They had bought themselves a lot of sunshine, at least. It was one of those cloudless true-blue skies that make even your confirmed New Yorker long for a day in the country instead of an afternoon in the park.

As the crowd thickened, I felt out of sync. Karen Newman in a black linen suit and snappy red blouse, headed for a seat on the stage, the audience below. My natural inclination ever since Victims Anonymous was to lose myself in anonymity.

Alan waved me over. He looked as if he needed moral support.

What I gave him and his colleagues on stage was polite chatter while I wrestled with a reckless impatience. When someone in the group complained about how the crime statistics were costing Legal Aid public support," I allowed myself a mild reproof. "Statistics? There are people out there getting mugged by your five-time losers."

No comment. Some people looked surprised. Not Alan, though. He had heard me express such sentiments ever since our daughter had been murdered.

"Looks like we've got ourselves a large audience," Alan observed, looking pleased.

I checked out the crowd. Maybe three or four hundred people. I took in the deceptive sight of people relaxed in jeans and shorts. In bright cotton blouses and T-shirts. A lot of faces were turned to the sun. The calm before the storm? This was to be Legal Aid's version of a Rouser, after all. Whatever Kagan had

EYE FOR AN EYE

planned, it was sure to be disruptive.

The first few rows of the audience had been reserved for Legal Aiders of high standing. Luke's wife Jan, her dark eyes snapping with enthusiasm and quick intelligence, was among them. I caught her eye and we exchanged nods and smiles. I hadn't really expected Luke to be here—not his kind of show—but there he was, milling around.

On duty or off?

"Well, what do you know," Alan said when I pointed Luke out. "Jan never told me."

On duty. No way an experienced detective like Luke, head of New York's investigative task force, would be relegated to crowd control in Central Park.

I shifted my attention to the podium. Legal Aid's executive director, who looked like everybody's version of Santa Claus, had left his center-stage folding chair to peer for a moment into the audience while he fingered his beard. Then he took firm hold of the microphone. Everyone stayed polite all through his obligatory introductions and public acknowledgments. He segued into a bit of Legal Aid history spiced with self-laudatory statistics. Since this was *old* history to me, I tuned out and looked around for Luke Cole. The watcher being watched...

"Santa Claus" handed off his microphone to the next speaker.

Alan was sitting back in his chair with a this-ought-to-be-good expression. And this particular speaker *was* good. I'd watched the man sway audiences maybe half a dozen times. Invariably, he was the "opening act" at your typical Legal Aid fundraiser. But today wasn't a fundraiser and the speaker sounded a touch defensive as, mike in hand, he swung into a long string of "or else" exhortations.

"—must rid ourselves of a primitive idea—

retribution—*or else* lose our grip on civilization. We must balance toughness with compassion—*or else* see that which we hold most sacred, our Bill of Rights, torn apart. We must stop balancing the budget on the backs of the poor—*or else* see them rise up in rebellion—"

"Thirty million bucks of our tax money ain't enough for Legal Aid?"

I saw Luke Cole's head snap around... but not soon enough to see who had spoken. Just an angry voice in the crowd.

One of Kagan's plants?

The speaker ran a hand through his dark shaggy hair. "*Or else*," he repeated, "risk a backlash of increasing crime. We must come to grips with the poverty-stricken—*or else*—"

"The poverty-stricken, my ass!"

Another voice. Another part of the audience.

A man who looked like a truck driver jumped to his feet, apparently not leery of being identified. "How about a little consideration for us *working-class* poor?" he shouted.

"They're not the criminals," someone else yelled. "Legal Aid is!"

"Don't lose sight of our Bill of Rights!" the speaker pleaded. "I can't believe you're saying that a man accused of committing a crime has no rights."

"What about the rights of the crime victim, you mealymouthed bastard?" *This* voice was harsher.

The crowd cheered.

The speaker was too experienced not to know when he'd lost his audience. He mock-bowed and yielded the floor.

My eyes darted back to Luke. I saw nods. Unobtrusive hand signals that meant "stakeout." How many plainclothes police were out there? No way that Luke's men would be able to identify a majority of the hecklers. A shout, an angry comment, then the voice cuts out. It was not unlike a telephone caller who hangs up too quickly to be traced.

The next speaker was a syndicated columnist of my acquaintance. A self-proclaimed expert on juvenile delinquency, she had flown in from Boston to attend the rally and given her reputation, I expected her to come out swinging.

She came out smiling, looking girlishly young, almost prim, in a full-skirted linen suit as pale yellow as her hair, which she wore Peter Pan style. I figured that she'd welcome the opportunity to lambaste the hecklers with your typical horror stories about crowded prison cells, homosexual rape, and the sheer inefficiency of a system that deprived the accused of a speedy trial. Wrong again. She began to spoon-feed this volatile crowd with the usual pap she dished out weekly to a loyal following.

Talk about misjudging your audience!

"Prisons degrade," she said, not bothering to get specific. "Let us not warehouse our children. Let us work shoulder to shoulder to help our more seriously disruptive teens," she told an increasingly restless assemblage. "We should focus our energies on positive solutions to crime. I, for one, cast my ballot for stable marriages and fewer working moms! I vote for less TV violence and more federal subsidies to help our children!" she enthused. "I vote—"

In time with her gasp, an apple core struck her cheek and rolled down, staining her pale yellow suit.

Alan was chewing his lip. "Here comes Matt to the rescue."

Whoever "Matt" was, he unfolded from his chair like a giant accordion and strode to the podium—a majestic figure well over six feet tall, with a shock of white hair and the kind of blunt features that remind you of Mount

Rushmore. His huge arms shot out, waving the unruly audience into silence. I thought of a spreading fir tree.

"Who *is* this guy?" I asked Alan.

"Not one of my favorite people," he whispered.

"You folks have gripes?" Matt said. "Fine with me. We want to hear them. But by God, we'll do it like reasonable men and women." He stared into the crowd. "Okay. I'll take one question at a time."

You have to admire a man for throwing down the gauntlet.

Some scrawny punk-rocker stood up. "I got mugged in the fuckin' park on my way home from a concert coupla weeks ago. Motherfuckers had on Calvin Klein jeans and gold neck chains," he said, his own collection of chains glinting in the sun.

"What's your question, fella?"

"You turned 'em loose on me, man. That's your job, ain't it?"

A hard hat, his sleeves rolled up to reveal muscular arms, shot to his feet like an exclamation point. "I read somewhere that Legal Aid defends seventy to seventy-five percent of this city's criminals and gets fifty percent of them off. True or false?"

True-blue Victims Anonymous figures. I had done the research.

Matt rumbled into the microphone, slipping into part explanation, part excuse. The questioner resumed his seat.

An old woman rose from the middle of the audience and waved her cane. She kept on waving until Matt saw her and motioned her forward. The audience murmured approval.

Points for fair-mindedness, Matt, but a strategic mistake just the same. Your audience is with the old woman now every faltering step of the way to the podium. Have you noticed how long it's taking her to get there?

The woman was handed the mike with deference. She gripped it with determination. Her hair was gray and her free hand shook. But not her voice, as she launched into an old story. Easy prey, our senior citizens—and not just from muggers. Defense lawyers were adept at cashing in on vulnerability. Old people whose memories were dimming, along with their eyesight, made lousy witnesses on cross-examination. But *this* old woman was a little too good to be true, and I was sitting close enough to confirm my suspicions. I saw subtle signs of premature aging and zeroed in on a first-class makeup job. It made me angry. I had wanted her to be real because old ladies really *were* being victimized.

Matt was all diplomat as he tried to close his Pandora's box, eventually moving the woman away from the podium. Another old lady in a yellow print dress sprang up in her place—a brassy big-bellied black woman with steel-gray hair. The complaints she made from fourth row center came gushing out as if she'd been damming them up for years.

"—and that girl confused me!" she wailed, jabbing an irate finger in the direction of the reserved section. "No way I'm not gonna know who cut me. I got eyes, don't I? I got the scars! She tripped me up with her fancy words, that young snip of a black girl." She spun around to a collective gasp. "You heard right. One of my own done it to me!"

More than a few Legal Aid lawyers were young black women, but only one of them was prominently featured in the front row of the audience. It was a moment of acute embarrassment for Luke's wife, Jan.

In the next moment, epithets were zipping like well-aimed arrows toward the stage.

Alan gripped my arm as if he'd been hit. "It's getting out of hand," he whispered.

But big Matt glowered, waving his arms, and the crowd—it was not yet a mob—surprisingly settled down to let the verbal sparring match go on.

It was going to be all right, I thought with relief. The speaker may have played into Kagan's hands, but Matt's approach—an air of no-nonsense bordering on impatience—was as effective a crowd-control measure as I had ever seen. Insults and smart retorts petered out in favor of some legitimately tough questions and thoughtful answers.

I asked Alan why this guy wasn't one of his favorite people.

"Too volatile," he said as Matt turned the mike over to a colleague, a man who turned out to be an articulate lawyer. He was followed by a succession of articulate lawyers.

Matt sat nearby, arms at his sides, long legs stretched out. But not as relaxed as he seemed... His eyes—his whole body—radiated tension.

The woman in the audience who stood up—a striking redhead—said matter-of-factly, "I was wondering how you people feel after springing a rapist. Or some pervert who stalks children. Would you comment please?"

Matt was out of his chair like a shot. He seized the microphone from the speaker like a man whose patience had been exhausted. "You want to know how I sleep nights, lady?" he growled. "Just fine. That's my job. Defend the accused no matter what—"

A piece of fruit smashed against the podium. Then a bottle. A whole series of bottles. There was a mad scramble as curse words gave way to screams. As screams competed with the eruption of fistfights and the sound of breaking glass. People were stampeding. Clutching each other. Rushing off in every direction.

Time to go, I decided, hoping to find out how Luke Cole and his men planned to handle what had turned into a serious outbreak of violence. Without uniforms, it was easier for them to blend in with a crowd. Luke was rounding up hecklers and askers of questions.

Maybe the foulmouthed kid with the half-shaved head and the the black lady in yellow print were legit. Maybe the hard hat and the old lady with the cane were not. He would sort it all out at the station house. Smart...

If he and his detectives made it to the station house in one piece, that is. A tight little crowd—a mob?—was moving in on them with "barricade" written all over their grim faces.

I fell back just as a black arm thrust a papier-mâché symbol in the air. As a white arm raised a fist. As voices rose in a chant—

"Fox! Fox! Don't let them take the Fox. Fox! Fox! Don't let them take the Fox!"

An anonymous voice shouted, "Victims Anonymous!"

The barricade expanded, surrounding Luke and his men as they shouted, "Break it up! Break it up!" Spreading out, they used their drawn weapons like cattle prods as they tried to cave a circle in on itself. The hecklers who'd been rounded up moved within the circle like the tail-end of a restless herd bumping against the gate.

I saw the brassy big-bellied black woman with steel-gray hair start to edge away from the others. Suddenly she bolted. As the mob made a hole for her, she dove into it with the agility of a young woman. She would have made it, too, if some hard hat hadn't deliberately stuck out his foot to send her sprawling. I wouldn't have given the man a second glance—too intent on the old woman—if something about his lean figure and the angle of his neck hadn't jumped out at me as he hurried off.

Kagan!

The black woman was up and running. Luke made a grab for a long yellow sleeve. I gasped. Cried out to stop him from bringing her down. Stop him, as her hand automatically shot out to break her fall, from seeing the sensuous entwining of jade and gold on her finger.

"Claudia... ?" Luke said with soft bewilderment.

She wrenched away like a wild creature tearing at the net and raced through the center of the chanting. Touching off chaos.

Fists. Screams. Bottles and bats. The hecklers who'd been chanting merged... fell back... blocked the police from stopping Claudia's desperate burst for freedom.

Kagan had created his diversion.

A glint of sunlight on metal caught my eye. Luke's too.

Someone—a sniper!—was positioned on a flat boulder above the rim of the mob. He was brandishing a weapon. Taking aim—

Luke and I must have had the same frantic thought. *Claudia, in the line of fire!*

He smashed his way through the mob to pull Claudia down while, behind me, I heard shouting and the unmistakable sound of gunfire. Saw one of Luke's detectives aim for the sniper just as the sniper simultaneously aimed for him. The detective spun to one side, his aim spoiled by a bullet in the shoulder—

I saw Luke take a fatal bullet in the back.

When I looked up again, Claudia was nowhere to be seen.

I stopped weeping long enough to do what Kagan had taught me so well. I vowed revenge.

CHAPTER 35

"COFFEE'S COLD. DOUGHNUTS ARE WARM," Angela said, and offered me one.

"Later. I want to try Claudia again."

I dialed the wall phone in Angela's pint-sized office to the background din of martial arts. I hung up. "She hasn't answered all night."

"When did you start calling?" she asked.

I sighed. "When did I *stop*? I gave up at midnight and took a cab over to her place. I'm assuming she never came home."

"I wish to hell I'd been there," Denzel muttered.

"Praise be to God you weren't," Angela told him. "Luke Cole wasn't tipped off. I was able to find out that much. He just went with the odds."

"So did Kagan." Denzel crushed a Styrofoam cup, leaking what was left of his coffee onto the table. "The bastard was hoping the cops would show so he could treat them to a display of public support for Victims Anonymous. Did Claudia see who'd tripped her?"

"I don't think so," I said. 'But if Luke hadn't been killed, he'd have spotted Claudia's wedding ring. She never took it off. "

"We'll find her. She just needs time to recover," Angela reassured me.

"What?" I said, picking up on her sudden look of determination.

"We have to get out."

Denzel pushed his chair back. "Of Victims Anonymous? It's Kagan who should get the hell out. He and his new pals are psychos. If we cut and run, we throw it all away."

"The body count is climbing, Denzel," I said. "That was a *cop* out there who was killed."

"Low blow, Karen. Committed cops like Luke Cole don't grow on trees. I liked him," he said softly. "Under different circumstances, we might have been friends."

"We won't just lose friends," Angela chimed in. "The violence is getting random and it's going to get worse. Civilians are bound to get caught in the crossfire."

"I've been doing a lot of thinking since my Judge Arthur Younger Mission, Denzel," I said. "Ever ask yourself what Victims Anonymous cashes in on? Weakness. People who turn bitter when the justice system lets them down. Even the best of us lose our perspective. But what about the *real* sickos out for kicks—or, in Kagan's case, the psychopaths?"

Denzel sighed. "All right, what makes sense here? Do we pick up our marbles and go home? Does Karen resign from the double-agent business without giving McCann so much as a 'fare thee well' and two weeks' notice? Do we stand by while VA rolls merrily along?"

"Or do we stick around long enough to help McCann bring it down," Angela said, following his train of thought.

"I think we have a consensus," I said slowly.

"Not so fast. You have a meeting coming up," Denzel reminded me. "We'd better see what's on Kagan's agenda first. What he wants you to take back to McCann. Between now and then, Angie and I will keep thinking."

"While we're at it, Denzel, we should think about how we get Karen out of this mess in one piece," Angela said, eyeing me as if she could already see my head on the block. "Up on your SIS training, kiddo?"

"Are you suggesting I fend off Kagan with a karate chop?"

"Funny. I'm suggesting something more reliable."

"Yeah, I've been thinking the same thing. I'll get you an unmarked gun," Denzel told me. "It'll increase the safety margin."

"You cops are all alike," I groused. "Do you guys keep a barrel of unmarked guns at the precinct that you dip into whenever—"

"Oh dear God," I said, bringing a chill into the room and a memory to Denzel's face.

My 'just in case' piece. Don't worry, it's an unmarked gun, courtesy of my ex.

"I'll call the building superintendent," Denzel said, his face tight.

I listened to his end of the conversation. Stared at the ash growing on my cigarette.

The last thing Denzel said was "You're sure?"

I breathed again because he was smiling.

"The super spotted Claudia coming home a few minutes ago," he said.

I gave her five minutes to take the elevator up. Five more while she opened Luke's formidable battery of locks and bolts. I dialed, steeling myself for what she would sound like when she picked up the phone.

I hadn't steeled myself for utter silence.

"Let's go, Karen. Stay put, Angie," Denzel said as she shot to her feet. "One cop on the scene is enough. If there's trouble, you risk being identified."

Angela nodded reluctantly.

Denzel and I went over our cover story in the car. I was the semi-hysterical friend who'd been trying to reach Claudia ever since the tragic death of her ex-husband last night. Denzel was a cop who happened to be passing by when I rushed into the street looking for help. He told me I was admirably calm. I told him hysteria lay close to the surface.

Tony was sitting on the doorstep of the building, looking scared.

I pressed an intercom buzzer. No response. "Claudia, buzz us in please."

"She won't," Tony said, wide-eyed.

"Is Claudia back in her apartment, Tony?"

"Yes, but—"

"Did you talk to Claudia?"

"No. But I talked to Jamie this morning. He said Kagan chloroformed her and brought her home right after the rally. I stole a motorbike. When I got here, Jamie said I could wait in the hall if I wanted—that he was going to stay up all night with her. This morning too. "

"She's okay then," Denzel said, breathing for both of us. "Jamie would never have let Claudia out of his sight if he didn't think she was stable."

"But how come she won't answer?" Tony persisted.

I held the intercom buzzer down.

"This is no good." Denzel was at the door with a credit card. The apartment house door swung open.

I followed Denzel and Tony up some stairs to Claudia's apartment. When we got there, I called out her name. I rang her doorbell once. Twice.

After the third time I screamed her name.

Denzel cut me off with a look. He made a calming gesture with both hands.

"It's Denzel Johnson, Claudia. Tony is with me. And Karen, of course. Please let us in."

Footsteps. Then, "Go away!"

Not her voice at all, not Claudia. Pure anguish.

Denzel's expression was more frightening than the silence that followed. He was staring at the locks on Claudia's door in an agony of frustration. He started at the top and worked his way down. Testing... probing...

makeshift tools useless in his hands. He went back to the top. "It's a barricade lock," he whispered. "The damn thing is anchored." He waved us back and took out a revolver.

I braced myself and heard a muffled shot. Then another—

I heard Denzel moan.

"Claudia?" I said cautiously. "Claudia? *Please Claudia!*"

When we found her, Denzel let me go on screaming.

CHAPTER 36

I TOOK ONE LAST LOOK IN the mirror. A composed woman stared back. I'd had a week and a half to work on her.

A week and a half since Claudia had committed suicide.

I left the apartment and got a cab. I told the cabbie where to go—an address new to me. I ran through my "emotional checklist."

Pain. It was jammed into my nerve endings, carefully hidden behind my wraparound dark glasses... but so palpable—like an aura—that it was impossible to hide. No problem. Kagan would expect that.

Rage. Invisible. Packed away for another day.

"Don't let them win," Denzel urged after the first wave of hysteria subsided and rage had taken its place. "Don't let Kagan know we know. Don't let him sense what we're up to. You want to avenge Claudia? Start with this meeting. Put the rage on hold."

Guilt. The hardest to bear.

"This outfit of Kagan's—it's bad news and you know it."

Luke and Claudia would still be alive if only I had listened...

Fear. None for myself. Guilt has its compensations.

Trepidation. One word—Claudia—not to be pronounced in the same room with Kagan or everything could come undone.

The building I entered was innocuous. A man I

didn't know in an office I'd never seen showed me to a room. It was dark. At the end of a long table was a single chair. I took it. Bright light in my eyes when I took off my dark glasses. Shadows with no faces at the outer edges of the room. An overhead light snapped on.

Kagan stood by the door. I looked around at the others. O'Neal. Polanski. Lee.

And Jamie in his Blackbeard disguise?!

"Spare me the melodrama," I snapped. "Let's get down to business."

O'Neal spoke up. "The FBI's section chief in criminal investigations is getting impatient. McCann had two months to get results. His time is almost up."

"If Bernard Rees doesn't get a bead on our leadership pretty soon, he'll be forced to consider alternative action," Kagan pointed out.

"We've decided to oblige him," Lee said. "The idea is to expand 'Operation Feeder.' You'll be given new information for McCann—just enough to keep him in the game. But the rules have changed."

"You're to tell McCann your cover is blown," Polanski announced. "If he should ask, you don't know how we got onto you but we figure you for an FBI stoolie. So instead of a roundtable discussion on PR tactics, we're turning you into a go-between."

"No more double-agent business, Karen. I've come up with a proposal," Jamie said, sounding please with himself. "The FBI has vastly underrated the size and scope of Victims Anonymous. You're about to educate them so they have a better idea of just how national our 'national conspiracy' really is."

"How do I go about doing that?"

"Using my updated figures," Lee said. "You give McCann hard evidence of VA cell activity all across the country. Small towns. The suburbs. What I call our big-city cells. I've included a rough approximation of our total membership, including the number of people who run things locally."

"Since the FBI wants only national leaders," Jamie pointed out, "we can afford to be vague about it. Lee's data will reveal our organizational clout. Once Max knows there are vast numbers out there and that we in New York control them, both he and Rees will realize they have only two options. Either the FBI stems the tide of vengeance in this country by filling prisons with the 'little people'—which is *not* their intention—or they do business with the leaders. With us."

"Only *we* can pull the plug," Kagan said. "You're to tell McCann that we're ready to strike a deal."

Even out of Kagan's treacherous mouth, the words touched off hope.

"Our proposal has two parts," Jamie continued. "Tell Max our people won't cease and desist until our list of demands has been met. Strike that. Our list of *proposed* reforms. Think Max will agree that our criminal justice system needs reforming?"

Jamie was grinning right through his bushy black beard.

I remembered what he'd told me a long time ago about glasses creating a barrier between people. I put my dark glasses back on.

He looked as if I had just slapped his face.

"Second," he said, all business now, "is the matter of incentive. There can't be a deal without complete immunity for the deal makers."

I couldn't help myself. "You're crazy—the lot of you!" I exclaimed.

"It's McCann who's crazy if he doesn't go for it," Polanski jumped in. "He's the one who keeps talking about wanting to wrap things up in a hurry."

It was true enough...

"There's nothing in my figures that will compromise

anyone," Lee said.

"You're a pro, Karen. We know what you must be going through," Kagan said.

Don't do it. Don't you dare say her name!

"What happened to Claudia was more than a tragedy. It was something none of us can avoid... our fate."

I was glad I'd put my glasses back on. If I hadn't, there was no way Kagan would have missed the depths of my rage.

Picking up Lee's folder, I walked out.

And barely made it to the ladies' room, where I threw up my lunch. When I came out, Jamie was waiting by the elevator. I hadn't seen him since before the rally. Hadn't heard from the bastard even after Claudia had killed herself.

I'd have brushed past him if I could. I couldn't because he was crying.

We clung to each other.

As we rode down an elevator together, he looked at me with a flagellant's eyes. "I misread the signs, God help me," he said. "I let her go too soon. What kind of psychiatrist does that make *me*?"

"The only kind there is," I told him. "Fallible."

"It was a hellish night. Claudia was inconsolable, but by morning I saw a surge of defiance Of strength. I thought it was the strength to go on."

I could see in precise detail what Jamie had misread. Claudia's typical stance—defiantly straight and poised for flight. Tough and tender as a young birch. Impossible to know the breaking point...

"You did the best you could," I told him.

You never had a chance.

* * *

I entered my apartment pressing hope in the form of a manila folder—contents unread—to my chest. Max wasn't due for an hour. I sat down to look through Lee's figures. After reading Jamie's list of "proposed reforms"—or, more precisely, Kagan's demands—I saw at once why everyone thought Max would be impressed with us as a national organization. The number of cells had increased tenfold, mostly in the suburbs and the small towns. While Lee's "big-city cells" had only gone up by less than fifty, every one of the existing units had expanded in size. I saw what everyone was hoping for. The FBI couldn't begin to nip this thing in the bud, let alone follow Bernard Rees's scheme of doing it in a hurry. Our cellular structure was much too diffused and widespread for that.

I studied Jamie's list. The first item was immunity for the leaders. I knew that neither Max nor Rees would go for it. Certainly not *complete* immunity for every leader. I scanned the other items and had to stop myself from rolling my eyes. Everything that was wrong with our criminal justice system was on it. Complex problems that were swelling the ranks of Victims Anonymous because even the well-meaning people in law enforcement hadn't been able to solve them.

But it wasn't so much that the demands were outlandish. It was the impractical notion that the FBI, even in the person of a sympathetic Max McCann or a Bernard Rees, could even meet them.

I picked a proposal at random. Eliminate parole. Great idea. A few states already had, and it looked as if more were ready to follow suit. But how was a federal agency supposed to eliminate it *en masse*? Realistically, any proposal for reform should include a proper remedy. In the case of parole, state-by-state legislation, or else it's doomed from the start.

I checked out another proposal. Prosecute violent juveniles as adults. Be nice if more states would follow New York's lead, but not many were that enlightened.

The rest of the list was no different—all pie-in-the-sky proposals. Overhaul the obscene pragmatism of plea bargaining? Clean up the bail situation? Standardize federal sentencing? So what if Max had genuine compassion for crime victims? So what if he thought parole boards like to play God at the public's expense? What could he *do* about it?

I tossed the list aside and made coffee.

As soon as Max arrived, I handed the list over without a word and followed him into my den, giving him ten minutes to respond.

He looked up at me in five. "You've read it?"

I nodded.

"This list of theirs—their demands," he said, calling them by their rightful name, they can't be serious about getting an answer to this nonsense in a week, can they? Unless we're dealing with a pack of fools."

He pondered the possibility. "It's not how I read them."

I knew what he was remembering. It wasn't how Jamie had described them.

"I need time to submit this to Rees and whoever else *he* needs to submit it to. None of this is going to get done in a week," Max said, reaching for his coffee.

I listened to him rummage through Lee's updated figures and some details about our cellular structure, his voice low and slow like a man sifting through gold dust...

"This stuff spells widespread cell activity, all right," he said. "Not to mention big-city strength. Won't Bernard Rees be surprised by the extent of it!"

Max followed me as I headed for the kitchen to make fresh coffee.

"The Bureau needs to keep them talking, Karen. We need to convince them that we're open to some sort of deal."

All that remained on my *personal* agenda was to wait for Max to press me on more details about the people I had allegedly heard but not seen. "I have an idea, Max," I said. I retrieved my sketch pad and went to work. "I'm no artist, but I do a fair imitation of a caricature. It wasn't as dark in that so-called interrogation chamber as they thought."

I started with my sketch of Kagan. "Not much to go by," I apologized, handing it to him, "but the angle of the neck rings true."

"The chauffeur at your daughter's funeral?"

I nodded. "This bozo," I said as Max studied a much more detailed sketch of Chuck Polanski, "had the bad judgment to hit the men's room just as I was leaving the women's."

Max frowned. "He might be an innocent bystander.".

"In case he *is* one of them, this guy was wearing a ring."

A "friendship ring" Lee had given Polanski. I followed it with a sketch of Polanski's height and brooding good looks.

I told Max I'd caught a glimpse of a very distinctive battering-ram shape—and turned in O'Neal.

Not Lee though. Not yet...

As for Jamie, I thought, not ever.

I tossed the sketch pad aside, feeling good. Max handed it back. "Do one of the guy who was spotlighted while the image is still fresh," he said. "The man with the black beard?"

"Why bother?" I stalled. "It was such an obvious disguise."

"Give it a try."

"One beard coming right up," I said.

Jamie's beard had been thick and bushy. I made it sleek and straight.

"And blue eyes." I drew buttons within buttons and

filled in the irises with blue ink.

Jamie's eyes were a penetrating brown.

Max studied my sketches one more time and was about to stow them carefully in his briefcase.

"Wait," I told him. "I just remembered someone else."

I drew a man sporting a Stetson hat.

Max studied his face. "He looks like a rodeo star."

He looks like Kagan's psycho protégé.

"Hey, watch it, Pola," Max said, grinning.

Pola had landed on my sketch of the psycho, sniffing it with disdain. But as soon as Max eased the sketch out from under her, she jumped down and began to dash in and out of corners. Pola has a real sense of drama.

Her brother Marco launched into his repertoire of late-night yodeling.

"Time for a drink." Max led the way to the living-room bar and poured me a brandy. "To be followed by one of your hot baths," he said. "Bubbles, perfume, the works. I'll run the water."

I frowned. "Don't get domestic on me, Max. I don't think I could bear it."

"Can you bear to lie in my arms for what's left of the night?"

Without wishing it would last forever? I don't think so, Max darling.

He took my untasted drink away.

I led him into the bedroom and loved him with a ferocity that rocked us both.

CHAPTER 37

MAX PLAYED MOCK INTERROGATOR WHILE I worked at my lines and smoked too many cigarettes—I was supposed to be nervous.

I tried to put him at his ease. "Stop worrying, Max. Either these so-called leaders want to negotiate or they don't. Rees is right and you know it," I said. "You can't afford to risk severing the lines of communication. These people are too good at picking up tails."

"Level with me, Karen. How worried *are* you?"

"Frankly, tonight's showdown bothers me less than stopping off first at Claudia's place. She'd jammed so much color and life into three and a half rooms that you forgot how small it was. Now, seeing it empty—" I shuddered.

He reached for my hand. "Must you go there?"

"Give McCann a plausible excuse about stopping off at Claudia's before you meet up with VA's leaders to discuss our proposals. If the FBI puts a tail on you when you pull away from her brownstone, we'll spot it and postpone the meet."

Kagan says I must...

"Just one last time. That sketch of Claudia her cousin promised me is my favorite."

"One of yours?"

"I'm not *that* good. Some offbeat friend of Claudia's managed the impossible in a caricature. Grace, not distortion, is the theme. Those striking cheekbones.

That face, growing out of a tiger lily...”

And that was how we said goodbye. Max kissing away my tears.

* * *

I really *did* love the sketch Claudia's cousin was waiting to give me. She told me how much her cousin would have wanted me to have it. I slipped it into my briefcase, wondering if I'd ever be able to look at it without weeping.

Minutes later, dry-eyed and depressed, I stood in front of Claudia's brownstone. A car pulled up. The two men in the car were strangers, but they said the magic words so I got in. Roughly forty minutes later, I was uneasy bordering on suspicious. What was taking so long to get where we were going? We pulled up finally in front of a small house. One of the men waved me inside. I opened an unlocked door with caution and found myself in a two-room cottage—a real charmer in tasteful French Provincial. I was wondering if the view would be charming too until I realized there was no way to tell. Not with the windows boarded up.

I did a quick inventory. Plenty of logs for the ceramic-tile fireplace. Soap and guest towels in the bathroom. Tiny kitchen, but with a well-stocked pantry. Mineral water in the fridge, and wine and brandy in the pantry. My brand of cigarettes lay in an open cigarette box on a table.

What the hell was going on?

I had just noticed the absence of a telephone when the door opened. In walked Kagan, O'Neal, and Polanski. Not a friend at court.

“Like it?” Kagan asked with an expansive gesture. “Our hideaway away from home, on loan from a fellow traveler.”

“We use it when security is top priority,” Polanski

271

said, as if that explained anything.

I filled them in on Max's compromises and counterproposals, hoping they'd think it was real. O'Neal looked skeptical. Polanski confused. Typically, Kagan was inscrutable.

"McCann is willing to go *that* far?" Kagan pressed. "He's faking. McCann doesn't deal. He's all wrong for this."

His words had an ominous ring.

"Wrong man, wrong FBI faction. I tried to tell Jamie, but he insisted we give McCann a shot. No, McCann's usefulness is over. He has to be discredited with his own people."

"That way, we knock the ball into another court," Polanski said, as if he'd just hit a home run with his clichéd metaphor.

"We'll find us some feds who'll go for our national-offensive-against-crime pitch," O'Neal predicted." He stuck one of his trademark Havana cigars in his mouth but he didn't light it up.

Why not? My aversion to his cigar smoke had never stopped him before.

I reached for the cigarettes they'd left for me on the table and, letting them see how calm I was, I lit up and blew smoke in their direction.

"I thought Victims Anonymous needed McCann as a way of stopping his publicity-hungry colleagues from putting out a dragnet," I said in a tone so reasonable even Kagan wouldn't sense my rising panic. I was remembering what Bernard Rees had told me about "certain factions" in the Bureau and what they were after...

"If we bring down Victims Anonymous with a series of big splashes, it could spawn that national police force we have every reason to be afraid of."

When Kagan didn't answer, I said, "What if the feds

you have in mind don't follow McCann's scenario? He and his boss have said all along they wanted to zero in on Victims Anonymous leaders, not the little guy running a five-man cell from Peoria."

Kagan saw through my facade. "What are you *really* afraid of, Karen?"

I answered with part of the truth. "That some new faction won't stop with us," I told him. "They'll drag things out for their own personal glory and go after everyone in sight."

"Not if they're willing to deal. Unlike McCann, the idea of a federal solution might appeal to them."

"Max is dogged," I shot back. "If he gets pulled off this assignment, he'll continue on his own."

"Special Agent McCann, an over-the-hill agent who gets so sloppy that he can't keep his adversaries from snatching his contact? I don't think so."

His contact?

"He'll look like a schmuck," O'Neal said through the cigar clenched in his teeth.

"In other words," Polanski said with a nasty grin, "you get kidnapped."

I shot to my feet, eyeing the front door.

"Don't force the issue, Karen," Kagan said as he nodded to Polanski and O'Neal. They backed out the door. "Unless you'd care to be responsible for the photographs of your two closest friends and allies being delivered to McCann?"

Angela and Denzel.

"How long will I be here?"

"A couple of weeks at the outside. Meanwhile, you have all the comforts of home." He took a last look around.

By the time I figured out what to throw at him, I was alone, the cigarette box cracking open on the thick-paneled oak of a door closing in my face. Closing and locking.

I sat on the carpet, cursing my dimwittedness as I fed cigarettes back into the broken bottom of the box. O'Neal's unlit Havana should have tipped me off. The bastard must have been forewarned not to foul my new living quarters with cigar smoke.

CHAPTER 38

A FLAME SHOT UP, HISSING, AND died—no contest against wet wood. Just my luck to pull five days of rain out of six in the first week of my mock vacation.

At least the weather took the sting out of being locked indoors. I looked around at what I'd dubbed my "enforced coziness." One more day of staring at cornices and a ceiling that looked like a giant upside-down tray and I'd be tempted to burn the place down.

I glared at the built-in bookshelves that lined the octagonal room, as well stocked as the pantry. But try concentrating on reading when all you want to do is think of what got you into the unholy mess you've made of your life and whether you can work your way out of it.

I thought about men and women who, like me, had lost someone in their family to violent crime. Decent people, most of them, who'd lived through the trauma of knowing that those criminals had served light sentences—or worse, were set free at the outset.

I thought about solutions to insoluble problems that always seemed to end up in the same place... stranded between Max's "I don't have the answers" and "Neither do they."

I thought about rage—how I'd let it consume me after Sarah's rapists and murderers went free. But what does one do with rage? Drive it inward and self-destruct?

Turn it over to vigilantes? Join a convent? What are the options? Eleven months ago, what were mine?

I thought about support groups and how-to-cope clinics for the victims of violent crime. But cope with what, the trauma? Go for a new lock on your front door? Hope that your luck holds and you get a chance to testify in court with indisputable facts? And even then, how do you keep your hopes up if people in the know warn you in advance, "Don't expect too much in court." God forbid you should expect justice!

Okay, you tell yourself, sign on with your neighborhood watch group. Go on patrol. But armed with what—a walkie-talkie?

Protest groups? They tend to fade in and out of the boldest headlines, the latest murder in the park.

Networking, then? I had read about quite a few senior citizens groups that regularly monitored criminal courts and private crime commissions. They also compiled statistics and recommended more cops on the beat. Good as far as it went, but local—hit-and-miss. Not like Victims Anonymous—big, national in scope. An organization run by thinkers and planners. It was *organized*. I'd never fully grasped the principle, Jamie had told me once. I grasped it now.

The door opened, catching me off guard.

Tony Montes came in, looking glad to see me. Kagan's messenger. I hadn't heard the car that regularly dropped him off. Twice in the past six days he'd been admitted into my cottage-prison.

Tony, my sole contact with the outside world...

"Kagan wants to know if you need anything."

"Nothing much," I said. "Fresh air, freedom, and your visits," I said lightly so he wouldn't know how much I really meant it. "Just don't tell Kagan," I added.

Big grin. "Yeah. He'd stop sending me."

He loved talking about it. How he'd "bad-mouth" me

every chance he got and how Jamie always backed him, saying Tony had a "problem" with me because of his sister Maria. That Tony could put even this much of his old conflict into words meant that he had stopped blaming me—and, more importantly, himself.

"You going to ask me about your FBI man?"

"I've been afraid to."

"Nobody told him you got kidnapped. Jamie wants to but he can't. He says McCann thinks you're dead."

I had to turn away so Tony wouldn't see the bitter tears.

"I have to get out of here," I whispered.

"I'll get you out. I *will*," he promised. "I'll think of something."

"Sure," I said, letting him see I was calm again. "Any other news from the front?"

"I heard something about a Mission. They're getting ready to go after some judge."

"Who's Kagan out to reeducate this time?"

"I didn't hear his name, but I heard something worse. I think they're planning to kill him!"

Two words jumped out—felony murder. Then an image, Judge Arthur Younger. If it hadn't been for Denzel and Angela, he'd have died from a heart attack.

I cross-examined Tony as if I were my trial lawyer friend, Jon Willard. Knowing that Tony had a taste for melodrama, I looked closely for any signs of it, but he stuck to his story. A Mission to kill a federal judge had been in the planning stages for at least a week.

I looked at four feet ten inches of stubborn determination in patched denims and matching denim jacket and, feeling like an enlistment officer who sends a child off to war, I explained what he had to do. Eyes solemn, Tony repeated his assignment to make certain he had it right. Get the name of the Target. Nail down the Mission—date, time, place.

As soon as Tony left, I filled the silence with the innocuous chatter of television as voices drifted in and out of my consciousness. Barely tasting a listlessly prepared meal, I half-listened as a popular talk show wound down the hour with the usual cheerfully brisk announcement of tomorrow's guest lineup.

I went to bed missing more than the comfort of Max's arms. Just as Angela was never without Joe's shield, I had always carried the memory-scent of my Sarah... her favorite perfume. It had faded by the end of my first day here—one more outrage of my confinement. At home in my bedroom, I'd never closed my eyes without looking at some photographs on my night table. Sarah as a child... Sarah on her wedding day... Sarah in the nursery that she'd decorated right after she and Peter had decided to start a family.

But when I awakened, it was Tony I had dreamed of. Tony, who was proudly holding up a photograph he had taken of me.

I didn't come fully awake until I was en route to the kitchen to make breakfast. I turned the TV to my favorite news channel and opened the fridge just as a commercial flashed on-screen with a list of scheduled guests for tonight's *David Brudnik's Headliners.* It read like a veritable Who's Who in criminal justice circles. One guest was an outspoken ADA from the Bronx. Another, the head of a prestigious fact-finding commission. The third was a prominent American Civil Liberties Union lawyer. Last but not least, a controversial state court judge named Kevin Reilly. "Tune in live at 8 P.M.!" urged the announcer.

I slammed the fridge and stared at the screen as photographs of Brudnik's four guests appeared on-screen. Reilly was a man out of central casting. Thick white hair... the kind that strikes envy in the hearts of middle-aged males. Puckish smile that slips easily into an off-color joke or a sly invitation to "meet me at the corner pub for a beer in, say, fifteen minutes?"

I was no stranger to what kind of judge Kevin Reilly was. He had a reputation for flexing his judicial muscles in the courtroom where he was king, and the bigger the clamor set off by his questionable—some said outrageous—edicts, the better he liked it. A month ago he had heroically—some said sanctimoniously— "struck a blow for overcrowded jails" by ordering the mass release of hundreds of felons awaiting trial in New York City. The reporter gave estimates on the ones who had already jumped bail or been rearrested for new crimes of violence.

I sat down at my kitchen table and drank some coffee while I filled in the blanks of the assignment I'd given Tony. Name of Target: Judge Kevin Reilly. Date: September fifteenth.

Tonight!

Place: an office building on the West Side of Manhattan.

I was startled by a knock on the door.

It couldn't be Tony. Not two days in a row.

But it was.

"I know the name of the Judge," Tony told me. "Kevin Reilly."

"I know. I just caught it on TV. If they're planning to kill Reilly tonight, we don't have much time."

"Jamie said McCann knows something's up, but he's expecting trouble at the Brooklyn House of Detention—"

I groaned. "When he *should* be expecting it at Brudnick's studio in midtown Manhattan."

"We gotta get out of here so you can tell your FBI guy," Tony said.

"But *how*?"

He smiled. "You'll see."

Before I could say anything, the driver stuck his head in the door and announced, "I'm going down the road to get some gas."

"He always does this," Tony explained. "He doesn't like to stop on the way back to Manhattan. He'll be gone about a half hour."

As soon as we heard the car drive off, Tony steered me outside—but not down the road. He cut through some trees.

"Where are we going?" I said uneasily.

"Ever since I been coming here, I check out the area," he said with a discernible touch of pride. "There's a trail down the other side of this hill." He shrugged. "Maybe it's for hunters. Anyway, it'll take us to a different blacktop road. From there we can hitchhike to a telephone."

* * *

It was five-thirty by the time we got to a phone. I rang Max's Manhattan office but he wasn't there. He wasn't in his hotel room either. I shook my head at Tony, who watched from the light and warmth of an adjacent booth.

I dialed again and got Jamie at home. I gave myself five minutes to bring him up to date. We agreed to meet somewhere near Brudnik's TV station. Jamie vowed to find Max and head off another wild-goose chase.

Tony waved me over to the other phone booth. He was dialing when I got there. "You the FBI man?" I heard him say.

Wordlessly, he handed me the telephone.

"... Max?"

There's one kind of silence I don't recommend. Once you hear it, you never want to hear it again. "Max," I repeated, "I'm all right. Dearest, I'm not hurt. But someone else is about to be. Listen. Listen to me, please."

"Oh God, Karen..."

After that he listened.

When he spoke again, the professional was back and events were taken out of an amateur's hands.

CHAPTER 39

I LET MYSELF INTO THE APARTMENT. My bedroom door was rattling off its hinges. That would be Marco. Pola's protest took the more delicate form of chicken-scratches. With a release-the-prisoners flourish, I opened the door and almost cried to see them race out, full of pent-up energy and looking none the worse for Max's devoted care and feeding.

"Ten minutes for the run of the premises," I warned them.

Ten minutes to get my house in order. To empty my safe of incriminating papers and emergency cash. To fill a hefty knapsack with essentials. To catch the cats and put them back in the bedroom, where they snuggled up on feather-down pillows.

I left my apartment in tight jeans, pea jacket, dark glasses, and navy watch cap, hit the street, and got lucky. The cab driver who'd picked me up tackled traffic like an inspired Grand Prix driver.

I arrived at my destination early. Only a handful of pickets? I'd expected a lot more. They were walking back and forth in the disorganized fashion of a New York labor dispute that's gone on too long. The object of their attention—a ten-story office building—was as far west as you could go in Manhattan without falling into the river. Behind revolving glass doors, a bored-looking guard presided over his round glass booth, the better to direct in-house traffic—not much at this hour.

The neighborhood was mixed. A cluster of automobile dealerships, deserted at this hour. Office skyscrapers competing with small brick buildings, their ground floors given over to a coffee shop. A seedy bar. A dry-cleaning establishment.

Construction was everywhere, promising a distant future to skyscrapers but filling the present with dust and debris. Adding drama to a darkening sky were eerie silhouettes of naked beams and cranes, one of them with a wrecking ball hanging from a chain.

I looked around for a friendly face. A recognizable enemy. A sign of foul play. Kagan moved in mysterious ways, but so far he was invisible.

The only thing that beckoned was your friendly neighborhood tavern—the Blarney Stone. It was where Jamie would probably think to look for me.

The bar crowd was watching television. A couple of big guys with shoulders that made you think "longshoreman" made room for me with more surprise than discourtesy, then promptly forgot me. I ordered a beer and zeroed in on an intricately carved mahogany bar. What made me look away was a noticeable dip in barroom banter at the sound of the familiar theme music of *David Brudnik's Headliners*.

Brudnik's crew cut was as dated as his trademark bow tie. He wore a sardonic smile that said he took pride in his reputation as a gadfly. Not for him the seamless delivery of a teleprompter-reading superstar like Cronkite or Rather. Brudnik served up controversy— red-hot and abrasive, starting with his format. A brief introduction all around. The ADA from the Bronx. The ACLU lawyer. The prestigious member of the fact-finding crime commission. His Honor Kevin Reilly. As soon as the camera had framed Reilly in a close-up, Brudnik snapped a question to kick off the theme and tone of the show.

"So-called prisoners' rights versus the public's right to be safe. Isn't that what your outrageous court order is all about, Judge Reilly?"

"Call me Kevin, David. Outrageous? That's not what my order is about. What's outrageous is the unconstitutional spectacle of prison overcrowding. It's gone on too long."

Brudnik's camera strayed from Reilly's bland expression to the flushed face of the Bronx ADA. "What about the outrage perpetrated on innocent people?" he snapped.

"Not to mention the so-called humane act of releasing murderers with a long record as repeat offenders," the silver-haired ACLU lawyer cut in, thin mouth twisting. "The public has a right—"

Brudnik's studio audience applauded. So did the bar crowd.

"And I have a *duty* to prevent the infliction of cruel and unusual punishment on our prison population!" Reilly snapped, anger reddening his already ruddy complexion.

The bar crowd reacted with bottle-smashing rage.

I was spun around on my barstool.

"You shouldn't be in here, love," Jamie chided.

He took firm hold of my arm and led me outside. "The Blarney Stone is one of Kagan's powder kegs."

"It's chilly outside. I figured you'd look for me here. What's with your buccaneer costume?" I said, thinking that he looked dashing in his disguise, complete with bushy black beard and blue contact lenses.

"Good question," Jamie said, but didn't bother to answer it.

"The picket line sure looks anemic."

"It won't be for too much longer," he replied, clearly distracted.

There were a few more pickets since the last time I had

looked. Men in windbreakers. Women in thick sweaters and slacks. Teenagers in tight jeans and T-shirts. They were walking back and forth lethargically in front of the brightly lit entrance to the building that housed Brudnik's studio. That would no doubt change as soon as Brudnik's show ended in roughly three-quarters of an hour.

For now, the only controversial thing about the pickets were their **Impeach Judge Reilly**! signs.

"The 'action' is on its way," Jamie told me, indicating the river. "A boat trip around Manhattan, courtesy of the Victims Rehabilitation League."

"Wasn't that the organization that picked up VA's expenses on Christmas Eve?"

"You have a good memory," Jamie said. "The people on that boat are planning to join the picket line along with friends, relatives, anybody they can recruit."

"To what end?" I said, puzzled. "Are they here just to protest Reilly's release order?"

"That's my guess. Maybe Kagan wants big numbers. VA's New York City cells—ten at last count—will be out in force. But since the fun won't begin until Brudnik's show ends, I doubt that these people have any inkling of Kagan's real intentions."

"An assassination," I said softly, still unable to make it real.

"Look over there," he said, pointing.

The Circle Line. It was crisscrossed with twinkling yellow lights. I had been aboard her a few times. Once with Alan. Several times after that during my affair with Jon Willard.

The large vessel headed in to shore.

"Kagan fed me a cock-and-bull story. Something about creating the impression of a spontaneous uprising with nary a fox symbol in sight," Jamie said. "Reilly was targeted so Victims Anonymous could tap into his national television coverage. On the surface, it makes sense," he admitted "A huge turnout. Crowds objecting to a bunch of felons being released in the middle of a crime wave. With VA keeping a low profile, tonight's orchestrated anger will be seen as a kind of People's Protest—a call to arms for reform."

"And for national solutions. Grist for the anti–McCann FBI faction," I said glumly.

"What puzzles me," Jamie said, arms widespread as he examined himself, "is why Kagan insisted that I disguise my identity when Lee Emerson is scheduled to address the crowd without any disguise whatsoever."

"Maybe Kagan doesn't want you anywhere near an assassination attempt."

"But it's okay for Lee?"

"Maybe she's expendable. Remember how cavalier Kagan was when I called his attention—and everyone else's—to a couple of her out-of-town Missions? I warned him. Hell, I warned Lee *and* Polanski."

"Doesn't make sense, does it?" he said, looking troubled.

"Let's think this through. Max was en route to the wrong location—Brooklyn—until I set him straight. He's probably on his way here as we speak. Suppose Kagan saw through Tony's alleged hostility toward me? What if he'd *counted* on Tony freeing me from that godforsaken cottage, deliberately giving me a chance to call Max? It would have given Max enough time to circle back. To spot Lee. To make a connection to the 'mysterious blonde' he's heard about."

"Can Max connect her to you?"

"Who knows? Max wanted a sketch of you. I changed as many details as I could. But if I were you, Jamie, I wouldn't set foot on the same stage with Lee."

I might have been talking to the moon. Jamie's preoccupation was impenetrable.

EYE FOR AN EYE

"What's Kagan *really* after?" he wondered aloud. "This People's Protest is a smart move—cash in on Brudnik's national publicity. But what does he *gain* by taking out Reilly?"

The Circle Line boat had pulled to shore. I dug into my knapsack. "I brought you some papers, Jamie. Incriminating stuff. Mind stashing them with your tapes?"

"I've already destroyed them. Give your secrets to Tony, love. He's holding some of mine."

He threw his head back and laughed. "Will you look at this magnificent sky?" he said, grabbing hold of my hand. "To see the moon and the stars in Manhattan!"

"Let the night be magnificent, Jamie," I whispered. "You be careful."

"Wonderful, witty, and wise," he said, fixing me with that penetrating gaze. I knew that about you from the beginning. I knew so much. And so little... Do you know that I love you?" he said with quiet pride. "That much I've managed to achieve. Don't worry," he said to the tears in my eyes. "The only role I want to play in your life is guardian angel. Yours and Max's," he said gently, touching my face.

I lost sight of him in a mad vortex of bodies. People pushed past me. All around me. Practically through me. Angular patches of white filled the air—their anti–Judge Reilly picket signs held high. Behind me a door flew open. The Blarney Stone bar crowd emptied, the wide avenue filling up with a rush. I looked at the river running parallel to it. Moonlight glinted off the water. A slow wind tugged at overhead clouds, teasing them into sensuous shapes. Like Jamie said, a magnificent sky.

A good omen?

The mob seemed to be settling down. A hot dog cart opened for business. It looked to me like good crowd control. Two policemen rode up on horseback—two helmeted boys in blue. Youthful and fit, they rode with the easy confidence of men who don't expect trouble but could handle it if it came. I smiled to see them living Max's childhood dream.

I glanced at the men and women still massing on the avenue who had begun to march. People with angry signs and protest banners.

Muggers and murderers belong behind bars.
Don't turn our streets into battle zones.
Let's jail all the judges!

The marchers walked ten abreast past tall buildings, construction sites, and the gaps in between.

They moved inexorably toward the entrance of the building that housed Brudnik's television station. I fell into step and got caught up in a vortex of SOUND—MOTION—MILITANCY. It seemed to reach out and pull me inside, making me an integral part of a strength of purpose infinitely more powerful than my own. I saw strangers who seemed familiar. Familiar faces blending into one another. Caught sight of one friend in particular. From this distance and out of uniform, Denzel was barely recognizable.

Look beyond the anger of the marchers. Can you sense the hope, Denzel? Do you see what I see? The opposite of a lynch mob. We don't have to give up what Victims Anonymous was trying to accomplish. Not all of it, anyway.

We halted before a wooden platform in front of an open construction pit adjacent to the targeted building. I cut around a tight concentration of bodies to move back for a longer view. A couple of portable floodlights appeared and lit up a microphone. Someone reached down to help Lee Emerson onto the platform. Lee, in a white leather trench coat, burgundy scarf caught in the wind, her hair a golden halo under the coveted spotlight.

You're a real showstopper, Lee. You're a damn fool, Lee.

The black woman who'd just joined her was holding onto a sign, but I couldn't make out the words. Lee turned, distracted. Looking for her co-speaker, perhaps? Come to think of it, she'd probably arranged it that way. Jamie was a hard act to follow.

At least the crowd was orderly—a couple hundred strong now. They stood clear of the front of the building, a stone's throw from the platform to its right. One of the cops urged his horse to the left of the entrance, giving him good visibility of the scene but practically on top of whoever would be coming out of the building—not a good idea. As for his partner, he looked a little too complacent as he hugged the rim of the crowd, opting for good visibility of the platform.

TV coverage arrived in the form of a three-man crew—cameraman, reporter, and someone fooling with lights he'd never need, Not when Kagan had had the foresight to set up floodlights.

Reaching for the microphone, Lee introduced herself in dulcet tones. Her introduction of the black woman was sparse: "A crime victim like so many of you," she told an audience straining to hear her every word. "For the past hour, ladies and gentlemen," she said, "a federal district judge has been trying to justify himself on national television. A judge who has unleashed countless muggers, rapists—and yes, murderers—on to the streets of our city and has called it *justice!*"

Typical Lee Emerson melodrama.

I relaxed my tense vigil over the building's exit just in time to hear a collective gasp before I grasped the reason. Before I saw that Judge Kevin Reilly had come spinning toward us through the revolving glass doors. He was preceded by one man and followed by another.

The first man out—was it Max? Even from this distance, it looked like him. No signal was needed for the black limousine parked across the street. It roared to life, negotiated a deft U-turn, and pulled up to the entrance.

Just as deftly, Lee jabbed a savagely accusing finger toward her adversary, booming out his name. *"Judge Kevin Reilly!"*

Impatient hands were edging Reilly toward the limo. He brushed them away, brushed thick white hair off his forehead as he turned to his accuser.

Could his anger match her rage?

Max kept Lee's audience from learning the answer, unceremoniously depriving it of the star of the show. Spinning Reilly around like a top, he shoved him into the waiting arms of a man who had leaped from the limo. It was over with the sound of a door slamming.

In the moment when I realized Max had been vulnerable to a sharpshooter's bullet, I spotted Kagan in his hard hat.

What chilled me was his expression when he spotted me. I saw no sign of surprise.

"We came here to protest, and protest we shall!" Lee spoke into the mike, eager to take advantage of exposure on nationwide television even as she simultaneously demanded on-the-spot attention from the crowd.

She got Max's attention, as well.

I couldn't see his features clearly, but I knew what he had to be thinking as he turned away from her and spoke to the nearest cop on horseback. Turning back, he moved swiftly toward Lee—and why not? She fit the FBI's description of a Victims Anonymous leader—a striking blonde woman. Max wasn't about to let her disappear before he'd had a chance to question her.

The cop bellowed into his bullhorn: "Let's break it up and go home, folks!"

Behind me, his partner took up the cry.

I wanted to seize the bullhorn and bellow a warning to poor Lee. I wanted to run away and hide. I let out a cry as someone—Jamie!—seized my arm. "Look," I said, pointing, "Lee's drawn Max to the platform like a magnet!"

Jamie's face was an agony of frustration. "Why did Kagan want *me* up there as well?"

My eyes flashed back to the platform. Max was in profile, a restraining hand on Lee's arm as she bent to him, gravely attentive. Max in a khaki raincoat, Lee in white leather, the two of them freeze-framed in floodlit relief against the yawning blackness of a construction pit and the deeper black of cranes and construction beams barely visible. Eerily still.

Not quite still.

I grabbed Jamie's sleeve. "Something's moving behind Max and Lee!"

He'd spotted it, too. "A revolutionary must have his martyrs," he said softly. "Kagan, you unmitigated bastard."

"BASTARD!!!!!!" he yelled, causing heads to whip around and people to back away. Their movement enabled him to carve out a corridor and dash through it. He ran straight to one of the cops on horseback.

"Look!" he yelled, pointing at nothing. One moment the cop was looking, the next he was out of his saddle. Astride the horse, Jamie maneuvered it to create a new corridor as people scattered out of his way to the sound of his piercing cry: "Hijahhhhh! Hijahhhhh!" He reined in to avoid a collision. The horse reared. Moonlight caught the moment. Jamie's head was thrown back, his magnificent torso taut with the strain and exhilaration of effort. One arm was raised. You could almost see a sword in it, or a banner...

Moonlight had also made him a target. I whirled

at the sounds of a scuffle in time to see an unhorsed policeman who'd gone for his gun hit the ground, tackled by a black cop.

"Denzel?" the policeman said, his anger turning into a question mark.

I ran through Jamie's corridor, my view of the platform spoiled by too many picket signs. Ran until I heard a gasp that rolled all the way back through the scattered remnants of the crowd. I saw a hot dog cart, climbed on top of it—

And saw death hurtling through the air as a giant ball dangling a murderous hook sliced through the sky. In the moment when I thought it would strike the two spotlighted figures—Lee and Max—as if they were pins in a bowling alley, a figure on horseback swept them out of its path and sent them sprawling to the sidewalk. In the moment when I thought I had lived through a surrealistic dream, I heard a sickening crunch. Saw the side of a building take the punishment intended for human beings—and recognized the stuff, not of dreams, but of nightmares. A steel wrecking ball.

A revolutionary needs its martyrs, and its Judas goat.

You didn't get yours, Kagan. Lee is up. She's on her feet. Jamie saved her. He saved Max. I fell for your phony assassination plot, but thanks to a guardian angel, I didn't lead the man I love to his death. Max is—

I heard a crack, heard it repeat itself, but for a second it didn't register.

What did was a splotch of red spreading across white leather, Lee, reeling like a drunk while a horse reared up in fright and threw Jamie off.

I leapt off the cart and took off running. To find bodies bending over bodies. Lee, dead from a sniper's bullet. Jamie, dead from a broken neck.

Max was bending over Jamie, his fingers exploring more than his broken neck. He was fingering a black beard that was peculiarly off center... a spot of blue crystal that lay on Jamie's cheek like a counterfeit tear. A fox medallion around Jamie's neck.

Tears streaming down my face, I slipped away.

CHAPTER 40

MY CHANGE PURSE WAS FULL of coins. I inserted some into a pay phone.

"How's it going?" Angela said, recognizing my voice.

"It's over," I told her. "One wrap-up session and I'm out of here."

"Two days early." Her voice had a fill-me-in sound.

I filled her in on ten days of carrot-and-stick activity—good news, mostly. Thanks to Lee's off-the-record list of "real administrative talent," culled from her trip to the provinces and liberated from my safe, I had tracked people down fast and met with most of them. The "chic blonde" who ran our Baltimore cell. A couple of "plucky" housewives from Atlanta and Detroit. A gingham-curtains-and-apple-pie lady from Houston who was a "crack shot" with a pistol. A "savvy" black woman from Charlotte.

Thanks to Jon Willard's help, I'd spelled out our options. One by one, everyone I had spoken to had come aboard.

"Five cities," I told Angela. "Tip of the iceberg. That's the bad news. But if we could get our hands on Lee's administrative records—the ones she'd compiled before I took over—and feed those names into a computer, I could *then* go to Max—"

Jon's a lawyer," Angela said, pointing out the obvious. "He's the one who should be negotiating with

McCann. What am I missing?"

"Don't blame him," I said. "He wanted to meet with Max but I wouldn't let him."

"Got it. Hold on a sec," Angela said. "I've got someone here who is eager to file a report."

"They get fresh water every morning and their teeth look great—People Crackers twice a day," Tony said proudly. "Pola never finishes her supper but she looks okay."

"Giving them plenty of hugs and kisses?"

"Yeah, sure. You coming home?"

Home. To whom and for what?

"Yeah, sure," I said.

"Where are you?"

"In an airport bar in Charlotte, North Carolina. You be good, Tony."

I hung up just as a woman, who moved with the confidence of the tough-minded, walked in. She bore an unsettling resemblance to Claudia. It wasn't just the dark eyes. There was a touch of the exotic in her bone structure, not to mention her name—Sulette. We took a booth and waited for our drinks to arrive before she gave me her report. Sulette's experience with VA's Charlotte contingent had been almost identical to mine in other cities. Shock. An initial show of resistance. A touch of false bravado. Then the slow realization that it was the only way to go. What invariably followed was a resolve by the cell leaders to make it work in their own respective territories, giving me the bargaining power I needed.

To most people, the FBI was a mythic organization, either dismissed out of hand as so much television melodrama or the source of instant fear. Like me, Sulette had made the threat overhanging every one of us real, but not overwhelming. Not yet.

"We're batting a thousand in Charlotte," she said

cheerfully. "Sensible people don't need much persuading if they're looking a prison cell in the face. By the way, have you seen this?" She handed me a press release that had all the earmarks of a Karen Newman knockoff that had been rushed to every Victims Anonymous cell in the country.

It was Kagan's version of the Big Lie, and a doubleheader at that. "Dr. James Coyne, revealed as the martyred leader of Victims Anonymous. Prominent psychiatrist lays down his life for the cause. Lee Emerson, heroine of the hour, who managed to stay one step ahead of the FBI only to die from a madman's bullet."

"Don't worry about it," I told her. Kagan's press release will give me something special to talk about when I get to Houston," I said drily.

* * *

Good to be back? Not when it means wearing a hair shirt. Not when I can't help reliving the death throes of a best-loved friend.

Back to Claudia's place, not mine. Three and a half claustrophobic rooms I couldn't bear to be in, but I had to admit that it was the last place Max would think to look for me.

"The lease is in my name?" I asked.

"Denzel and I thought better of it after you left." Angela said, handing me half a driver's license, a supermarket charge card, and a lease.

"Mrs. Rosa Ramirez. So Rosa's generosity extends to my borrowing her identity," I said with a faint smile.

"I picked out a few pieces of furniture. Items small enough to fit in these cramped quarters until we know our next move." Angela pointed out a couple of sturdy chairs and a square box-like job that opened into a twin bed on springs. "For Tony," she said. "Some kid he's been living with picked him up earlier and drove him to the Bronx to pick up his gear."

"Tony's idea." Denzel offered me a cigarette. "Take a look at the lease."

The name on the lease was "Mrs. Rosa Ramirez and son."

You're not too late, Jamie had assured me. You're too early.

"Angie and I figured Rosa's name was quicker and safer than manufacturing a new identity," Denzel said, pretending not to see my tears. "We have more pressing matters to risk our necks over."

"Were we right about O'Neal?" I asked.

Angela nodded. "He was the brains behind the wrecking ball, all right. Mind if we change the subject? It's depressing. Given the space limitations, the only other furniture I could fit into Claudia's bedroom was your bed, a dresser, and one night table. Denzel's contribution was to buy the smallest desk he could find. There's plenty of room for your clothes. The closet is surprisingly spacious."

Not surprising to me. I pictured one breathtakingly lovely outfit after another during Claudia's seemingly endless quest to get Luke back...

How do I look?

Menu and décor, a ten. Ten-plus for the hostess, who looks sensational in billowy cocoa and cream topped off by an exquisite turban.

"—kitchen appliances all in good shape," Angela was saying.

I thought of Luke's all-time favorite—oyster stew. Of spinach lasagna and lemon meringue pie.

"Thanks," I said. "I can't begin to tell you how much—"

Angela's eyebrows shot up. "Then don't."

"Okay, consider yourselves thanked. No trouble with my boss?"

"Not after your letter arrived. He's on hold."

On hold while I "recuperated." But not from one week of kidnapping and two more on the road. My excuse had been a new strain of flu.

"By the way, Jon Willard picked up your office computer. It's in the bedroom."

"You up for a small piece of good news?" Denzel asked. "A fence-sitter by the name of Timothy yielded to his better instincts. He's with us—at the moment just in spirit. Safer for him that way."

"A businessman with a penchant for fund-raising *is* good news," I said, sinking into the couch. "We're going to need him."

The sound of the buzzer lit up smiles all around.

"One orphan coming in out of the storm," Angela quipped.

Tony came in with a load of camera equipment and a noisy carrying case. Marco and Pola seemed to be protesting their confinement in one case—no doubt as cramped for *them*," I thought, as Claudia's three and a half rooms were for me.

Denzel went for Tony's suitcases. Angela tousled his hair. I was content with his solemn watchfulness whenever he looked at me. Jamie had told me that he had looked at his sister Maria that way.

As we helped him unpack, everyone exchanged high-spirited "Mrs. Ramirez and son" one-liners, climaxed by an ID card that Tony proudly produced from his pocket: TONY RAMIREZ. "I forged it," he said, the way a kid might say "I got an 'A' on my math exam."

"You dropped something, Antonio." Denzel reached for a folded envelope that had fallen out of Tony's pocket.

Tony colored. "I found it under the door where I was living."

The letter was addressed to me. I pulled it out of the envelope and read it. I read it again—this time out loud.

"Forget trying to take over Victims Anonymous and

turning it into something it was never intended to be, Karen. Picture five items delivered to McCann. A photograph of you killing your daughter's murderer. A bullet from the same gun. The gun with your prints on it. Another bullet—but this one belongs to a rifle with a telescopic sight. Could it be the one fired at poor Lee Emerson? A photograph of someone in navy cap and pea jacket kneeling on top of a panel truck. Could that be you, taking aim with a rifle? Thanks to me, McCann got a tip about a mysterious blonde—a Victims Anonymous leader. Just as he was about to question Lee Emerson, she's shot to death. Very convenient if the *real* administrative head—that's you—wanted to deflect suspicion. *I have a lot more to say to you, but not in writing. I want to see you in twenty-four hours. Polanski will arrange it."*

Denzel spoke for us all. "Sonofabitch. He's trying to frame you for two killings. You *have* to get McCann's help."

"I wish to God I could but I have no leverage—not once Max recognized Jamie. I'd need his help not only with Kagan. But I also need to make a deal with the FBI if *somehow* I'm going to get immunity from prosecution for the well-intentioned people who got caught in the web of Victims Anonymous. I can't do that until I have Lee's VA files—names, dates, places, cells. Polanski must have them. But don't worry, I'm not going anywhere near Kagan."

CHAPTER 41

THE INTERCOM RANG.

"I'm waiting downstairs," Polanski said.

I walked out of the building and over to a tan Chevy.

"First things first, Polanski," I told him. "I want you to hand over Lee's VA files."

He laughed.

"What's so funny?" I snapped.

"I don't have them anymore. Kagan does."

"Wait here," I told him, and went back upstairs.

"What's going on?" Denzel asked.

"Polanski just told me Kagan has Lee's files."

"What if he's lying and Kagan intends to kill you?" Angela asked.

Tony put his two cents in. "What if it's a trap?"

"If I don't go, there's *no* chance to get my hands on those files. Without them, I won't have what I need to negotiate with the FBI."

"If you're going to see Kagan you better be armed," Denzel said. "Where's your handgun?"

"Locked up at the gun club."

"Then you'd better take this," Angela said grimly.

"This" was a small .38 caliber revolver.

"What do I need a gun for? He just wants to talk!"

"Don't be naïve. If he's willing to frame you for two murders, who's to say he wouldn't kill you?"

"He'll search my purse."

"Not if I strap the .38 to your ankle," Angie said. "You're right-handed so it goes on your right ankle. Lucky you're wearing slacks."

I sighed and let her do it.

* * *

Polanski gave me a hard-edged nod. I gave it right back.

He held open the passenger door. My stomach lurched when I noticed how he was holding it—like he was a hair's breadth away from slamming it against my body. I recovered in silence as he drove east through Central Park and pulled onto the drive heading uptown.

"Just so you know, Polanski, I've never fired a rifle. I don't know how."

"You could have learned," he said. "Kagan says you're one smart lady."

"Not so smart," I said faintly into the raised collar of my camel's hair coat. I had just noticed my surroundings... crumbling buildings and vacant lots. We were heading toward the Bronx.

Murky twilight descended. Traffic was thinning out. Cabs mostly. They'd be running a race with their meters. Drop off the fare, then get the hell out before dark. I saw one off-duty light that had been with us since the East River Drive in Manhattan, but I lost it when Polanski turned onto a side street. As soon as he pulled over, I reached for my purse. He got to it first. "Waste of time," I said drily as he reached inside. "It's too small for a rifle."

He handed it back. "Time to go."

This time he let me open my own door. When I got out, he pressed a gun to my ribs.

"Lucky I don't kill you first," he told me.

First. Before Kagan?!

I made myself go limp, mentally reviewing Angela's basic strikes, kicks, and escapes. He grabbed both my

301

hands in one huge paw and started to drag me forward. We passed hollow-eyed buildings and empty lots, took a few sharp corners.

"We're here, Polanski said.

He must have noticed something in the corner of his eye because he turned.

"What the hell you doing here, kid?" he said as Tony stepped out of the shadows.

"I don't trust Kagan anymore than Karen does," Tony said.

Polanski waved his gun back and forth, indicating we should enter the building ahead of him.

"Up the stairs. Five flights. Stop on the sixth-floor landing."

We trudged to the second floor, Tony in front of me, Polanski behind, his gun poking me in the back. Steep staircases... three... four. As soon as Tony reached the sixth-floor landing, I pushed him forward, whirled, kicked Polanski in the gut and sent him flying down the stairs.

"He's not moving," Tony whispered. "Is he dead?"

"If he's not, do something to keep him down there while I deal with Kagan. Then grab his gun, come back, and wait outside the door. But don't come *in* until I call you."

Apparently hearing the noise, Kagan opened the door. He spotted Polanski's body on the fifth-floor landing, Tony hovering over him.

"Stay there, Tony," Kagan ordered. Come in, Karen."

Still rail-thin and laconic, I thought, but *this* time I knew how to read tension in those smoke-gray eyes. With a half-turn of his angular neck, Kagan gestured me inside and invited me to look around. Instead of bathtubs full of gold and silver, garment racks of clothing, and furs serving as bedspreads for sagging-mattress-draped beds, I saw desks, file cabinets, a safe, charts on the walls, and drapes across the windows. The den of thieves had become an office.

Kagan headed for his safe, spun the dial a few times, and removed a metal strongbox. "My little black box, you called it."

"Let's cut to the chase, Kagan. The only reason I'm here is to collect Lee's files. Turn them over and I'm out of here."

Kagan smiled. "What makes you think *I* have them?"

"Polanski told me."

"Thanks to you, it looks like he's in no position to tell anyone anything."

He dug deeper into the safe, pulled on a pair of gloves, and removed a handgun. He put it on the desk.

I had waited too long to go for mine.

"I gather this is the one I used on Indio," I said, letting him hear hardness in my voice, not sinking despair.

"The very same. There's one round left in the cylinder for the suicide victim," Kagan said. "You."

Denzel and Angela were right. I'm not going to get out of here alive!

"You won't get away with it. I've been in contact with Victims Anonymous cells in five cities so far—people who will realize what you're up to and guess what happened to me. How will you explain it?"

"I won't even try. Victims Anonymous will have a titular head shortly after I *appear* to disappear, the victim of stepped-up FBI activity. Democratic of me, becoming one of my own fall guys, don't you think?"

"Imaginative as always. So the law closes in while you cover your tracks with fall guys. You're not really out to make a deal with the FBI, are you? You never were."

"Sounded good, though."

I bent over double, my head in my hands. "Oh God, I don't want to die," I moaned, hoping to distract him as, slowly, I slid my right hand down to my ankle—and instantly came up with the .38.

It took him by surprise.

What took *me* by surprise was his next move. He laughed at me as his arm reached for a light switch by the door, plunging us into darkness. Frantic, I pulled the trigger. This time, his laughter came from behind. I turned on a dime and fired two shots behind me to the sound of breaking glass.

The silence afterward was as mocking as a Kagan smile.

I felt myself falling into a deep pit of fear... a frightened amateur, pitted against a professional killer.

I backed into him. He pulled me into a bear hug.

"Have you counted your bullets like a good girl should?" he teased in my ear.

Three? Four? I wasn't sure!

I squeezed off another round over my shoulder in the direction of his voice. As he laughed, I smashed my foot down on his left instep and broke free. I thought I heard his breathing off to my left, and fired again. Darkness swallowed us as I tried to fire another shot. Nothing happened.

Kagan flicked the light back on, all smiles. "I never trusted you," he said. "I sensed what I would be up against in a showdown... a formidable adversary."

A dubious tribute. At least it kept me from sagging. What kept me from screaming my head off was the neighborhood—the lack of one. All I knew to do now was keep the conversation going as long as I could until I could think of something.

"Kagan, the man with the soul of a revolutionary," I said, tossing my useless gun aside while he left his on the desk. "What did Jamie mean by that?"

The question seemed to startle him. It was as if he'd heard it before but had never tried to answer it for himself. "I think of myself as a professional soldier," he said finally.

"A mercenary? You have all the earmarks. Join the cause. Insinuate yourself with its leader. Work tirelessly until you're indispensable. But did you ever get *genuine* pleasure out of what we were doing? A mercenary is a man with a price. What's yours? What are you greedy *for*, Kagan? If we rule out the obvious—money and macho—what are we left with? What do you get out of life?"

I'd done that much, at least. I'd wiped the smile off his face.

He shrugged. "Like you, animals give me pleasure."

"You're no animal lover," I said, sure of my ground. "It's not the same thing, being comfortable with them. I wonder about a man with no friends, no home, no woman. Does a man like you find the *human* animal threatening? As for the cause, Victims Anonymous was full of worthy goals and good intentions. You saw how contagious Jamie's sense of justice could be. Did you care one way or the other? Do you give a damn even now, with everything you helped to build on the verge of collapse and—"

"I care about the fight, you fool! I *am* a revolutionary."

"*Any* revolution?"

"As long as it's in ferment"—his eyes flattened as he considered his own statement—"and against established order," he said with the slow reflection of a man in the process of discovering and enjoying a personal revelation.

"And if your revolution succeeds?" I pressed, feeling close to a discovery of my own.

"You mean, what if Victims Anonymous had turned respectable and ushered in a New Order?" He shrugged. "How long before the whole thing turned sour?"

"Before *what* turned sour? What are you saying?"

"No revolution ever succeeds, not for long. There's

always something new to rebel against. That's where people like me come in. We go to ground. Organize the opposition—"

"You rebel... for the sake of rebelling?"

We stared at each other.

I was thinking of a man who lacked the antennae to tune in to people except for his own limited purpose.

"I'm what society spits up after a gluttonous meal," he told me, still thinking about rebellion. "The indigestible man."

"But you're *invisible*," I said as I groped to understand. "Don't you have any desire to take credit? To seek notoriety for—"

"You do things wholesale and in the dark. *That's* the secret formula. Shoot a subway mugger, take out the neighborhood bully, and what have you got? A feeble isolated 'protest.' But take your time—organize the shooters—and you can pull it all down."

I knew him then. A man with no goals but one—tear down what others build. His is a darker need...

"You were born into the wrong century," I said. "The pillaging hordes that destroyed entire civilizations would have suited your purpose far better than a sorry mix of misguided crime victims and assorted neurotics. The breakdown of a criminal justice system—"

"Is as good a cause as any." He looked amused.

"You're in no danger of running out of causes, are you?"

What do you know about a man with no discernible values who derives his sense of identity not from anything he is or wants, but from what he does to other people's values?

I didn't dare say it aloud, afraid Kagan would kill me on the spot.

But I'd run out of options. "Victims Anonymous never stood a chance, did it?" I said. "The good guys can never do business with the bad and come out ahead. People like you contaminate everything you touch. You're worthless, Kagan. You lack even the nobility of the animals you pretend to love. People like you are subhuman."

The back of his hand across my cheek sent me reeling across the room to crash-land against the door. I slid to the floor, not as dazed as I looked, and told myself he wouldn't shoot from this distance—not with one bullet. Not if he wanted my death to look like suicide.

I yanked the door open. Tony stood there, Polanski's gun in his hand.

I snatched it.

Kagan looked stunned.

"Back up and sit down," I told him.

Moving cautious steps away, hands raised above his head, he retreated to his desk.

"Nervous, Tony?" Kagan said.

Kagan obviously wasn't. The drapes behind him added a bizarre touch, stirring in the breeze from the glass I'd shattered with a bullet.

Tony was fingering the camera strap around his neck.

He *wa*s fidgeting with the portable heater next to his chair. "The streetwise kid who never goes anywhere without a camera is a boy with a guilty secret. May I tell Karen your secret?"

Tony flushed. Putting down his gun, he took Kagan's picture.

I had the distinct impression that if the gun weren't aready back in Tony's hand, Kagan would have ripped the camera off his neck and smashed it.

"Tony, our pint-sized co-optee. How grateful you were to the boy who'd risked his life. Who'd helped identify your daughter's killers with photographs so devastating they distracted you," he said, swinging around in his chair, one hand dropping below the desk. "You never asked yourself a key question. Where did Tony get the photographs? *How* did he get them without being Johnny-on-the-spot?"

"Kagan!"

Tony's scream mingled with Kagan's laughter.

"Tony, all dressed up in a Halloween Muppet costume—Kermit the Frog, wasn't it?"

Would you believe old-fashioned ghosts outside my door? Oh, and one modern touch—an adorable little Muppet frog.

Tony had turned into a statue.

So had I.

I don't know how long I stared at him, screamed at him, before I realized I was staring into a conflagration. The bottom of the drapes were in flames from the portable heater Kagan had been fiddling with.

If I hadn't been mesmerized by the flames crawling up to the ceiling, I might have been able to shoot Kagan in the back as he climbed out of the window onto the fire escape.

I rushed to the window, not knowing what I'd find. Kagan was descending the fire escape. He glanced over his shoulder and said cheerfully, "There will always be a Victims Anonymous!"

There will always be a Kagan.

When I ran for the door through the smoke, Tony was gone.

CHAPTER 42

"NOBODY HOME. TONY HASN'T BEEN back," Angela said, sounding uneasy.

I followed her inside. "Good riddance," I said. "By tomorrow morning I'll have all the locks changed. When can you get his stuff out of here, Denzel?"

"Karen, can't you at least—"

"Not another word. I need a clear head to deal with the FBI. According to Polanski, Kagan had the files and his place when up in smoke."

"I never believed either one of them, Karen," Denzel said. "So while you were with Kagan, I jimmied the lock at Lee Emerson's apartment, searched the place, and found her files in, of all places, her clothes dryer!"

"Bless you!" I told him, breathing a sigh of relief.

How long before you lay it on the line with McCann?" Angela asked.

"A week at the outside now that we really have bargaining power. Jon Willard advised me not to stretch it beyond that."

I lit a cigarette. Mashed it out. The quicker I got Tony's things ready, the sooner Denzel could take them away. I carried a couple of cartons to Tony's room, ready to go through the drawers in the dining-room cabinet that served as his bureau. The first drawer was filled with T-shirts The second was a tangle of socks, underwear, and whatever else could be jammed in. The bottom drawer was a surprise. Under a top layer of neatly folded sweaters was a small recorder and a couple of cassettes. Attached to one of them was a note addressed to me in Jamie's familiar script. It was dated shortly before he had unhorsed a policeman in a vain effort to protect Lee Emerson, even as he had saved Max's life at the expense of his own.

Give Tony your secrets, love. He's holding some of mine, he'd told me.

I was hoping this would never be necessary, Karen, although I sensed that someday it would. Forgive me the half-truths and the method I've chosen to see you through the bitterness and pain. It's Tuesday, the day after Labor Day. So much left undone. After what's happened, I dare not put it off any longer. This tape is for you in the hope that Tony listens to me one last time and gives it to you. Tony Montes was not one of the Savages who raped your Sarah. Nor was he there to vandalize and rob. Do you hear me?

I'm afraid to hear you, Jamie. I'm afraid to hope...

Remember New Year's Eve, after I'd persuaded you not to give yourself up to the law? I talked you out of it.

Take a life to protect a life. I remember.

The law is just as savvy when it comes to "duress"— unlawful constraint. Forcing someone to do something he wouldn't do of his own free will. Are you with me? Do you see what I see? A boy short on stature, trapped in a nightmare not of his making. Now let me correct some half-truths in the nightmare he's been living with—the one you sat in on. Remember where it begins? Crashing cymbals. Screeching violins. People in uniform. Tony was reliving a terrifying threat. Indio and his gang had cornered him. Had tapped him for their Halloween robbery binge. If—

But why Tony?

—asking 'Why Tony,' think back to the drowning incident in that nightmare and how he described being

surrounded by worm-like fish—by tadpoles? Indio and his gang had gone looking for a kid and forced him to wear a disarming costume—a real door-opener. A literal one, as it turned out.

Would you believe old-fashioned ghosts and an adorable little Muppet frog!

Tadpoles, in aquatic terms, are the larval stage of the frog. Bear with me now. This is going to be painful. Remember in the dream when Tony is hiding in the woods? There's a full moon. A wolf pack is closing in on him—all that howling.

I hear it, Jamie, especially when I try to sleep— Sarah screaming as they rip off her clothes. As they cut off her finger...

Tony's subconscious was in play again in a desperate effort to absorb the shock and horror of Sarah's mutilation.

Suddenly he's at a dance hall. Scantily dressed women slide down poles while men slip money into their tights. He's ashamed of his beloved Maria—part Madonna, part whore. But she's also—hang in there— she's also your Sarah in the first stages of her defilement.

Gang rape... Hang in there, Jamie? I'm hanging by a thread!

Remember whenTony grows smaller and smaller by the minute? He's running and shrinking—but from what? From helplessness and fear. From guilt. Because—and this is the worst of Tony's ongoing nightmare—he blames himself for being on the other side of the room when it happened. The fatal stabbing. Somehow he should have been able to prevent Sarah's murder. Once you two had met, once he'd come to love you, that unearned guilt was close to unbearable. The conflict over you and his sister wasn't the true source of Tony's nightmares. He was terrified you might find out how he'd come by the photos.

It came back to me in disconnected pieces right before Kagan had set fire to the drapes... how Kagan had distracted me as he talked about his "pint-sized co-optee." The streetwise kid who never went anywhere without a camera. A boy with a guilty secret.

Jamming my eyes shut, I heard it again—

"Kagan!"

I heard Tony's scream mingling with Kagan's laughter.

I've left the worst for last—the reason I took refuge in a tape recorder. To confront the look in your eyes when I can barely confront myself? Unspeakable. I made Tony my responsibility. I've helped him, it's true. But I used him too. The photographs he gave me led straight to you. Oh, he was willing enough to cooperate in return for the sanctuary Victims Anonymous offered him. But with Indio out of the picture, Tony became the boy who knew too much. I capitalized on his growing attachment to you, calling him Tadpole in your presence from time to time just to remind him that we had mutual secrets to guard, he and I. It kept him in line... but it was blackmail, God help me.

Tony didn't hold it against me even before I apologized—he's that kind of kid. At least I had the wits to recognize a mutual need. To sense what you two could mean to each other. I nurtured that.

Each of us has our nightmare. This ends mine. You helped end Tony's by sitting in with us that day while we played a trick on his psyche, giving him the illusion that you had learned his secret but hadn't rejected him. But his improvement is temporary, and only you can make it permanent. Get Tony to describe what went through his mind as he sped toward Westchester, wedged between the bodies of those vicious predators. How he had turned the camera he'd been forced to bring along into a tool—a distraction. How it became just that when he used it to help Sarah. How he blames himself for not resisting harder, sooner. For not running away before Sarah opened her front door. Convince him that it wasn't his fault... unless you really believe that a terrified boy, armed only with his camera and his courage, could have stopped the carnage.

"Leave her alone! Don't hurt her!"

What Tony needs so desperately, Karen, I need it too. Can you forgive me?

"For everything but dying on me," I whispered.

The tape ran out.

* * *

"Sorry I'm late," Angela said.

"No problem. Dinner's in the oven, not on the table. Denzel is making drinks."

"You set a nice table. How about laying on another plate?" Angela said.

"Tony?" I whispered.

There'd been no word for almost a week.

"He showed up this afternoon, right in the middle of a martial-arts session. What happened to those cartons you packed?" she asked with a casual look around.

"Still in the closet. Angela, I—"

"Tony Montes alias Ramirez. Runaway kid, waiting to be found," she said. "Have we found him?"

I closed my eyes. "Where is he?"

"In the hall. Maybe you can make him come in."

In the hall.

I went out, apron and all. Behind me, the door clicked shut.

His eyes were wide... as dark and solemn as a boy-priest.

I was hollow, as empty as the hallway.

But only for a moment.

When I opened my arms, Tony walked into them.

CHAPTER 43

I WALKED THROUGH THE ROOMS OF my Central Park West apartment, but not like someone who'd been away for a month. Like someone who didn't live here anymore.

For Marco and Pola, it was part homecoming, part familiar space to run around in and a lot more places to play hide-and-seek.

For me, the hiding was over. Max was due in twenty minutes.

I checked the mirror. Big mistake. Max had liked my hair long. A few weeks ago I'd opted for a short no-nonsense cut.

As for my makeup, it was wasted effort. Nothing can disguise that puffy look—a dead giveaway for periodic outbursts of crying.

You grab hold of a cat and make him purr if you want to lower your blood pressure.

Marco obliged. Pola had already slipped into her typical languid windowsill stretch and stayed put, a lovely addition to my park view.

When Marco bolted out of my arms, it occurred to me that a doorbell is its own kind of mirror. It can be cheerful, annoying, tense, violent. This one suggested that someone had barely touched the bell.

What greeted me was flat and empty. A face devoid of everything but recognition.

I said his name. He nodded.

I said, "Let's go into the living room, Max."

He followed at a discreet distance.

I gestured at the couch.

He sat on the arm of a chair and unbuttoned his raincoat, as if to say, "I'll give you the courtesy of an explanation, lady, but make it brief. I'm a busy man."

No surprise when I offered him a drink and he turned it down.

I took the couch he'd rejected. Took a deep breath.

"Max, I'm so sorry," I said. Empty words under the circumstances, but I had a year's worth of explanation behind them and maybe fifteen minutes to pull it all together. There was so much to be sorry for where Max was concerned. I started with that. How he had a right to be angry, disgusted, betrayed. I spoke slowly the whole time so that part of me could watch for a hint of emotion in his face. But after a while I stopped watching—that's what can happen when you plunge into an inferno. At some point you stop explaining the events that have consumed your life and start to relive them.

I came back to the present at the sound of contempt in his voice.

"Dr. James Coyne," he said. "My good friend Jamie."

"He *was* your friend. What I'm trying to say—"

"You had a few laughs at my expense, did you? You and your vigilante lover?"

"You think so? Then choke on this," I lashed out. I reached for an envelope on the coffee table—one more secret fished out of Tony's bottom drawer—and tossed it at him. "Go ahead, open it. It's for you."

"From whom?"

"The man who died saving your life."

Poor Max. It was a losing battle. Even from the other side of heaven, Jamie could work his magic—but not with charm, this time. With a passionately truthful account

315

of our relationship, from Jamie's initial Svengali efforts to recruit me to my actual role in Victims Anonymous and my valiant attempts of late to thwart Kagan and his minions.

True to form, Jamie rose to a dramatic climax.

Max, I never slept with her. Karen never loved me. But we both loved you.

Pola chose that inopportune moment to break off her toilette. Jumping down from the windowsill, she ambled over for a greeting. Max never could resist her any more than he could Jamie. As she brushed against his legs, defrosting that rigid countenance, he bent to stroke her.

"Vigilantism is loose in the land," I said—a flat quotation from a recent headline in the *New York Times.* "Ignore the little people and take out the leaders. If Bernard Rees meant what he said, tell him I can deliver. Tell him I've cut off the head of the snake. You need visible leaders? Lee Emerson is one. Jamie is another."

"Any live candidates?" he said acidly.

"Brian O'Neal, construction business. The man who almost succeeded in having you crushed to death while you were interrogating Lee Emerson. A couple of sniper protégés of Kagan's. And Kagan, of course. No known first name."

"The man with the forgettable face. Proof?"

"The only known photograph in existence, finally captured on film."

I handed him Tony's handiwork.

Dipping into Kagan's little black box, I extricated a few more photographs. "Here are a couple of Kagan protégés who turned that Legal Aid rally into a shooting gallery. One of them is a blond guy—looks like a rodeo star, you told me once. The other is short and dark-skinned—Hispanic maybe? Color them snipers."

"And all the rest—just 'little people'?" Skepticism in

those narrowed blue eyes.

"Not quite. But it's all you're going to get, Max."

"Right," he said, pulling a notebook out of his raincoat pocket. "Something for us, something for you." He made a few notes. "It's not enough."

"I'm well aware of that," I said, following Jon Willard's advice to the letter. "I'm in a position to identify every Victims Anonymous cell in the country—a complete membership list." I took my time lighting a cigarette. "Since we don't expect the FBI to trust the word of a bunch of lawbreakers and co-conspirators, I'm authorized to offer you that list."

I saw a flicker in his eyes—the equivalent of "*Now* you're talking."

"Since it's nowhere in evidence," Max said, "I assume we're getting to the heart of the matter. The list in return for what?"

"Complete immunity from prosecution for every member—every decent person—who wants out. Their numbers are considerable."

He wrote in his notebook. "*How* considerable?"

"Every cell leader has been contacted—some in person, the rest by phone. A solid majority—maybe as high as eighty or ninety percent—are ready to renounce their vigilante activities in favor of operating within the law. There are bound to be a few holdouts of course — especially with Kagan still on the loose—but not many."

"And the list?"

"It would enable you to keep tabs on whoever hasn't gone to ground. It would help you make sure they lived up to their end of the deal. Nobody likes living under glass. But I reminded everyone I talked to that far-flung surveillance costs a lot of money and manpower, and the FBI is no exception. You can't keep it up forever."

"That's it?"

"Not quite. Before you huddle with Rees, you should

know that I've stacked the deck against you. Every cell has—let's call it a blackmail box. They're incriminating photographs of members who were 'making their bones'—a Mafia expression I'm sure you're familiar with. Almost all of the women in Victims Anonymous—they were called 'Passives'—never killed anyone. Unless, as in my case," I couldn't resist adding, "they were tricked into it."

"But there *were* people committed to literal revenge. An eye for an eye. A tooth for a tooth. I'm putting you on notice that, by now, every cell leader has destroyed the evidence. You won't be able to prove a thing."

"And without your list, we won't even be able to keep tabs." More notes. "If I were to tell you it's no deal—"

"I would have to tell you when you asked, '*What* list?'"

"Someone has been talking to a smart lawyer."

Someone named Jon Willard who, unlike Jamie, really had *been my lover...*

Max put his notebook away.

"The little people," he said caustically. "The good vigilante versus the bad. Nice euphemism."

"It happens to be true. Only a small percentage of the people in Victims Anonymous reveled in the violence. The rest were victims of violent crime in more ways than one. When revenge permeates your life—"

"It brings out the worst in you?" he said, making it sound like the cliché it was.

"More precisely, it destroys the best. Wipe the blood of a killer off your hands and then go home and try to bake a cake, tuck in the kids, water the plants. There's something else Rees should know. Ninety percent of crime is handled locally, he said. But with every major failure on the part of the cops—every breakdown in the system—we hear repeated cries for national solutions. Some of us are convinced that the way to respond is through a national organization which works to keep things local. Arm people with facts and figures. Spell out the strategy and skills needed to fight parole boards and politicians."

I leaned forward, warming to the subject. "All those fragmented, disorganized efforts could be turned into a unified whole. The structure is already in place, don't you see? If we were to build on the ruins of Victims Anonymous with cells—let's call them chapters—in every major city, we could—"

"*We?*"

So there it was. Max, the company man, who would never cut corners, not even for me, Jamie had predicted.

Especially not for me.

I shrugged. "A figure of speech. The foundation exists. Any number of people could head it. You want one more head on the block, Max? Will it cinch the deal if I cut myself out of it?"

It would cinch the deal. I saw it in his eyes.

"You'll hear from me." He stood up.

"How soon?"

"A week."

I went with him to the door. Watched the knob turn in his hand. Saw it stop.

That should have been signal enough, giving me the opportunity to close my eyes—turn away—flee into the next room—jump out the window—rather than see what was happening to his face.

A ghastly jigsaw puzzle, every feature cracking to pieces.

"Don't you know what it means to me, your 'deal'? What an agony of indecision? I loved you!"

I was almost glad I hadn't turned away. Glad he'd let me see what I had done to him. It would give me the strength I needed to "close the books" on this chapter of my life.

CHAPTER 44

IT TOOK A WEEK, JUST as Max had promised. The message Jon Willard delivered to my apartment five days ago said, "Offer accepted."

That wasn't all it said. Whether Karen Newman was or wasn't part of the deal was still "under consideration."

It went on, the agony of indecision.

For Max, but not for me.

"McCann hates you that much?" Denzel wondered when the message arrived.

Angela knew better. "He loves her that much. McCann is straitlaced and by-the-book. Had Karen meant less to him, he'd never have risked a good deal like this slipping through his fingers."

"Change of subject," I announced. "Let's get started on the party preparations. We have a lot to celebrate. Who's doing what? I can order in or—"

"I'll be the chef," Angela volunteered. "Just get me an accurate head count."

"I'll be bartender," Denzel jumped in.

"Where does that leave *me*?" I protested.

"How about turning this lovely penthouse apartment into something festive and fun?"

I smiled faintly. "Why not?"

* * *

Festive and fun it was. I'd decided on an Art Deco theme with background music to match. Everyone heaped extravagant praise on the chef and drank wine and beer between courses. We saved the champagne for last. We toasted with undiminished joy and passed hugs and kisses around the table like party favors.

The one person everyone toasted with special fervor was Jon Willard. I had put Jon's place setting at one end of a long table, with me at the other. When someone turned up the music, Jon stood, reached for my hand, and swept me onto a makeshift dance floor.

A memorable evening.

After everyone had left, I stood before my park view, staring at a three-quarter moon tinged with a russet-colored sunset and a breathtaking sprinkle of stars. It reminded me of the night Jamie died. The night he had saved Max's life.

Stop stalling, I told myself. It's time.

I repaired to the den and sat down at the desk to write my "Dear Max" letter.

It began with "I'm not asking you to forgive me, Max. Not now, not ever. I will never forgive myself. Knowing how much pain I've caused you is truly devastating. As for your contempt, I've earned it. There were times when close friends told me I was being too hard on myself, but they were wrong. I realized—too late—that I wasn't being hard enough.

"I've lost so many people I loved. Sarah. My son-in-law Peter. My dearest friend, Claudia, who'd be alive if I only I'd heeded her warning not to join Victims Anonymous. My dear friend and ally, Jamie, who'd launched Victims Anonymous with the best of intentions, only to be sidetracked by a man whose intentions couldn't have been more lethal."

I paused. Chose my words carefully.

Forced myself to keep writing.

"I plan to spend the rest of my life pulling together a national organization of people, all of whom are eminently qualified to channel the cellular structure of Victims Anonymous into a unified whole. State by state, we intend to push for legislation. To work at educating people on how to reduce violent crime.

"I hope you realize that what I'm telling you is not an excuse, but an explanation. You might say I fell victim to the 'law of unintended consequences.'"

I poured myself a brandy. Started to reach for a book. Put it back again

I knew this particular poem by heart.

Before our lives divide for ever,
While time is with us and hands are free,
(Time swift to fasten and swift to sever
Hand from hand, as we stand by the sea)
I will say no word that a man might say
Whose whole life's love goes down in a day;
For this could never have been; and never,
Though the gods and the years relent,
Shall be.

OTHER BOOKS BY THE AUTHOR

Freedom Bridge

Ayn Rand: My Fiction-Writing Teacher

Fake Warriors: Identifying, Exposing, and Punishing Those Who Falsify Their Military Service (With Henry Mark Holzer) (Second Edition)

Fake Warriors: Identifying, Exposing, and PunishingThose Who Falsify Their Military Service (With Henry Mark Holzer) (First Edition)

"Aid and Comfort": Jane Fonda in North Vietnam (With Henry Mark Holzer)

ABOUT THE AUTHOR

Erika Holzer received her B.S. from Cornell University and her law degree from New York University.

For several years following her admission to the New York bar, she practiced constitutional and appellate law with Henry Mark Holzer. Their clients included Soviet dissidents and defectors, and other lawyers for whom they prepared appellate briefs and Petitions for Certiorari with the Supreme Court of the United States.

One of the Holzer firm's clients (and later friend) was novelist Ayn Rand. Because of Rand's literary influence, Erika Holzer switched careers from law to writing.

With Henry Mark Holzer, she co-authored *"Aid and Comfort": Jane Fonda in North Vietnam*, proving that Jane Fonda's trip to Hanoi during the Vietnam War, and her activities there, constituted constitutional treason.

Again with Henry Mark Holzer, Erika Holzer co-authored the first and second editions of *Fake Warriors: Identifying, Exposing, and Punishing Those Who Falsify Their Military Service*.

Her other nonfiction writing consists of essays, articles, reviews, and political and legal commentary.

In addition, Holzer is the author of the memoir *"Ayn Rand: My Fiction-Writing Teacher: A novelist's mentor-protégé relationship with the author of Atlas Shrugged."*

Erika Holzer can be contacted at erika.holzer@erikaholzer.com and through www.erikaholzer.com

ACKNOWLEDGEMENTS

I'll always be grateful to Nelson DeMille, who took the time to read a neophyte's novel and recommend it for, among other things, my "vividly created" and "impassioned" prose. My "sharp terse writing and snappy dialogue."

As for my longtime friend and talented novelist, Robert Bidinotto, it was Robert who, early in my career, wrote in the *Boston Herald* that my first novel, *Double Crossing*, was "both grand entertainment and grim education in the realities of Soviet-American relations, with all the excitement that fans of a Robert Ludlum or a Ken Follett could ask for.

My thanks to Mary Higgins Clark, who said of *Double Crossing* that it was a "splendid espionage story with high suspense, good writing, believable characters"— and that it make her very glad she'd been born in a free country.

And thanks to Rita Samols (jejeune@mail.com). Copy-editors (with or without a hyphen) don't come any better than you!

Glendon, you are a marvel. No one—and I mean no one—can compete with your magnificent award-winning covers!

Finally, thanks to Hank. Every manuscript I've ever written has been filled with editing suggestions which greatly improved the novel.

ERIKA HOLZER

COMING IN LATE 2014

A new novel by Erika Holzer

Readers who have just finished *Eye for an Eye* will recall that when protagonist, Karen Newman, faced legal trouble, she relied on her former lover, attorney Jon Willard.

Although he had only a cameo role in *Eye for an Eye,* Jon Willard is the hero of Erika Holzer's new series. It stars a lawyer whose practice is devoted to seeking—and hopefully obtaining—justice for his clients.

No "hired gun," Willard takes on the government as well as powerful individuals in his representation of those whose supposedly inalienable rights have been violated.

ERIKA HOLZER

Made in the USA
Monee, IL
09 January 2020